THE VEGAS BLUFF

A SINFUL CHRISTMAS ROMANCE

AJME WILLIAMS

ALSO BY AJME WILLIAMS

Ajme Williams writes emotional, angsty contemporary romance. All her books can be enjoyed as full length, standalone romances and are FREE to read in Kindle Unlimited .

Books do not have to be read in order.

Heart of Hope Series (this series)
Our Last Chance | An Irish Affair | So Wrong | Imperfect Love | Eight Long Years | Friends to Lovers | The One and Only | Best Friend's Brother | Maybe It's Fate | Gone Too Far | Christmas with Brother's Best Friend | Fighting for US | Against All Odds | Hoping to Score | Thankful for Us | The Vegas Bluff

Billionaire Secrets
Twin Secrets | Just A Sham | Let's Start Over | The Baby Contract | Too Complicated

Dominant Bosses
His Rules | His Desires | His Needs | His Punishments | His Secret

Strong Brothers
Say Yes to Love | Giving In to Love | Wrong to Love You | Hate to Love You

Fake Marriage Series
Accidental Love | Accidental Baby | Accidental Affair | Accidental Meeting | Accidental Daddy

Irresistible Billionaires
Admit You Miss Me | Admit You Love Me | Admit You Want Me | Admit You Need Me

The Why Choose Haremland
Protecting Their Princess | Protecting Her Secret

Check out Ajme's full Amazon catalogue here.

Join her VIP NL here.

DESCRIPTION

I was right all along...
Amelia was just like *all* the other women I never wanted to see
again after spending one night together.

In fact, she turned out to be worse than them.

Let me backup...

It's true when they say that Las Vegas should be burned to the ground.
I'd burn it myself after ending up married to a woman and having no
memory of it.
Was Amelia playing me?
Judging by the way she was sweating and yelling in shock, I didn't
think so.

My heart lied to me and begged me to believe in her authenticity.
You know, maybe she wasn't after my money or prestige, after all.
Maybe her gorgeous body contained a heart that I could actually love.

Boy was I wrong.

Instead of finding an honest heart, I discovered a nasty secret that made me want to rewind time and undo the moments I'd spent with her inside the bedroom.

She was a devil in human form.
A devil that was now wearing a wedding ring... *and* carrying my baby.
Could this Christmas bring me any more surprises?

PROLOGUE

Amelia

Slowly, I awoke from a heavy sleep. The fog in my brain was thick, making it difficult to fully come awake. At first, I was disoriented, not sure where I was. But then a heavy arm draped over my hip and a warm body spooned around me, bringing a memory and a smile back to my face.

Max.

Max with the large hands and an amazing expertise around a woman's body. Enough of the fog lifted that I was able to open my eyes. I frowned as I realized I was still dressed. Why was I sleeping in my clothes?

I scanned through my brain, trying to recall last night. Max had asked me out again, surprising me because I thought the night before had been a one-night thing. And while I wasn't interested in a relationship, I had to admit that I was happy to have another opportunity to spend the night with him. There was no danger of an entanglement because he was from New York and would leave today to return home.

I could recall a lovely dinner, and then a driver taking us through the city as we drank champagne. Had we drunk so much that when we got back to the hotel, we crashed out?

Max's large hand slid down my hip, over my thigh, and up again. His lips pressed to the back of my neck, nibbling, sending a delicious shiver through me.

"I think I drank too much last night," he murmured against my neck.

"Oh?"

"It's the only thing that can explain why we're in bed and still dressed. If I'd had my wits about me last night, we would be waking up naked."

"I was just thinking the same thing."

"Were you now?" His lips continued to trail kisses along my neck. "How do you feel about sleepy, slow sex in the morning?"

"I feel pretty good about it." Already, my body was flushed in anticipation. My nipples were hard and my pussy quivered, knowing the pleasure Max could bring.

He tugged the zipper of my dress down and pushed it from my shoulders. With him still spooned behind me, I shimmied out of my dress. He unclasped my bra, and I tossed that aside. Last, I divested myself of my panties.

He tugged me to him, his slacks-covered dick pressing against my ass as his hand slid over my belly and then down into my nest of curls.

"You're not going to join me?" I sighed against him.

His lips were on my neck again. "I will. But first, you." His fingers found my clit, gently rubbing it. I closed my eyes and sank into his touch, into the warmth of his firm body.

It didn't take long for my orgasm to wash over me. Only then did he undress. Naked, he spooned around me again, lifting my leg to make room for him. He slid inside me, and even though I'd just come, my body responded, my blood heating again.

Like he'd promised, he moved slowly and languidly. His lips kissed my neck and shoulder as he rocked in and out of me. It was sweet and lovely, and a part of me would miss him when he left. I'd never met a man like him. Oh, sure, there were plenty of good-looking, rich guys in Las Vegas. But Max was more than that. There was a down-to-earth feel about him that made me think he grew up in a good family, unlike mine. He wasn't necessarily open about his feelings, but that reservedness gave him a shy factor that was sweet. He was smart and interesting. And he knew how to have a good time.

He groaned against me. "I'm close." His whisper tickled along my neck. He reached over my body, pinching my nipple as he picked up the pace.

"Oh!" I cried out as my orgasm flowed through me, just like he'd described, sleepy and slow.

He thrust again, emptied, and then held me spooned against him as the last waves of pleasure flowed through us.

When our heart rates settled, he gave me one last kiss on the neck and rolled onto his back. I turned onto my back as well.

He slid his hands over his face as if he was still feeling foggy from last night. A flash of light from his hand caught my eye. A ring on his left hand.

In an instant, the languid warmth of my orgasm was gone, replaced by shock and anger. I scrambled out of the bed, grabbing the sheet and tugging it to cover my body as I stood next to the bed.

He brought his hands away from his face and looked at me with concern.

"You're married."

His expression morphed into confusion. "No, I'm not."

"You're wearing a wedding ring." How was it that I didn't notice that before? I wasn't against an occasional hookup with somebody from out of town, but I drew the line at married men.

He frowned and looked at his hand, the confusion remaining on his face. He looked over at me, his eyes squinting, hovering near where I clutched the sheet around my breasts.

I was about to take offense at his ogling me when his gaze returned to my eyes. "So are you."

"What?"

"You've got a ring too."

My head jerked down, looking at my left hand, and sure enough, there was a gold band around my finger. My brain ceased to function. It didn't make any sense. And then it did.

"Oh, my God." I turned and sank onto the bed. How did this happen?

"Care to fill me in?" Max's tone had gone from confused to suspicious.

I shook my head, still not believing I could've done something so stupid. "I've become a Las Vegas cliché."

The bed shifted, and I glanced back to see Max getting out of bed, finding his boxers and his pants and slipping them on. "What does that mean?"

"We must have gotten drunk-married last night."

His hands on his belt buckle stilled as his gaze jerked to me. "What?"

"It's the only thing that explains this."

He shook his head, finishing with his belt. "That doesn't explain this. First of all, no one in their right mind would marry two people who were incoherently drunk."

I arched a brow. "We're in Las Vegas, Max."

"Even so, there would have to be paperwork, right? A marriage license. Marriage certificate."

He pulled the ring from his finger and tossed it onto the pillow. I had no illusions that Max and I were going to have some great love affair. Still, it hurt a little bit the way he yanked the ring off and tossed it away.

Even so, he was right. I pulled the ring from my finger and leaned over to set it on the side table. That's when I saw the papers. I scooted closer to the side table and picked them up, studying them. "Oh, God."

"What?" Max rounded the bed, buttoning his shirt.

I held the papers up. "Marriage license and certificate."

He snatched the papers out of my hand, and again the force of it and the look on his face made me flinch.

His gaze moved from the paper to me. "Is this some sort of joke?" He tossed the papers on the bed, much like he had done with the ring.

Incensed, I stood up, gripping the sheet around me even tighter. It was hard to believe that just a few minutes ago, I was wrapped up in this man. "You think I did this?"

"The proof is in the papers, sweetheart."

I was shocked at his derision. I wished I were fully dressed because I felt vulnerable in just the sheet. But maybe it was just as well because if my hands were free, I might've slapped him. "Your signature is on there as well, slick."

He reached over, picking up the papers again, looking at the signature line. For a moment, he stood, looking utterly confused. The anger and accusation dissipated as he sank down onto the bed. "We'll be able to get this annulled."

"Being drunk doesn't constitute being incapacitated to get an annulment in Las Vegas."

"Sounds like you have experience with this." A hint of his derision returned.

"This is Vegas, Max. I know about gambling and showgirls, but that doesn't mean I gamble and dance."

He set the paper on the bed and scraped his hand over his face again. "Not being able to read or understand what I was signing would be a reason to grant an annulment, wouldn't it?"

"I suppose, but I don't remember reading or signing it either, and I'm not so sure that being too drunk to read and sign will work."

He turned to look at me, and for the first time, I saw vulnerability in him. Like he was going to confess something he wanted to keep a secret. "I have dyslexia. It's often hard enough to read legal papers when I'm sober. I can't imagine I could do it drunk."

I was no lawyer, but his reasoning made sense to me. I sat on the bed next to him.

He looked at his watch. "Fuck." He turned to look at me. "I don't have a lot of time before I need to catch my flight." He shook his head. "I guess I could take a later flight. I can move my schedule around."

"I'm not sure how to go about this in the first place. Why don't you let me research and get whatever paperwork we need, and once it's together, I can let you know? Maybe we can do this long distance and you don't need to return to Las Vegas."

He nodded. "But if I do need to be here, I can come."

I hadn't thought much about being married since I left the romanticism of fairy tales behind me when I was a teenager. But I never could have imagined that on my wedding day, my husband would be eager to divorce me.

CHAPTER ONE

Max—two days earlier.

I walked my twin brother, Sam, out to the charter flight he was taking home to Los Angeles. Yesterday, when we flew to Las Vegas, he was despondent and pissed off at the same time because the woman he loved wouldn't forgive him and love him back. His plan in Las Vegas had been to forget her through booze and women. It had been a bad idea all around because I knew that any chance that he'd have to win Kate back would be gone if he followed through and slept with another woman. Granted, they weren't technically together, mostly because Kate was still pissed off at how he'd left her five years ago. But after seeing the two of them together, I was sure if Sam could stay the course and continue to fight for her, she'd come around. She had a lot of walls up, but I felt certain that deep down, she still loved him too.

He had hit on a couple of women last night, but he hadn't brought any of them back to our suite. He told me this morning that he'd nearly gone to a woman's room, but in the end, he knew I was right. So now I was putting him back on the charter plane to return to Los Angeles so he could try again.

My plan was to head over to the regular terminal and catch a commercial flight home to New York. But with him on his flight heading home, my thoughts turned to business. Sam was in L.A. because we planned to expand our club enterprise out west and he was in charge of putting the deal together in California. Once that was done, I planned to do the same in Las Vegas. Our plans were that I would do it next year, but I was in Vegas now, and our business was doing well. Why not begin scouting and planning a club location here?

I had made it over to the commercial part of the terminal when I made the final decision to stay another day or two. I pulled out my phone to order a car. When the car arrived, I stepped outside. Walking over, I reached for the handle to open the door when a feminine hand reached for the handle as well.

I stepped back. "Oh, I'm sorry. I thought this was my car." I looked down at the app and then at the car and felt pretty certain this was my car.

She looked down at her phone and then the car. "Oh, you're right. I'm sorry."

I smiled at her. She was beautiful, with long, red, curly locks that I could picture my hands getting lost in and hazel eyes that today veered toward green. Probably because of the green silk blouse she wore. I wasn't a lech or even a playboy, but I liked women, and whenever possible, I enjoyed spending time with them. I studied her, feeling like the sparkle in her eyes suggested she liked the way I looked too.

"How about we share?" I opened the door and extended my hand, motioning for her to get in. "I'm sure the driver won't mind." I would pay him whatever it took for him to agree to drive us both.

"That's very kind of you, but I'm probably out of your way. I'm heading home."

So she lived in Las Vegas.

"Well, if that's the case, maybe you'd be willing to be a tour guide for me."

She arched a brow, and I could see the speculation in her eyes. I didn't blame her. Women needed to be careful these days about who they spent time with. Even a good-looking guy like me could be a serial killer.

I thrust out my hand. "I'm Max Clarke. I'm from New York, and I'm here scouting a business location."

Her eyes still held skepticism, but she extended her hand to mine. It was warm and petite, and the man in me couldn't help but imagine it wrapped around my dick.

"Amelia Dunsmore. From Las Vegas. I'm home from a business trip to Southern California." She took her hand back and tilted her head to the side. "I'll tell you what. Let's share this ride to your hotel, and I'll let you know when we get there whether or not I'll be your tour guide."

I nodded. "Fair enough."

I had already indicated where I was heading in the phone app when I ordered the car, so I didn't have to tell the driver where to go. I had the trip from the airport to the hotel to convince Amelia to spend the day with me. Perhaps even the night.

"So, Max Clarke from New York, what sort of business are you scouting for here in Las Vegas?" she asked as we rode from the airport toward the Vegas strip.

"A club."

She laughed. "Of course. You do know that restaurants and clubs are a dime a dozen out here, right?"

I arched my brows. "You doubt my business prowess?"

She shrugged. "Las Vegas has ruined a lot of successful people."

"Well, she won't ruin me. At least not business-wise." I gave her a flirty grin. I wouldn't mind being ruined by her in bed, but I was smart enough not to say that out loud.

"What makes you think you'll be successful?"

"Well, for one, my brother and I already have three successful clubs. Two in Manhattan, and one out in the Hamptons."

"And two?"

"And two, our clubs are a little different from most."

She smirked at me skeptically.

"No, really." I pulled out my phone, going to the website for one of our clubs in Manhattan. "My brother and I like to combine business and technology, along with a whole lot of fun." I handed her the phone to look at the club's website. "My brother, right now, is scouting locations in Los Angeles. We're looking at putting in a noir prohibition-type club there."

She handed the phone back to me, and the skepticism was gone. She almost looked impressed. "They didn't have much technology back then."

"No, but we have some interesting ideas. I was thinking of doing something similar to that here, but having a prohibition gangster theme is a little on the nose for Las Vegas, don't you think?"

She nodded. "Absolutely."

"What about old Hollywood? You know, the glitz and glamor and music of the Rat Pack."

She shrugged. "That's not hard to find here, either."

She was probably right, but still, I felt Sam and I could put an interesting twist on it. I could already envision having our guests doing karaoke with a hologram of Frank Sinatra or Dean Martin. I wondered what the licensing fees for that would be.

"It's your turn, Amelia Dunsmore, from Las Vegas. What sort of business do you do?"

"I have a social media marketing agency."

"No kidding?" I pulled out my phone, opening Instagram to see if I could find her on it. Sure enough, she was there and clearly knew what she was doing. She had all the coordinated colors and filters that professional Instagrammers used. I stopped and poked one photo to get a larger view of it. In it, she wore a deep purple bikini with a large, brimmed hat and fifties-style glasses while lounging in a chaise by a pool. I shifted in the seat as my dick took notice of her fantastic curves as well.

"Is that the only thing that interests you about me?"

I shut the app, feeling like an asshole lecher. "No. But I won't deny that you're very attractive. What sort of businesses do you work with in your social media agency?"

14

She smirked, clearly enjoying that she had caught me being a base, primal male. "I work with boutique hotels and a few clubs. In Los Angeles, I just signed a contract with a celebrity-owned restaurant."

I grinned. "Congratulations." Seeing that we were about to pull up to my hotel, I knew I had to make my move. "We should celebrate. Why don't you let me take you out for dinner?"

"You don't need a tour, then?"

I nodded. "I'd very much like a tour, but I didn't want to push my luck, especially after my ogling faux pas."

She laughed, and it was light and lovely. I felt it flow through my chest in the oddest way.

"I'll tell you what, Max Clark from New York. I need to go home and check on a few things, but I'll meet you back here at your hotel at, say, two o'clock?"

I looked at my watch. It was barely eleven. Two o'clock seemed like an eternity away, but it was closer than dinnertime. "I'll be ready."

In the hotel, I rebooked a suite and headed up to take care of my own business. I started by checking in with our New York office to make sure all the clubs in New York were running as usual. Sam and I had business educations from college, but the most important parts of our knowledge came from our dad and uncle and other members of the family who were in business. From them, we learned how to hire the best people, so I wasn't worried that something would be going off the rails while I was away.

Next, I tapped into our network to get a referral for a commercial real estate agent in Las Vegas. Once I got a name, I called her up, told her what I was looking for, then made arrangements to meet her tomorrow to preview possible club locations.

When I was done with that, I thought I should call Sam and tell him I changed my plans, but hopefully, his plane was landing in Los Angeles and he was on his way to make another bid for the woman he loved. I prayed she would finally forgive him.

At two o'clock, I was standing in front of the hotel like an eager teenager going on his first date. I laughed at myself for feeling like that. I enjoyed women, but it'd been a long time since I'd been excited about spending time with one. I couldn't pinpoint what it was about Amelia that was drawing me in. Yes, she was beautiful and sexy, and she clearly was her own woman. It had to have been more than her musical laugh, but damn if I could figure it out. The reason didn't matter. I hoped we would have an enjoyable afternoon and evening, perhaps even night, then tomorrow, I would do my business and plan to return to New York.

As Amelia approached, I felt a whoosh of excitement. Her long red curls were blowing in the wind as she pulled up in a Mini Cooper convertible. I'd never been in a Mini Cooper. I hoped I could fit my large frame into it.

As I approached her car, she said, "Your tour carriage awaits. I hope you weren't expecting a limousine or a fancy Hummer or something."

I opened the door and climbed in. "Not at all. This is perfect."

For the rest of the afternoon, she drove me around the city, pointing out the major tourist spots but also bringing me to lesser-known, off-the-beaten-path locations. All of them were great to see, but the best part was talking to her. We talked about anything and everything and laughed a whole hell of a lot. I couldn't remember the last time I'd laughed so much.

When dinnertime rolled around, she was comfortable enough with me to let me take her out. I ordered the most expensive champagne to celebrate her getting the celebrity client in Los Angeles.

During dinner, I learned more about her business and how she had started off as a social media influencer and then, after college, built her own business. She not only had clubs and hotels in Vegas but was expanding, including the celebrity restaurant in Los Angeles, and she was hoping to get a vineyard up in Northern California.

She didn't speak much about her family, except for her brother she said she was close to. I learned enough to know that she wasn't very close to her father and that, like me, she came from money, although probably not as much money as I came from. I got the feeling her father was a big fish in a little pond.

I shared a little bit about my family, including my twin brother

Sam's woes with women. We made a toast to Sam and Kate, hoping they would find their way back together again.

When dinner was over, I didn't want to let her go. And it wasn't just that I wanted to have sex with her, although I really, really did. I was enjoying spending time with her.

I convinced her to go dancing, and the first time she was in my arms, it felt like a puzzle piece snapping into place. It was disconcerting even as it was welcomed. For a moment, I thought I should end the date because the last thing I needed was to fall for a woman. Then I remembered she lived here, whereas I lived in New York. We could have this one night together, and after that, we'd go our own ways.

Thank fuck, she was in agreement. By the time we returned to my suite, I needed her so badly it was like I was a starving man given a feast. And feast I did. The door was barely closed when I pushed her against it and drew my tongue over every inch of her skin I could get to. I divested her of her blouse and bra, burying my face in her tits. Good God, they were perfection, round and soft, with hard pink nipples. I sucked one deep into my mouth, loving the sound of her moan.

But my journey had only just begun. I got her skirt and panties off, dropping to my knees to discover the secrets of her womanhood. She was a woman who liked to keep things tidy down there, but the small nest of red curls told me she was a natural redhead, not that I questioned it. I inhaled the scent of her sex, loving how her wetness glistened on her pussy. Then I ran my tongue through her pussy lips, and it was like drinking the nectar of the gods. I lapped and sucked and tasted until her body was shaking and she cried out. Her juices flooded my mouth, and I wanted more.

I picked her up and carried her to my room. I laid her on the bed and loved how her hazel eyes watched me as I tore my clothes off. I shoved my pants and boxer briefs down, my dick springing free, hard and aching.

I grabbed the condom from my wallet, but before I could roll it on, she knelt on the bed and wrapped her hand around him.

"Fuck."

She licked her lips, and I was a goner.

I removed her hand. "I'm going to come, and I want to do it inside that sweet pussy of yours."

She feigned pouting. "But I want a taste too."

I rolled the condom on and then pushed her back on the bed. "Sorry, sweetheart." I settled on my heels, kneeling between her thighs. I pulled her body to me until my dick was resting on her belly.

I waited to make sure she was okay with this. After all, she'd just said she wanted to suck my dick. Maybe that meant she didn't want to fuck.

She arched a brow. "Is there a problem?"

I looked down on her sexy body, her cheeks still flushed from her orgasm, and something in my chest clenched tightly.

"No problem."

She took my dick and brought it to her pussy opening. "Well, then."

Holding her hips, I rocked forward and filled her with one hard thrust.

She gasped, arcing off the bed.

Shit. Too much, too soon. I withdrew. "Are you okay?"

"I won't be if you don't fuck me."

She didn't have to tell me twice.

CHAPTER TWO

Amelia

Oh. My. God. I'd only had a moment to see and hold and admire Max's dick. I wouldn't say I was a connoisseur of dicks. I'd only seen a few. Max's wasn't much longer, but good God, was it thick. When he entered me, all the breath whooshed out, replaced with the most amazing erotic sensations. My pussy throbbed in a good way.

When he withdrew, I wondered whether he'd changed his mind. After all, he'd been hesitant for a moment. But when I told him to fuck me, he didn't hesitate then. His green gaze watched me as he sank inside and then methodically moved, in and out, in and out. My pussy had never had it so good.

As he fucked me, his hand slid over my belly and squeezed my breast, his palm rubbing over my nipple. I felt like I'd been plugged into a light socket. My entire body was zinging with electricity.

"How's this?" he asked.

I managed to open my eyes to see a cheeky grin on his face. He knew he was lighting me up.

"Make me come, and I'll let you know."

He picked up the pace, and holy moly if his dick wasn't still expanding. The friction was beyond anything I could have imagined. With each thrust, he sent me closer and closer to the edge. I knew that when I came, it would be the best, hardest orgasm I'd ever had.

He licked his thumb and rubbed over my clit, and that was it. I went blasting, flying, soaring . . . all of it. The pleasure rocketed from my pussy throughout my body. I think my cells were orgasming.

"Oh, fuck . . . fuck, you're tight." Max shifted, his body coming over mine, his hand finding purchase on the mattress next to my head, his other hand holding my hip as he drove into me again and again and again. He threw his head back and growled as he slammed into me, grinding against me as his orgasm crashed through him. He continued to move, and my pussy continued to quiver and quake until he collapsed on me.

Wow was the only coherent thought I could form for several minutes. I finally understood what it meant to have your world rocked. Max definitely rocked mine.

He withdrew and took off the condom, tying it and tossing it in the trashcan near the bed. I didn't know how he could move because I was boneless.

But as my jellied limbs began to solidify again, I knew it was time to get up and leave. As much fun as we had today, there was nothing more to us than just two people enjoying each other. Still, I wouldn't mind staying a little bit longer and perhaps having another go at him. I definitely wouldn't mind sucking that magnificent dick. But that wasn't how hookups like this worked.

I turned and sat up on the bed, pulling my hair back, thinking it probably looked like a wild, knotted mess.

"Leaving so soon?" His finger drew a line down the center of my back, sending a whole new wave of erotic sensations through me. I turned my head to look back at him lying on his side. His head was propped up on one hand. His other hand was teasing the skin just above my ass.

"That's usually how these things work."

He grinned. "Whoever has been teaching you about *these things* hasn't done a very good job."

I cocked my head. "Really? What am I missing?"

"Well, when the sex is spectacular, you don't just settle for one time. Unless you have somewhere to be now or if you have to get up early, why not stay and we can do it again? In fact, if you're willing to stay the night, we can do it again several times."

My body flooded with excitement. My nipples hardened and my pussy, already wet from the first time, got even wetter. "I have nowhere to be now, and my first appointment isn't until ten tomorrow."

"Well, then, it's settled." He reached out, taking my wrist and pulling me back into bed with him.

"You can recover that quickly, and that many times?" I asked.

He gave me a wicked grin. "When adequately stimulated."

This was my opportunity to really get a good look at him. I pushed him onto his back and straddled his thighs, running my hands down his chest. I wanted to take in every inch of him, savoring this because it was going to have to last me a lifetime. He would become the star of my erotic fantasies when I had to take pleasure matters into my own hand. Maybe I'd buy a vibrator. I wondered if they came in Max's girth.

His chest was hard with smooth skin. It tapered down into abs with the coveted six distinctive packs. Below that lay his dick, not full, but not flaccid either, on his belly.

I drew my fingers down over his stomach and to his hips and then brought them back over the tops of his thighs. Then I teased the area around his dick, but never touching it, watching each time my fingers drew close to his dick how it would twitch and thicken.

"You like teasing, don't you?" he asked.

"Is this teasing? I'm just getting the lay of the land." I bent over and drew my tongue from root to tip, then sucked the velvety soft head into my mouth.

He groaned, his fingers threading through my hair. "Jesus, yes."

"It's Amelia."

I heard the rumble of his laugh. "Amelia. Yes. Use that sexy mouth on my cock."

He didn't have to ask me twice.

I woke the next morning, at first disoriented, wondering where I was. But then the night before came flooding back. I'd never before had a night filled with so many orgasms. We'd fucked again after I sucked him off, and then he woke me twice in the middle the night with sensuous touches that led to more orgasms.

I looked over to the other side of the bed, but it was empty. From outside the room, I could hear the murmur of a voice. I checked the clock on the side table, noting it was only seven in the morning.

As much as I hated to admit it, my time with Max had come to an end. I'd never before been so disappointed to have my time with a man come to an end. I rose from bed and noticed a robe lying across it. I considered slipping it on thinking perhaps we could have one more morning interlude, but it was best not to prolong things. He might even be annoyed if I expected more today.

I tied my hair up and jumped in the shower, washing quickly, then getting dressed.

I stepped out of the bedroom into the main part of the suite.

Max stood at the window in one of the complementary robes with a phone in one hand and a cup of coffee in the other.

He turned toward me, his gaze scanning my body from head to toe and back up again. He gave me that sexy smile of his.

"Everything sounds like it's going well, Douglas. I'll be returning to New York tomorrow. I've got to go now." He pulled his phone away, tapping the screen, presumably to end the call, and then set it on the table. "Good morning, gorgeous."

It was ridiculous how much my heart fluttered in my chest at the way he looked at and spoke to me. If I were a woman looking for happily ever after, I'd grab onto it. It was a good thing that I wasn't a woman looking for a relationship because as sweet and sexy as Max was, I was pretty sure his words and looks didn't mean anything beyond the obvious attraction.

"Do you have to run off, or can you have breakfast? I've already ordered coffee but was waiting to see what you might want for breakfast before I ordered."

I needed to add *thoughtful* and *generous* to the list of quality characteristics Max had. "I don't want to be in your way. It sounds like you were on a working call."

"That was just a quick call to New York to let them know what I was doing today and when I'd be back. I'm done until ten."

Darn it. I should've put on the robe because that would've given us time for another round of great sex.

"I wouldn't mind a cup of coffee."

He poured me a cup, and when he handed it to me, he leaned over, giving me a quick kiss on the lips. My heart did that flippy flip thing again, and I followed it with a reminder that he was just being nice.

"I'm going to order eggs and bacon. Can I order you something too?"

Tell him no. Tell him you have to go. The more I was around him, the less I wanted to leave, and that wasn't good. "I guess I could have some breakfast."

His smile suggested he was pleased by my answer. "What would you like? Eggs, pancakes?"

My eyes lit up. "I like pancakes."

He laughed and shook his head.

"What's so funny?"

"Nothing. My brother, Sam, is a pancake fanatic. I always joke with him that it's a breakfast for eight-year-olds."

I arched a brow. "I am not eight years old."

His gaze took a heated inventory of my body again. "No, you're not."

My nipples had gone hard, and I looked down to see if he could notice. Yep. Yep, he could. But maybe that could work in my favor.

We stood staring at each other for a moment, and I wondered if he was contemplating skipping breakfast and going back to bed. But finally, he gave his head a quick shake and went to order breakfast.

While we waited, he hurried to the bathroom to shower and get dressed. I guess that answered the question about whether there would be more sex before we parted ways.

He returned to the main living area of the suite just as our food arrived. Once our dishes were served, we sat at the table. He had a nice view of Las Vegas out toward the mountains. The day was clear and bright, making it a lovely spot for a morning after breakfast.

"So, what's on your schedule today?" he asked.

"I have a video conference call with my virtual staff at ten. I have several campaigns I need to review, and then later today, I have a meeting with a local client." I didn't mention it was my brother.

"What time does your day end?"

I looked up from the pancakes I'd smothered in butter and syrup, wondering why he was so interested in my schedule. Deep down, I hoped that he wanted to see me again.

"Officially, I end around five, but I often work later. My office is in my home, which makes it easy to continue to get things done."

"Or work too much."

I stuffed pancakes into my mouth so I didn't answer.

"When Sam and I started our business, we worked out of our residences as well. Of course, we don't have a virtual staff, so getting office space was necessary when we started to grow."

"That's one of the benefits of having a digital agency. I can hire the best from anywhere in the world. And work with anyone in the world."

He nodded. "But again, you risk working too much. You know what they say about all work and no play."

It was an odd conversation, but I stayed with it. "I wasn't a dull girl last night, was I?"

His grin was wide and wild around a piece of bacon. "Not at all." He picked up his glass of orange juice, taking a sip. "Which brings me to wondering if perhaps you would want to repeat it tonight. I have some business things to take care of during the day, but my night is free."

Inside, all my girly parts were screaming *yes*. But a part of me cautioned me against having another night with Max. I liked him and could see that if I spent more time with him, I might not want to stop. That was problematic for two reasons. The first was that while my agency was successful, I still needed to dedicate all my time and resources to keeping it that way, especially if I wanted to grow. The second reason was that being who Max was, and the family that he was from, my father would probably concoct a cockamamie idea to try and get an investment or something out of Max. Along with building my business, my other goal in life was to keep out of the reach of my father's tentacles. He was ruthless and had no scruples about hurting anyone who got in his way.

Max tilted his head to the side. "Unless you didn't have as good a time as I did yesterday."

"I'm pretty certain I had a better time."

"What do you say to one more night? I'll be leaving before noon tomorrow."

I wasn't sure if he was saying that to make sure that I understood that we were just talking about another fun day and a hookup. Whatever his reason, it alleviated my concern, because that's exactly what I wanted.

I nodded. "I can meet you here, or anywhere, at six."

"Perfect."

When I left Max's, I headed home and prepared for the meeting with my virtual staff. I wasn't one of those bosses who micromanaged the people who worked for me, but I learned early on that not everybody had a good work ethic. So once a week, I had a group call where we would all connect together, and then during the week, I had a standing time with each of my staff simply to check in. At first, a few of them resented it, feeling like I was looking over their shoulder. Eventually, they weeded themselves out, and now everyone who worked for me worked as a team. Because they were so good, there were times that our one-on-one calls were mostly talking about things other than the job like their lives, their children, and in the case of my staff who were digital nomads, learning about whatever spot they were in at that time.

After the call, I reviewed the campaigns that were waiting to start and then went through existing campaigns to make sure that they were getting results for our clients. Next, I started brainstorming ideas for the celebrity-owned restaurant in Los Angeles and then continued to work on my presentation for the vineyard I hoped to obtain as a client in Northern California.

At two thirty, I left my home office and headed to the Dunsmore Investment offices to meet with my brother. When I started my business, my brother was my first client. Or rather, I should say my father's company was my first client because my brother, who someday would be taking over the company, hired me.

I arrived, and as usual, I took the long way to my brother's office to avoid seeing my father. He was unscrupulous and manipulative, so I did everything I could to stay out of his way. I think my brother felt the same way, which was why his office was in a totally different part of the building.

When I arrived, his secretary announced me, and I went in. My brother looked up from the desk he'd been hunched over.

He grinned when he saw me. "Hey, how did the trip to Los Angeles go?"

I grinned. "Signed, sealed, and delivered."

He stood up and gave me a hug. "You're a rockstar."

I was on the verge of doing well enough that I could dump my father's company as a client, but because my brother had been so supportive, I wasn't sure I would do that. Plus, these bimonthly meetings gave me a chance to spend time with my brother. There were times when we would see each other a couple of times a week and other times we wouldn't see each other at all for months if it weren't for these meetings.

He motioned for me to sit on the couch, and he went over to his coffee machine, putting in a pod for my favorite—mocha. When it finished brewing, he put in a pod for himself and then brought them over and sat next to me on the couch.

I opened up my laptop to show my brother how the business campaigns were going. My family's business was a real estate investment firm. If it weren't for my brother, I wouldn't have taken the company on as a client. I knew that sounded bad, but I wouldn't put it past my father to run a Ponzi scheme. My brother's involvement ensured that wouldn't happen.

I showed my brother what was working and told him areas I thought we should change to improve results. He nodded, and I appreciated that he deferred to my expertise.

When I finished, we entered sibling mode to catch up. I gave him more detail about my presentation in Los Angeles, and he let me know that he discovered his most recent girlfriend was stealing from him.

I winced.

He didn't seem distraught, but I could see it bothered him. "I need to learn that women only want me for my money."

I shook my head. "What you need to do is stop picking up women at casinos. Most of those women only want to find a sugar daddy." He did have horrible luck in choosing women.

"I'm not sure if you've noticed, Amelia, but we're in Las Vegas. Where else would I find a woman?"

I nearly told him to go to the airport. Perhaps there was a woman there like Max.

He shrugged it off. "Her leaving means I'm free this evening. Do you want to meet me for drinks?"

I shook my head, unable to stop grinning and hoping that the warmth in my cheeks didn't mean I was blushing. "I've got a date. And by date, I mean a hot date."

My brother's eyes lit up. Most of the world saw my brother as serious, bordering on grumpy, but with me, he was different. Ever since we were little and figured out that our parents didn't have much interest in us, my mother even less so once she left my dad and went off to who knows where, my brother and I had stuck together.

"And who is this guy? Is it serious?"

I shook my head. "It's not serious. He's in town on business and will be leaving tomorrow."

"You know I support you, little sis, but big brothers don't like hearing about their little sisters hooking up."

I shrugged. "That's a double standard. I thought you were more enlightened than that, James."

James's secretary poked her head in the door. "I'm sorry to interrupt, Mr. Dunsmore. I'm heading down to take these drafts to the printer."

"Thank you, Mrs. Curtis."

"I thought she was retiring," I said when she left.

"Next year. I don't know what I'll do. Don't tell anyone, but I think she really runs the show."

I laughed. "You have a year to learn the ropes."

He smiled. "Enough about Mrs. Curtis. Tell me, why are you so excited about this date tonight if it's just a one-time thing?"

I looked down at my coffee, trying to figure out how to articulate what it was like being with Max. "It's hard to explain. I mean, of course, he's really good-looking. And smart and successful. He's just fun to hang out with. I don't know, I guess we just clicked."

My brother cocked his head to the side. "So tonight won't be the first night, I take it?"

"No. But it will be the last."

"And does this Mr. Wonderful two-night-stand have a name?"

"His name is Max Clarke. He and his brother have opened a couple of clubs in New York and are looking to open one in Los Angeles and one here in Las Vegas."

My brother's brows furrowed as if he was trying to place the name.

"I don't know that you would know of them, but you might know of his family. His uncle is Daniel Clarke. And his dad is Drew Clarke." Before I'd met with Max last night, I Googled him, out of curiosity and for safety. I was surprised to learn that I knew of his family. Both James and I knew Drew Clarke because we'd both been marketing majors in college and had studied his marketing methods. Especially my brother James, because the Clarke family was in real estate, making Drew's marketing plans a good matchup for my father's real estate investment business.

"No shit? How did you meet him?"

"I almost stole his car at the airport when I arrived back yesterday."

He laughed. "And you're sure this will be over tonight? If he is handsome and nice, and comes from the Clarke family, he's quite a catch."

I glared at my brother. "First of all, I am my own woman. I don't need a good catch to fulfill my life."

He held his hands up in surrender.

"And second, keep your voice down. That's just the sort of thing I don't want our father to know about."

James nodded. "No doubt, he'd try and find a way to take advantage of that."

I nodded. "So, mum's the word."

"Do you suppose he and his brother will need any money for this club?" James asked.

I rolled my eyes. "I doubt it."

He nodded and shrugged. "I had to ask."

The door opened, and my father walked in with a smarmy smile. My guard went up immediately. It was no fun to be around my father when he was his usual asshole self, but the smarm scared me the most. That was when he was in manipulation mode.

"How come I'm never told when you two are meeting? I don't get to see you two together nearly enough."

I wanted to barf. My father didn't give a fig about seeing my brother or me. For a moment, I worried the sudden act of paternal attention meant he'd overheard me talking to James about Max. If that was the case, I would have to cancel our date. It wasn't that I didn't think Max could handle any antics from my father, but he shouldn't have to. Not for a two-night stand.

"Why don't you come over for dinner tonight? I'll have Alice make both of your favorite dishes."

It was just like my father to force his cook to make two different meals for us, three if we counted Dad who didn't like my favorite, fettuccine Alfredo, or James's favorite, sushi.

I stood, ready to make my exit. "Sorry, I have a prior engagement tonight."

My father arched a silver brow. "Oh?"

"Yes, she's having a business meeting with a club owner out of New York."

I wasn't so sure I liked James sharing that much information about Max, but at least he said it was a business meeting, not a date.

"New York, eh? Your business must be doing really well, kiddo."

There might be some twenty-six-year-olds who found their fathers calling them kiddo endearing, but I hated it. I knew it was his way of dismissing me as being a child.

"Speaking of which, I need to go get ready for my presentation." I turned to my brother. "I'll let you know about those changes in the campaign."

"Good luck tonight."

I hurried out of James's office and to my car as quickly as I could. Once I was on the road heading home, I let out a breath. I'd just dodged a bullet.

CHAPTER THREE

Max

I wanted more than anything to take Amelia back to bed and drown myself in her body one more time. After the first time, it was clear that once wasn't enough, but even after the second and third times, it still wasn't enough. If she hadn't walked out of the bedroom fully clothed, I definitely would have tried to take her back to bed.

But she was dressed and ready for the day and perhaps that was a good thing. The fact that I couldn't seem to get enough of her could be problematic if I continued to indulge myself. But even with that kernel of concern, it didn't stop me from asking if she would spend tonight with me. I was leaving tomorrow, so I'd be safe from getting entangled with her beyond just enjoying her company and the physical aspect of our relationship. I got the feeling she felt the same as I did, wanting to indulge the attraction but not wanting to get emotionally entangled.

When she left, I did my best to focus on the whole reason I was in Las Vegas. The real estate agent that I had contacted picked me up outside the hotel to show me a few properties that might work for the club Sam and I planned to build in Las Vegas. Thinking of Sam, I wondered how things had gone with him and Kate when he returned home yesterday. I hadn't heard from him, and I decided to go with the old adage that no news was good news.

My agent, Carlyn, was a thirty-something professional woman. She reminded me of my uncle Zack's wife Eleni, who exuded power and fierceness when she was in work mode. Carlyn was attractive and clearly spent a lot of time and money to get that way. It made me think of Amelia who dressed nicely and wore makeup, and yet came off as natural. Maybe it was because she let her hair hang with all those wild curls. My hands definitely didn't get to spend enough time tangled up in all that lovely hair.

As Carlyn drove us to the first location, she went through the list of prospective properties that she'd selected for me. As she rattled off all the features and benefits, I looked over the paper with the same information that she'd handed to me when we got into her car.

When we arrived at the first spot, I felt certain that it would not be the place for us. It was too far away from where I believed our market would most likely congregate. But I toured it anyway on the off chance that it provided something in the building that would make up for what the location lacked. It didn't.

The second location was much improved, closer to all the action in Las Vegas. Sam and I weren't looking at building a club for locals. We liked to create places that were destinations in and of themselves. Putting them close to other destination spots ensured that we would be where the market could find us. At the same time, I didn't want to compete with the hotel casinos. Too many of them were like all-inclusive resorts, where everything and anything a visitor would need was provided on the spot, which meant they didn't venture out. This second location seemed to fit the bill.

"This location was built back in the early days of Las Vegas. For a time, it was mobster central," my realtor said as we approached the front of the building. The style and the tiredness of the building showed its age.

What I didn't understand was why a building that was mobster central would be empty and rundown. "Seems like a place like this would have some historical interest. But what I'm seeing here looks like it's been abandoned for a while."

"Some of that has to do with people wanting to be closer to the center of things as well as the economy. For all the tourist money that comes into Las Vegas, clubs and restaurants come and go on a regular basis here."

"Those are the only two reasons?" There had to be more to it.

She opened the door to let me in. "Well, the building also has some disturbing history. Some say it's haunted. Others feel like it just has bad juju. The truth of the matter is that once the casinos and other clubs went in, this location suffered. No one who has bought it has been able to make it a success. With that said, the past incarnations have been a restaurant, bar, and liquor store, but not a club."

It was never a good idea to invest in a location that had a history of bankruptcy. Particularly over fifty years of it. But I was intrigued by the history of the building and of the idea that it could be haunted. Its terrible history meant I could probably get a really good deal on it as well.

The inside was even more rundown than the outside suggested. In the corner, a dusty neon sign saying *Desert Oasis* was propped against the wall. I'd definitely need to get an inspector in to check out the structure and systems of the building. But what I could see with my eyes only needed a good scrub and cosmetic fixes. Any place Sam and I bought would undergo renovations, so the work needed here wasn't a big issue.

"The history is a little disconcerting, but I actually like this place. I'd like to get as much information on it as I can."

"I would be happy to pull together information about the building's history, if you'd like."

"I would like that."

"I have two other locations for us to look at, but I'll keep this one on the list."

The next location was automatically out because it was smack dab next door to an all-inclusive casino resort. The next location wasn't perfect as it was very close to the Bellagio Fountains. But the realtor pointed out that many people come to the fountains who are not staying at the Bellagio, and the building itself was pretty good, so it went on the list as well.

I got to the hotel at just before three and decided I would get some exercise before my date with Amelia tonight. After running five miles on the hotel gym's treadmill, I returned to my suite and took a shower. As the water washed over me, I imagined having Amelia there with me, seeing all that gorgeous red hair, wet and sticking to her creamy, smooth skin. Of course, my dick rose to the occasion, and I considered giving him some relief but then opted not to. He'd just have to wait till later tonight.

Once I was dressed, I gave my mother a quick call just to check in. She reminded me for the umpteenth time not to forget about Thanksgiving. She asked about Sam, and I only gave her the basics. I figured all the craziness with Kate was for Sam to tell her about, not me.

When I got off the phone with her, I considered calling Sam again, but to be honest, I didn't want to hear if things had gone wrong. I felt a little guilty about that, but I had a night with Amelia to look forward to and I didn't want to be bogged down by my brother's disappointment.

When it was time, I headed down to the lobby, my excitement growing with every second I came closer to seeing Amelia. I felt like a fucking kid on Christmas morning about to discover what Santa left under the tree. It was a good thing that I was going home tomorrow. Otherwise, this could be a real problem.

When I got to the lobby, she was already there waiting for me. She smiled brightly, and I smiled back, pretty sure I looked like a lovesick loon. No. Not lovesick. Not that.

When I reached her, I pressed my hand against her back and pulled her close, giving her a quick kiss. "You look great." I wasn't kidding. She wore a sexy dress that was somewhere between blue and green that looked amazing with her red hair and ivory skin.

"You don't look so bad yourself, slick."

I didn't think I looked any different than usual. I wore a pair of charcoal gray slacks and a white shirt. I omitted the tie but did wear a jacket.

"Do you know where you want to go tonight?" she asked.

"I was thinking I'd take you to the Roarke."

She fanned her face. "Ooh, la-la. Someone wants to spend big money tonight." She leaned a little closer to me. "But you don't have to spend a fortune to get lucky tonight, just so you know."

My dick twitched to life at her flirty, sexy words. I laughed. "Good to know."

"I hope you don't mind. I didn't drive. I got a rideshare here and figured I would take it home whenever our date finished."

I nodded. It was probably a good idea. I imagine she spent a fortune in parking last night. Perhaps I should've offered to have paid for that.

We ordered a car, and a few minutes later, we were in the backseat heading toward the restaurant. The Roarke family was world-famous for their upscale restaurants. They also had amazing clubs located around the world.

Amelia glanced over at me. "Are you going to brag about how you're connected to the Roarke family?"

I felt my cheeks heat. I wasn't sure whether I was embarrassed that she knew of my connection or worried that she thought I was trying to show off. "How do you know about that?"

"You don't think I didn't do my research on you before I had sex with you, do you?"

I laughed. "I guess I should've considered that."

"So, tell me about the Roarkes."

"My Uncle Daniel married Brianna Roarke. She's not with the Rourke company. She decided to go out on her own, and like me and Sam, she owns a few clubs. Her brother Devin has expanded the Rourke restaurants and clubs. I haven't been to the one here in Las Vegas and figured now was a good time to check it out."

She studied me for a minute. "You're close with your family, aren't you?"

It almost sounded like she was surprised. I knew there were lots of families that had dysfunction and chaos, but it was hard to believe that my family was the only one that for the most part got along well. My Uncle Daniel and Brianna were happy. My Uncle Zach and his family were happy too. But I'd once overheard my dad and uncles talk about their father, who sounded like a miserable fuck. I wasn't sad that I never got to meet him.

"Yeah, I guess we are. My brother and I are twins, so we're definitely close. I have a younger sister who is great. And our parents are happily married. It's all pretty boring, actually." This time, I studied her. "I get the feeling it's not the same for you."

She shrugged and looked out the window. I was about to change the subject because I didn't want anything to sour the mood of our date, but then she said, "I'm close to my brother too. We're not twins. It's been more like me and him against the world. Or in our case, against our dad. Our mom took off, so I suppose I should give my dad some credit for sticking around, but he's not a great person."

I reached over, taking her hand and giving it a squeeze. "Well, as far as I can tell, his daughter is a great person."

She gave me that lovely smile again.

We arrived at the Roarke, and although it was difficult for most people to get reservations, one of the perks of coming from an affluent family, particularly one who knew Devin Rourke personally, I was able to get one. It wasn't just any table, either. I imagined it had to be the best table in the place. Like the Roarke restaurant in New York, this one was high on the top floor of a skyscraper. The difference was that this one rotated, giving us a 360-degree view of Las Vegas.

Of course, nothing beat the view of the woman who sat across from me. Yep. If I were like my brother and prone to falling in love, this woman could quite possibly be the one I'd tumble for.

CHAPTER FOUR

Amelia

It was laughably nuts how nervous I was for my evening with Max. I felt like I was in high school, finally landing a date with the most popular guy. When I left my townhome to meet him, practically every dress I owned was lying on my bed after having tried them all on to find the best one. Ultimately, I decided on the teal dress, which wasn't necessarily as sexy as some of my other dresses, but the color looked great on me, and while it wasn't snug, the cut did accentuate my assets. Not wanting to deal with traffic or parking, I decided to get a rideshare to Max's hotel. Whether I left later that night, or hopefully the next morning, I'd be able to order another ride home.

When Max exited the elevator and made his way toward me, his gaze scanned my body. The smile on his face told me that I'd chosen the right dress. He wore the typical suit a man on a date might wear, dark gray slacks and a crisp white shirt, but he wore them very well. He looked like he'd stepped out of an ad in a men's magazine.

When he said we were going to the Roarke, on the one hand, I wasn't surprised since I knew his connection to the family, and yet on the other hand, I hadn't expected that he would go all out for dinner.

It was likely to cost several hundred dollars by the time we were done. Of course, to someone like him, the money was a drop in the bucket. My father was rich, but not the kind of rich that Max was. My business did very well. I expected to finish the year in the high six figures. But I also had quite a bit of overhead. I'd been supporting myself from the time I graduated from high school because my father never gave anyone anything without wanting something in return, and I didn't always like or trust the price my father wanted me to pay when I asked him for money. All that to say, having dinner at the Roarke wasn't on my radar in my modest life.

When we were seated at the table, the only thing that was able to take my eyes off Max was the view. I grew up in Las Vegas, so I knew it well and was rarely impressed anymore. But I had to admit, the slowly rotating restaurant with the three-hundred-and-sixty-degree view of Las Vegas was spectacular. I made a mental note to create a savings pot to come to the Roarke for breakfast or lunch so I could see the view when it was light out.

The only thing that could make this dinner dour would be having to talk about my family, so I was glad when Max dropped the subject in the car on the ride over.

"Shall I order a bottle of wine? Do you prefer white or red?" he asked.

"Either, or both, is good for me."

He flashed me a grin. "Both? You can drink an entire bottle of wine on your own?"

"I imagine I could, but it might also put me to sleep." There was no way I would fall asleep before having him touch me again.

"We can't have that." He winked.

When our server arrived, Max ordered a bottle of red wine, which a quick look at the wine list said was over $800. My father had ordered some expensive bottles of wine before, but I'm pretty sure none of them were $800.

"So, how did the hunt for your Golden Age of Hollywood club go today?" I asked once the server brought back the wine and poured us each a glass.

"Not bad. I walked away with two possibilities. One of them I really like, but it has a dismal history for businesses."

"Really? Where is it located?"

"I was told it was one of the first clubs in the city, way back during the Bugsy Siegel days."

"You mean the Desert Oasis." The building looked like a wreck, but it was famous for being old and cursed.

He nodded. "I think that's what it was called."

I sat back and grinned with amusement. "Some people think that place is haunted."

"I know. That's part of the draw."

"Most business owners stay away from it now because they also think it's cursed," I said. Rumor had it that no business ever succeeded in that location since the club closed down about sixty years ago.

He arched a brow. "Do you believe in curses?"

"I don't believe in voodoo witchcraft type curses, but I believe there are locations that people don't want to visit, which makes them very bad places to run a business. That building is one of them."

He thought for a moment. "I know what you're saying because that's what I'm telling myself."

"And yet . . . "

"And yet, I'm drawn to it. It has a ton of historical significance, and while it's tired and rundown, it retains much of its historical architecture and design. It has ghosts and gangster lore. It's in a location that I think would be ideal for what we want to do—close enough to the attractions of Las Vegas and yet enough away to sit on its own and not get lost in the glitz of those big hotel resorts."

"I imagine others have thought the same thing."

He shrugged. "I've asked my realtor to do some research to see what sort of businesses have been in there that have failed."

"Well, you're braver than I am. I suppose the good news is you'll be able to get a good deal on it."

Our server returned, taking our orders. Max ordered the prime rib, while I opted for the Irish stew. It seemed like an odd item to have on a menu at a place as fancy as the Roarke, but rumors were that it was the best Irish stew anywhere in the world, including Ireland.

"Maybe I should order you a Guinness," Max said after I ordered. "The stew is best with Guinness."

"That doesn't quite fit with this fancy wine you got us."

"There are no rules when it comes to eating and drinking." He raised his hand, and our server returned. Max ordered us each a Guinness to be brought with our meals. I wasn't really a beer drinker, but my understanding was that Guinness wasn't like regular beer.

The stew and Guinness were excellent, and the company was even better. The night was ticking away faster than I wanted. I wished it would slow down, giving me more time with Max. That sort of thinking was a little disconcerting, and while I wanted to spend more time with him, I was glad he was leaving the following day. I needed to focus on my business and finish the year strong, not be distracted by a handsome New Yorker.

When we finished, we took the elevator down. It was a long enough ride, and we were alone, so I was pleased when Max took the opportunity to tug me in close and plant a heated, hot kiss on me. Thank God he was holding me because my legs immediately turned into Jell-O.

When the elevator stopped, Max lifted his head, his green eyes filled with erotic promise. "You're more intoxicating than Guinness."

"And here I thought it was you."

The elevator opened, and we stepped out, walking through the lobby of the building out front.

"Is there something to look at within walking distance from here? Or should I order us a car?" he asked.

I was about to suggest ordering a car and finishing the rest of the night in his room when a gentleman dressed in a suit called his name.

"Mr. Clarke. I've been sent by the hotel to be your driver this evening."

Max looked at me with the same quizzical expression that I looked at him with. Why did the hotel send a car? Then again, hotels were known for taking care of their big spenders.

"I think they're hoping you'll gamble away some of your wealth," I said.

"That could be fun." He leaned closer to me. "But I like sure things better."

All my girly parts flared to life. "I'm a sure bet, slick."

He grinned wickedly.

"There's champagne and other drinks in the back for you. We have a great Vegas by night tour."

"Is there a privacy shield?" Max asked the limo driver.

The man's lips twitched slightly, clearly knowing why Max wanted that, but he pulled his expression together. "Of course, sir."

Max looked at me. "What do you say? Champagne and a Vegas tour by night?"

I nodded, even though I couldn't imagine there'd be anything I'd see that was impressive. Hopefully, with the privacy screen in place, I wouldn't be looking at the scenery. I would be looking into Max's gorgeous green eyes.

Max helped me into the limo and pulled out the champagne, popping the cork and pouring us each a flute.

The driver got into the front seat, and before raising the privacy screen, he asked, "Would you like me to point out attractions on the tour, or should I just drive?"

Max looked at me and said, "Just drive."

I wanted to down the champagne and then rip his clothes off and straddle him in the back seat of the limo. It was crazy how this man affected me. I've been in a limo before, once with another man, but I never wanted to jump him.

Max held up his glass of champagne. "To Vegas by night with the most beautiful woman in Vegas."

A woman could get used to a man speaking to her and looking at her the way Max did to me. *Too bad he's leaving tomorrow.* No, I couldn't think that. Instead, I had to focus on this being a lovely moment in time.

I clicked my glass against his. "And with the sexiest tourist in Vegas."

He sipped the bubbly, his green eyes sparkling at me over his glass. When he pulled it away from his lips, he said, "So, you think I'm sexy?"

I waggled my brows. "I know you are."

We drank our champagne, and then Max leaned over, giving me a kiss.

I felt warm and sensuous, and yet at the same time, my head was foggy and I felt tired. I suppose it wasn't unexpected with half a bottle of wine, a glass of Guinness, and now a glass of champagne. I felt okay getting in the limo, but perhaps the champagne was too much?

Max gave his head a quick shake and pressed his thumb and his forefinger to his closed eyes.

"Are you okay? I asked.

He looked at me and smiled. His eyes were slightly glazed. "Sure. All of a sudden, I feel a little tired. I guess that champagne was one glass too many."

"I feel the same."

He tugged me close, pulling me onto his lap. "Being tired hasn't dimmed my need to taste you."

His lips were on mine, sweet and soft. I could taste the champagne even as the fog seeped deeper, denser into my brain. I was vaguely aware of his erection pressing against the back of my thighs as I sat on his lap.

Max pulled away from the kiss. "Maybe we should go back to the hotel."

I nodded, even though I wasn't sure if he meant we should go back to the hotel because I was very nearly half asleep or to have sex. Either reason worked for me.

As Max reached over to press the intercom button to tell our driver to take us back to the hotel, I rested my head on his shoulder. Then everything went black.

CHAPTER FIVE

Max

Slowly, I awoke from a heavy sleep. It felt like my head was full of cotton. As awareness came to me, I opened my eyes. Amelia was asleep next to me. I was spooned around her luscious body and my arm was draped over her.

I frowned as I noted that she was dressed. In fact, I was too. I scanned my brain for memories of the night before, but my mind was blank. I took her to dinner at the Roarke, ridiculously happy that she'd said yes to the date, even as I told myself that it didn't mean anything more than two people enjoying time together.

Afterward, we were in a limo, and I had visions of fucking her as the lights of Las Vegas drifted by. Had we done that? I couldn't remember. In fact, I couldn't remember anything after pulling her into my lap. I must have drunk more than I thought. I hoped she wasn't mad. Geez, had she been the one to drag me up to bed? How embarrassing.

Maybe I could make up for it now. I ran my hand down her hip, over her thigh, and up again. She had great curves.

I leaned forward, pressing my lips against the back of her neck, nibbling. She shuddered, making me smile.

"I think I drank too much last night," I murmured against her neck.

"Oh?"

"It's the only thing that can explain why we're in bed and still dressed. If I'd had my wits about me last night, we would be waking up naked."

"I was just thinking the same thing."

"Were you now?" I continued to trail kisses along her neck. "How do you feel about sleepy, slow sex in the morning?"

"I feel pretty good about it."

Hallelujah. I tugged the zipper of her dress down and pushed it from her shoulders. I stayed spooned behind her and helped her shimmy out of the dress. I unclasped her bra. She tossed it aside. Lastly, she pushed off her panties.

Was there anything better to wake up to than a warm, soft woman? I tugged her to me, my dick, constrained in my slacks, pressed against her ass. I slid my hand over her belly and down to the curls between her thighs.

"You're not going to join me?" She sighed, softening even more. There was nothing like the powerful feeling of having a woman surrender her pleasure.

My lips were again on her neck. "I will. But first, you." I found her clit and gently rubbed it. It didn't take long before her breath caught, and then her orgasm washed over her. Only then did I undress. Naked, I spooned around her again, lifting her leg to make room for me. I slid inside her body, her pussy quivering and squeezing around my dick.

I took my time, moving slowly and languidly. I kissed her neck and shoulder as I rocked in and out of her. It was sensuous and sweet. I wasn't looking forward to leaving and never having this again. It was an unsettling thought.

I continued to move as if I had all the time in the world until I hit the edge of pleasure. I groaned. "I'm close." I reached over her body, pinching her hard nipple as I rocked faster, deeper, harder.

"Oh!" She cried out as an orgasm flowed through her again. Her body gripped mine, and with one more thrust, I emptied. I held her against me as the last waves of pleasure flowed through us.

When our heart rates settled, I gave her one last kiss on the neck and then rolled onto my back. She rolled onto her back as well.

Still feeling a little bit cloudy but oh, so good, I slid my hands over my face.

An abrupt movement on the bed had me opening my eyes. Amelia stood beside the bed, her eyes angry as she gripped the sheet around her body.

"You're married."

Huh? "No, I'm not."

"You're wearing a wedding ring."

What the hell was she talking about? I looked at my left hand, and sure enough, there was a wedding band. I looked up at her, confused. That's when I noticed the gold band around her finger.

"So are you." Something was wrong here. Maybe it was a dream. A nightmare. A warning about why I couldn't let my emotions get tangled up with her.

"What?"

"You've got a ring too." I pointed to her hand.

Her head jerked down, looking at her left hand.

For a moment, she looked as confused as I felt.

"Oh, my God." She turned and sank onto the bed as if something dawned on her.

"Care to fill me in?" Something about this wasn't right. What had she done?

She shook her head. "I've become a Las Vegas cliché."

All this was starting to feel like déjà vu. I was about to be made a fool. I rose from the bed, grabbing my underwear and pants and slipping them on. "What does that mean?"

"We must have gotten drunk-married last night."

My hands stilled on my belt buckle as my gaze jerked to her. "What?"

"It's the only thing that explains this."

I shook my head, finishing with my belt. "That doesn't explain this. First of all, no one in their right mind would marry two people who were incoherently drunk."

She arched a brow. "We're in Las Vegas, Max."

"Even so, there would have to be paperwork, right? A marriage license. A marriage certificate."

I pulled the ring from my finger and tossed it on the pillow. Doing so made me feel like a jerk.

Amelia took my lead, pulling her ring from her finger. She leaned over to set it on the side table, stopping as she saw papers. She scooted closer to the side table and picked them up, studying them. "Oh, God."

"What?" I rounded the bed, buttoning my shirt.

She held the papers up. "Marriage license and certificate."

No fucking way. I snatched the papers out of her hand. I scanned them, but I was too out of sorts to decipher the words. All I could think was, *so this was the joke*. I looked at her, so disappointed. Sure, I didn't see a future for us, but I'd really thought she was different.

"Is this some sort of joke?" I tossed the papers on the bed.

Amelia's eyes flared with heat. She stood, gripping the sheet around her tighter. "You think I did this?"

"The proof is in the papers, sweetheart."

Her mouth gaped, and she stared at me like I'd grown a horn, and then said angrily, "Your signature's on there as well, slick."

What? I reached over, picking up the papers again, looking at the signature line. For a moment, I stood, utterly confused. She was right. That was my signature, or at least what it would look like if I were drunk.

My anger lessened, and I sank down onto the bed. I was a party to this. I couldn't figure out how, but it was clear that I'd been a part of what we'd done.

Now I needed to undo it. "We'll be able to get this annulled."

"Being drunk doesn't constitute being incapacitated to get an annulment in Las Vegas."

Annoyance flared as I again wondered if this was some sort of joke. "Sounds like you have experience with this."

"This is Vegas, Max. I know about gambling and showgirls, but that doesn't mean I gamble and dance."

I set the paper on the bed and scraped my hand over my face again. She seemed to be as annoyed as me. I wasn't helping by accusing her.

It was strange that being blackout drunk didn't constitute grounds for annulment. It meant we couldn't consent to the marriage. So what would constitute grounds for an annulment? Not being able to understand what I was signing would meet the requirements, right? God. That meant I'd need to tell Amelia and a judge about my reading challenges. I wasn't ashamed, but still, I didn't need people knowing my challenges.

In this case, I didn't have a choice. "Not being able to read or understand what I was signing would be a reason to grant an annulment, wouldn't it?"

"I suppose, but I don't remember reading or signing it either, and I'm not so sure that being too drunk to read and sign will work."

I turned to look at her, wishing I didn't have to tell her this. "I have dyslexia. It's often hard enough to read legal papers when I'm sober. I can't imagine that I could do it drunk."

She sat on the bed next to me.

It was then I remembered I had a flight to New York today. I looked at my watch. "Fuck. I don't have a lot of time before I need to catch my flight." Except I couldn't leave now. I had to take care of this. "I guess I could take a later flight. I can move my schedule around."

"I'm not sure how to go about this in the first place. Why don't you let me research and get whatever paperwork we need, and once it's together, I can let you know? Maybe we can do this long distance and you don't need to return to Las Vegas."

I hate how relieved I felt. It was cowardly and unfair to put this on her. "But if I do need to be here, I can come."

I had never been one to wear my feelings on my sleeve. My brother was an open book when it came to feelings, even if he wasn't expressing them verbally. One look at him and I knew exactly what he was feeling. Perhaps he could do the same with me since we grew up together and were twins, but it wasn't because I was as open and expressive as he was. When it came to my feelings, I kept them to myself. A shrink could probably figure out why, but mostly, I just thought they were no one's business. Especially the bad ones where people might take pity on me. Or the ones that made me vulnerable, giving somebody access to a part of me they could break.

While I kept my feelings to myself, I could almost always determine what they were. But as I sat in the first-class seat on my flight back to New York, I couldn't figure out what the hell I was feeling. Was I a fucking idiot? I mean, who in reality ended up accidentally married in Vegas? Sure, there were tons of people who got married on a whim and discovered the next day that it was a mistake, but they'd still known they got married. How could I have done it and have no memory of it? The only thing that made any sense to me was either I drank too much or I was drugged and somehow coerced into it. If that was the case, that would mean that Amelia had to be a part of it. But to what end? She hadn't asked me for anything, and in fact, seemed just as eager to get unhitched.

But among those feelings of stupidity and suspicion, there were other feelings. Like guilt for leaving Amelia to fix an issue that I was a part of. Disappointment that I wouldn't see her again unless, of course, we had to go to court together.

Somewhere over the Mississippi, I realized that it was the feelings of disappointment that were really fucking me up. I really didn't like the idea that I wasn't going to see Amelia again.

By the time I arrived in New York and made it to my apartment, the practical adult side of me had finally won over. My time with Amelia was awesome. I would remember it for a long time to come. But these feelings I had for her, whatever they were, weren't love, and the way we were together wasn't sustainable. It was like going to an amusement park and riding all the best rides. You could do it for a day, but you couldn't live there day after day.

When I went to bed that night, I had finally understood what it meant when they said what happens in Vegas stays in Vegas because that was how I was thinking about Amelia. It was a wild and raucous time that I would never forget, but now I was home and in the real world.

CHAPTER SIX

Amelia

I should have said no to Max's idea of another date yesterday at breakfast. If I had, we wouldn't be in this predicament. Funny how my hesitation at the time was due to the fact that I liked Max a lot but wouldn't be able to commit to anything. As it turned out, my worry should have been accidentally ending up married. But what was done was done. Going back over what I should have done wasn't going to fix what I did.

I turned my attention back to my computer where I was supposed to be working. Unfortunately, I couldn't stop thinking about my predicament and what Max and I were going to do about it. When I arrived home after he left for his flight, I began the research for the annulment, and while the process was straightforward, it wasn't without its complications.

At first, I thought it would be easy enough when I saw that if the other party didn't show up for the annulment hearing, the judge would automatically grant it. I could file, and if Max didn't come, it would be done. The only problem was that I needed to meet one of the grounds for annulment. The closest was "want of understanding", which basically meant I didn't know what I was doing. But I wasn't sure drunkenness counted. After all, people who got drunk married usually did it because it sounded fun at the time. Clearly, that suggested knowing what was going on.

But I had no clue what happened. The last thing I could remember was sitting in Max's lap in the back of the limo. To have gotten married, we would've had to have gone to the County Clerk's office to get a license, and then to a chapel to get married. Surely, I would've remembered doing either of those two things. While I'd never blacked out before, what else could it have come from except drinking too much? There was no other explanation.

Thinking about it, how did Max and I get from the limo to the bed? Under normal circumstances, I might have thought Max drugged me, but for one, he didn't need to do that to get lucky with me, and he knew it. And two, he seemed as shocked as I was to discover we were married. In fact, he practically accused me of duping him into marriage. So, what the hell happened last night?

Since I didn't think I had the grounds to say I was incapacitated simply from drinking too much, Max would have to be the one to file the papers. He said he had dyslexia, and being drunk would have made it impossible for him to read and understand what he was signing. That gave him better cause to claim a want of understanding than I had. I wasn't sure the judge would accept that, but it was worth a try if Max was willing to file the papers instead of me.

Researching the filing process, it looked like he could obtain and fill out the papers online, but he'd need to be here to file them unless, of course, he got a local lawyer. But Max and I agreed that the fewer people who knew about this, the better. Lawyers were bound by attorney-client privilege, but still, I didn't think either of us wanted to risk it. God, if James found out, he'd probably laugh his ass off.

Continuing to read through the annulment information, I learned that once the papers were submitted and the other party was served, it was just a matter of waiting for the court date. According to this website, it would be sometime within ninety days. Ninety days? That could put us to February. Getting a marriage annulled on Valentine's Day. How depressing was that?

Thanksgiving and Christmas were coming, and while my family wasn't big on the holidays, we at least got together for dinner. How was I going to face my family with this hanging over my head? My father was a shrewd man who knew how to read people like no one else. I wasn't sure I had a good enough poker face to keep him from noticing that something was up with me. And of all the people who could never know about this marriage, my father was top of the list. Dammit, I should have said no to the second date.

Unable to continue to work on it, I pushed this marriage and annulment business to the side to focus on my clients.

When I closed up business for the night, I left my home office and headed to the kitchen, pulling out a bottle of white wine. For a minute, I second-guessed whether I should have any wine or alcohol considering what happened last night. It still made no sense to me how I could have blacked out like that. Yes, I'd had several glasses of wine and that Guinness, so I was feeling warm and loose, but I wasn't staggering drunk. Could that one glass of champagne really have tipped me that far over the edge?

"What the hell. I'm home." I poured myself an ample glass of wine and went to sit at my kitchen table to psych myself up for contacting Max. Only then did I realize two things. One, it was after nine o'clock there. Was that too late to call?

The second issue was that I didn't have his number. I'd been the most intimate with a man that one could be, but I didn't have his phone number. What did that say about me?

I pulled out my phone and did a quick search online for his number, but deep down, I knew I wouldn't be able to find it. Someone like Max Clarke didn't have his private number on display for anyone and everyone to call. The only answer was to call him at work tomorrow. He'd probably hate that because the mistake in Las Vegas would be intruding into his work life in New York, but what other choice did I have?

There was a knock on my door, and my heart leapt in my chest as I imagined Max on the other side of it.

Ugh! Why would I think that? It was another reminder that I really should've said no to that second date.

I went to the front door and opened it.

"Hey, little sis." James's head tilted to look behind me. "Am I interrupting?"

I stepped aside and opened the door. "Nope. I'm here all alone."

He stepped in looking at the wine I still held in my hand. I was clutching it like a lifeline.

"There's something about drinking by yourself that isn't good."

"Well, I'll pour you a glass and then I won't be drinking by myself."

He grinned. "I thought you would never offer."

He followed me to the kitchen, where I got another glass and the wine out of the refrigerator.

"So, how did your date go last night?" he asked, leaning against the counter.

I stilled mid-pour of the wine. "Why? What did you hear?" God. Had I made a fool of myself during the forgotten part of the night?

When he didn't say anything, I glanced over my shoulder, my panic rising.

His head tilted to the side and his eyes narrowed in question. "That sounds bad. What did you do that you think I heard about your date?"

Okay, so maybe he didn't hear anything. I finished pouring his wine and handed him the glass. "It was fine. I just thought maybe Dad told you something." I hoped he bought that excuse.

"Why would he say anything?"

I shrugged, unable to come up with a good answer to that.

"Besides, Dad went out of town last night."

"Where to?" I always liked it when my dad was out of town because I felt like I could move through life not wondering if he was one step behind me.

"Who the hell knows? You know how he is. He's off with his cronies, gambling or carousing or whatever."

God, I hoped he hadn't gone to Atlantic City. That was way too close to New York City for my comfort.

"I think he went with Georgie, so they're probably on some yacht off the coast of Catalina or something." James sipped his wine.

I breathed out a sigh of relief. I hoped that was true. "Let's sit in the living room." I led the way.

My brother joined me, making himself comfortable on my couch. I sat in the wingback chair across from him.

"So. Tell me about the date," he said.

"Why are you so interested in my love life all of a sudden?" I wanted to talk about anything else but my date with Max.

"Hmm, so it's love?"

I growled in frustration. "No, it's not."

He grinned. "You doth protest too much."

I took a long gulp of my wine, resisting the urge to throw my glass at him. I had to believe he was just teasing me like big brothers did and that he didn't know anything specific.

Then again, I wished he did know something. Maybe he would've been able to fill in the blanks from last night.

"You're not one of those dumb shmucks who accidentally ended up married, are you?" He laughed.

I finished the rest of my wine, hoping my face didn't give away the truth. At the same time, I wished I could tell him. I trusted James and knew he would help me, but I swore to Max that I wouldn't say anything, so I kept mum.

"What did you do last night?" I asked, hoping to change the subject or at least take the spotlight off me.

"Nothing as interesting as you, I bet. Come on, what did you guys do?"

"He took me to the Roarke, and then we had a nice tour of the city." All that was true. Technically, I wasn't leaving anything out because I didn't remember getting a marriage license or getting married.

"The Roarke is nice, isn't it? I took Kaley there once."

Kaley was his latest love interest who had apparently stolen from him.

He shrugged, his jovial expression falling. "The food was good, so there was at least that."

I didn't want to spend a lot of time talking about our personal lives, so I said, "Are you hungry? Maybe we could order some take-out."

His expression perked up. "Thai? It seems like forever since I've had Thai food."

I nodded. "Thai food it is."

For the rest of the evening, we were able to avoid discussions about Kaley and Max. When he left, I got ready for bed, hoping that I'd be able to fall right to sleep. Of course, that didn't happen. Thoughts of Max and our annulment crowded my brain.

It seemed like I had just fallen asleep when my alarm went off at five in the morning. I didn't normally get up that early, but five in the morning out here was eight in the morning in New York, and I figured it was best to call Max first thing in the morning.

After getting coffee, I sat at the dining table and dialed Max's office number. An efficient sounding woman picked up the line in New York.

"Is Max Clarke in, please?"

"He's not in yet today. Can I take a message?"

Crap. Should I leave a message? Maybe I should just try again later. But if I kept calling back, that might look suspicious too.

"My name is Amelia Dunsmore, with Dunsmore Media Management Services. I'm following up on a discussion we had while he was here in Las Vegas."

I practically patted myself on the back. No one would be suspicious of a business call. And it would make sense that Max would consult a social media marketing agency while entering a new market, right?

"Is there a number he should call?"

I rattled off my number, and she assured me that he would get the message. I thanked her then hung up and blew out a breath. For a moment, I tried to imagine him getting the message. Would he smile at seeing my name because he remembered the good times we had?

Or would it irritate him because the issue of our marriage hung over him? I supposed I'd find out when he called me back.

While I waited, I went to work on my own business, doing my best to push Max and my marital status out of my mind.

CHAPTER SEVEN

Max

I woke up the morning after returning from Las Vegas hoping that it had all been a dream, or maybe a nightmare. Accidentally getting married in Las Vegas was something Sam would do. Or maybe my sister, Vivie.

Then again, it was hard to regret the time I spent with Amelia prior to waking up married. I couldn't articulate what it was about her, but whatever it was, it awakened something inside me. For a moment, I pondered whether I was missing out by not allowing myself to develop a relationship with a woman. But then I remembered Candace in high school cheating on me with a jock and Lauren, my college sweetheart, making fun of the adaptations due to my dyslexia that I needed in the classroom at college to be able to do well academically. And now, blacking out and waking up drunk married to Amelia. I'd been rip-roaring drunk a time or two in my life, but I couldn't ever remember blacking out. Of course, that was the issue. For all I knew, I had forgotten things while drunk. Still, I'd always been able to remember at least bits and pieces of the night before. But everything after the limo drive, up until waking up the next morning beside Amelia, was a complete blank.

I got out of bed, hit the shower, and dressed. I gathered the clothes to go to the dry cleaner, checking to empty the pockets. I pulled out the wedding band. When Amelia had gone to get dressed, I found it on the bed where I'd tossed it like it was the plague. I was trying to figure out what to do with it when she emerged. It felt rude to throw it out even though she didn't want to be married either. It seemed like it might be construed as I was tossing her out, and that wasn't the case. Yes, our affair was over, but still. Ah, hell. I don't know what I was thinking. All I knew was that I shoved it in my pocket.

Once I'd taken care of my clothes for the dry cleaning service to pick up, I headed out. Instead of heading straight to the office. I went by my parents' house. With Thanksgiving just around the corner, I needed to check in with Mom to see what, if anything, she wanted me to do.

When I got to the house, I found my mom in the sunroom drinking a cup of coffee and reviewing something on her tablet. My mom had been a career woman when we were growing up, but once Vivie was born, she switched to working part-time and mostly from home. When Vivie was old enough that she could go back to a regular office schedule, she'd been so used to working from home that she decided to stay there. Today, working from home was no big deal, but she was a pioneer, one of the early work-at-home moms.

Her smile brightened when she saw me. "Oh, hey. You just missed your dad." She rose from her chair and gave me a hug. "How are things out west?"

"Well, an earthquake hasn't sunk it into the ocean yet."

She laughed. "How about I get you some coffee? You can tell me how Sam is doing."

I didn't know how Sam was doing. I planned to stick with the no news is good news theory.

My mom returned to the sunroom having refilled her cup and getting one for me. I sat in one of the wicker chairs while she took her regular seat in a rocking chair. She got the rocker five years ago when

Sam had come home after graduating from college with his ex-girl-friend, Sandra, and a baby. All was not as it seemed, but Mom and Dad took in Sam's ex and the baby as part of the family. Recently, the two of them had moved to Boston, and I imagined my mom missed them. Especially little Chelsea. Hopefully, things between Sam and Kate would work out and they'd be able to give Mom and Dad a real grandchild. Hell knew I wasn't gonna give them one. I had a flash of the other morning waking up next to Amelia and making slow, slow love her. Did I use a condom?

"Max?" My mom shook me out of my thoughts.

"Yes?"

"How is Sam doing?"

I shrugged. "Fine, as far as I know."

She arched a brow, while at the same time, her eyes narrowed. It was the look she gave us when she didn't believe us.

I held my hand up in surrender. "I swear to God. He seemed perfectly fine the last time I saw him." That was true. He had gained a second or third . . . maybe it was a fourth wind in his pursuit of Kate. The fact that Mom didn't know about Kate being back in his life meant he hadn't told her, and I was a good enough brother not to be the one to spill the beans.

"Do you think he'll come home for Thanksgiving?"

"I don't see why not." I suppose if things were going well between him and Kate, maybe he'd stay behind and have Thanksgiving with her family. But Kate was so resistant to him, even if she was going to give him another chance, it seemed like a holiday family meal would be too much, too soon for her.

"You don't think he's going to stay out there to live forever, do you?" she asked.

I couldn't answer that. If he and Kate did reunite, she had a business out there. He was building a business out there. It seemed unlikely that he would move back to New York.

"I don't know, Mom. That's not the plan, no." That was true too. Our goal had been to spend time at the new location to get it built and running, but then hiring a great staff to keep it going with a few trips a year out to check on things. Of course, if Sam did stay out in Los Angeles, that could be good because it wasn't far from Las Vegas, which means he could check on both locations. Then I'd have no reason to go back there.

An image of Amelia lying underneath me, all that wild red hair fanned over a pillow, her cheeks flush and her lips red and ripe, flashed in my mind. My dick twitched in my pants. I crossed my leg, not needing my mother to see my reaction to thoughts of Amelia. But because I did think of her, I wondered how things were going with the annulment. I felt bad leaving her to take care of it herself. Maybe I should call her. Then it occurred to me that I didn't get her number. I supposed it wouldn't be too hard to find. I just need to look up her business.

I decided it was time to change the subject. "When is Vivie going to be home?"

My sister had graduated from college back in June, and she was taking a gap year traveling before settling into a job. What that job would be, no one, including Vivie, knew.

"She'll be here for Thanksgiving as well. And you'll be here too, right?"

"Yes, Mother."

Her expression was asking me to sympathize with her. "Someday, when you have children and they all grow up and leave you, you'll know how I feel."

I was smart enough not to tell my mother that I didn't plan to have children.

I visited with my mom for a little longer and then headed out to the office. It was around ten when I finally entered the building. Although I'd been gone for a while, everything looked the same. Everyone was exactly where they should be, doing exactly what they should be doing.

I headed to my office, stopping by my administrative assistant's desk. Mrs. Critzer was a retired Army officer, and she ran my office like I imagined she ran her troops. It was awesome except for the times when she treated me like I was one of her troops instead of her boss.

"You had several calls this morning," she said, handing me a stack of message papers. "There was an incident at the Hamptons club last night. The police were called, but Mark says everything is handled. He says he's emailed you a report."

Owning an establishment that served copious amounts of booze always ran the risk of bar fights and other activities that led to the police showing up. Interestingly enough, the Hamptons club held the record for the most police calls even out of the clubs here in Manhattan. Usually, they were around college breaks. "Are college kids off for Thanksgiving yet?"

She shrugged. "I don't know. I haven't had a kid in college in ten years."

I nodded, taking my messages into my office. I tossed the messages on my desk as I took off my coat and hung it on the back of my chair. I sat down, turning on my computer, and then thumbed through the messages. Most of them were from alcohol distributors, and one was from the manager of one of the Manhattan clubs. The last one stopped me in my tracks. *Amelia Dunsmore.* Her phone number. *Following up on a discussion in Las Vegas.*

I studied the message, having one of those weird feelings that I couldn't quite define. Why was she tying me up in knots? It had to be because of this marriage hanging over my head. As I studied the message, it occurred to me that the information she gave suggested that it was a business call. I breathed out a sigh of relief. It was stupid of me not to give her my direct number before I left. It was a testament to how freaked out I was at waking up married with no memory of it.

I needed to call her, but doing it here in the office wouldn't be wise. I folded the paper and stuck it into the pocket of my slacks. I'd call her later tonight. I set about getting to work, but the paper in my pocket continued to call at me. It made getting anything done nearly impossible.

I left a little early and headed out to visit the clubs in Manhattan.

Sam and I trusted the people who worked for us, but that didn't mean we didn't show up unannounced every now and then just to make sure everything was running well.

When I arrived back at my apartment, I poured myself several fingers of bourbon and took the glass out onto the terrace. I pulled Amelia's number from my pocket and studied it. Our time together was supposed to be over and done with. But as I studied the paper and got ready to dial her number, I had to admit, I was glad for an excuse to call her. It was a dangerous feeling, and if I could have, I would have resisted it and not called her. But I figured if she took the effort to seek me out and leave me a message, perhaps there was something important she needed to tell me. Maybe, if I was lucky, she would say we weren't really married, after all. Someone played a practical joke on us or something. I could totally see Sam doing something like that. Of course, Sam would've had to have known I was in Las Vegas and had met Amelia. That seemed unlikely because he was one hundred and ten percent focused on Kate.

I dialed her number, glancing at my watch to figure out what time it was in Las Vegas. It was just about seven here, which meant it was nearly four there. Hopefully, I wasn't interrupting a meeting.

"Max?"

The sound of her voice floated through my chest. It reminded me of the time I heard her laugh. "Yes, it's me. I'm sorry I wasn't around to get your call earlier."

"I'm sorry I had to call you at work. I hope they think you're getting a consultation for social media services."

It pleased me that she was looking out for me, and at the same time, there was a wrongness to keeping her a secret. I wasn't embarrassed by her, and despite how it might have looked, our time together wasn't sordid. The problem was the accidental marriage.

"I think that's exactly how my assistant took it. Is everything okay?"

She let out a long sigh, which told me that no one had played a practical joke on us. We were really married. She went on to explain the process of an annulment and how it might be better if I filed since

62

I had a stronger reason for saying I was incapable of entering into a marriage agreement. I'd been fortunate, as a kid having dyslexia, to have had supportive parents who advocated for me in school. Plus, my father had it as well, and he helped me develop coping skills and adaptations so I could be successful. But that didn't mean that I didn't sometimes feel cursed by it. Dyslexia is a processing disorder, not an intellectual one, but people often believe that a person who had difficulty reading couldn't be smart. Once I became an adult, I did everything I could to keep anyone I worked with from knowing I had dyslexia. The growth of technology made this much easier because most businessmen I knew dictated notes and recorded meetings, all things I did when I was in school and now in my career. It looked like for once, having dyslexia was going to be helpful, although it still made me look stupid. I mean, seriously, who accidentally got married and then didn't remember it?

"I guess that means I need to return to Las Vegas." The idea of that wasn't entirely unpleasant. Oh, sure. My mind was a little bit annoyed by it, but all my body could think about was being with Amelia again.

"I'm sorry, Max. I know that's not what you wanted to hear."

"Don't be sorry. This predicament is as much my fault. It was wrong of me to put all this on you to deal with in the first place. I'm sorry for that."

The line was quiet for a moment. "Even with all this, Max, I don't regret spending time with you."

To be honest, I didn't regret our time together either, but I couldn't admit that to her. These types of words carried more meaning than what we'd agreed to.

Still, I'd be a jerk by not saying anything. "I had a really nice time with you too, Amelia."

She was quiet for a couple more seconds. Finally, she said, "I guess you will let me know when you can come to Las Vegas?" Her words signaled the end of our call, and for a moment, I panicked because I wasn't ready to stop talking to her.

But I couldn't find a good reason to stay on the call, so I said, "It probably won't be until after Thanksgiving. In fact, I'll tell my brother that I'm going to return to him to check on the club's progress in Los Angeles after Thanksgiving. Then I'll be able to hop over to Las Vegas to meet with you and file whatever I need to file."

"Okay, that sounds good. I'll talk to you after Thanksgiving."

"Okay."

There was another long pause. "Have a nice Thanksgiving, Max."

"You too, Amelia."

When I hung up, I kicked myself for being such a blithering and insensitive idiot.

I looked at my calendar, noting that Thanksgiving was just over a week away. That meant in just over a week, I'd be seeing Amelia again. How was it that I could both be excited and dread it at the same time?

CHAPTER EIGHT

Amelia

When I saw Max's name pop up on my caller ID this afternoon, happiness filled my chest. There was no reason for that to happen. Our little tryst was over, and now we just had this hassle of an unexpected marriage that we needed to get annulled. But when I eagerly poked the answer button, I had to admit that I was dying to hear his voice again.

Unfortunately, the call was awkward. The moment we had met at the airport, we had clicked and conversed easily, but this call wasn't anything like that. I supposed that was a good thing because Max and I were done, even if somewhere inside me, I didn't want us to be. At least he hadn't sounded angry or irritated. But it was clear that he still didn't want anyone to know about us and our situation. He wanted our marriage annulled, but he also didn't want to raise any eyebrows by immediately flying out to take care of it. His trip west would be under the guise of meeting with his brother about their club in Los Angeles.

Honestly, I didn't much like feeling that I was a sordid secret. Then again, I didn't really want people to know what happened, either. I was still baffled by how our marriage came about. It was so odd. Quite frankly, it was suspicious that we both had no memory of the night. How had it all played out? It wasn't like we could stumble into a chapel and get married. We would've had to have gone to the County Clerk's office and gotten a license first. While Las Vegas made it easy to get married quickly, I couldn't imagine they would give a marriage license to two people who were so out of it that they wouldn't remember it the next morning, right? Furthermore, chapels weren't supposed to marry intoxicated couples.

But even without the marriage, having no memory between the limo and waking up the next morning was disconcerting. How did we get into the clerk's office and fill out an application?

I pulled out the paperwork that I had put into my desk to study it. It looked like a drunk version of my handwriting.

I sighed. It didn't matter how it happened, only that it did happen. Clearly, we had gotten a license because I was staring at it. How else would we have gotten it or the marriage certificate? There was no other explanation than we got drunk-married.

I put the papers back in the drawer under the ring I'd woken up wearing. I'd looked for Max's but didn't find it. Either he tossed it or took it with him. I couldn't imagine him doing the latter.

It occurred to me that our limo driver would be able to give me all the answers to that night. I wondered if he'd told his colleagues about it. Probably not. Crazy marriages happened every day in Vegas. There was nothing interesting about it to talk about.

I scanned the cobwebs in my brain of that night to remember who he was. I hadn't caught his name. He'd said that the hotel had sent him as a courtesy to Max. Hotels could be very generous to guests that they considered to be whales, the term they used for rich big spenders.

I wondered if the hotel would give me the name of the driver they sent. Probably not. Maybe they'd give it to his secretary. I could call pretending to work for him.

I did a search on my computer to find the number for the

concierge at Max's hotel. I wasn't sure if they were the ones that sent the car, but perhaps they could tell me who I would need to talk to.

I dialed the number, and when the woman answered, I said, "Hello. I'm calling from Max Clarke's office. He was a guest of yours for a couple of days recently."

"Yes, we remember Mr. Clarke."

That was a good sign. "On Mr. Clark's last night, the hotel sent a limousine and a driver to give him a tour of the city. He really enjoyed the ride and didn't feel like he'd adequately thanked the driver. I was hoping you could give me his name as Mr. Clarke would like to formally thank him."

"Hmm. We don't normally send a limousine, but let me check."

I waited as she looked at whatever she needed to refer to. A few moments later, she said, "No, I don't see a request for a limo from Mr. Clarke on the last night of his stay."

"Oh, no, he didn't order it. He was told it was sent courtesy of the hotel."

"Really?"

Her surprise at that wasn't a good sign.

"We don't normally do that."

Thinking she was just referring to the concierge desk, I asked, "Who at the hotel would do something like that to take care of your VIP guests?"

"I suppose you could talk to Guest Relations. They're usually the ones who organize special packages for our most important guests. I've never heard of them sending a car out for someone on a whim, but who knows?" She gave me the number for guest relations.

It hadn't occurred to me that the hotel hadn't sent the car, but her response had me wondering. But if the hotel didn't send the car, then who did, and why?

I called Guest Relations, but I got an answering machine and didn't feel comfortable leaving a message. I hung up, deciding I would try again later.

The concierge's answer to my question was unsettling, but in working through the events of the night, she must've been right and

Guest Relations was looking out to make sure Max had a good time and hopefully would spend some of his fortune in their casino. There really was no other explanation.

Accepting that the hotel had to have sent the car, the only thing left to do was to have Guest Services tell me who the driver was so Max and I could figure out what happened. Although, knowing that didn't matter in the scheme of things. We were still married and needing an annulment. Knowing how we got into this predicament wouldn't change that. Still, I wanted to know about the missing hours of my life. It was unsettling not to remember getting married.

After that, my evening progressed as usual. I finished up some client work, answered a few emails to my staff, and then quit for the evening. I scrambled myself a few eggs with a piece of toast, poured myself a glass of wine, then plopped down in front of the TV to catch up on a baking show. I was three episodes behind, and by the time I finished all three, it was time for bed.

The next day, I went about my work as usual, but at eleven, I took a break to call the hotel again, and again, I pretended I was Max's secretary, asking who had been driving the car they sent the other night. Unfortunately, she told me she wasn't able to give me guest information. I hung up feeling frustrated.

Maybe I should let it go, but it was really bugging me that I couldn't remember the night. I waited until the afternoon to call back, and this time, I did something that I never, ever liked to do and that was use my name, or more exactly, my relation to my father, to get information. For one thing, it felt a little shady. Dropping names and acting important were the type of things my father did. Plus, I didn't always like to be associated with my father. In fact, I had spent a lot of my adult life trying to distance myself from him. I doubt it ever worked because my father was very well known in Las Vegas. But still, I liked to keep a quiet profile when it came to admitting I was related to him. With that said, because he was well-known and somewhat feared, I figured it might work to get me the answer I needed.

I called again and tried to change my voice so if the same person picked up, she wouldn't know it was me again.

"Hello, this is Amelia Dunsmore." I waited to see if the person on the other end would make the connection between my last name and my father's.

"Ms. Dunsmore. How can I help you?" Her tone told me she did.

"The other night, I was with a client at the Roarke, and a limo was sent to pick us up. I was hoping you would be able to tell me the name of the driver."

"I'm not sure how we would know that. Did you check with our concierge?"

"I did. The driver told us that the hotel had sent him. He made it sound like you were taking care of a VIP guest. Isn't that something Guest Relations would do?"

The woman made a *hmm* sound and was quiet, presumably looking up information about Max.

A few moments later, she said, "I don't see us sending a limo to Mr. Clarke at the Roarke. Although we made several offers of VIP options, he didn't take advantage of any of them."

Okay, that was weird. "Are you sure? The driver was clear that he was sent by the hotel."

"Well, if we sent it, it wasn't registered in our system. To be honest, it's not something we would just do. Normally, guests would ask us or take us up on a package we offered. We don't normally send out cars without being asked."

I liked it better when I didn't know what was going on and I could pretend that the only thing that made sense was that the hotel had sent the car and that Max and I got drunk-married. But the concierge and Guest Services were both telling me they didn't send the car. If it wasn't them, who was it?

I got off the phone trying to make sense of it all. That's when I remembered that both Max and I couldn't remember anything from being in the limo up until the time we woke up the next morning. That meant the driver had to have been the culprit. But why would he want us to get married? How would he know that we would drink enough to black out? How could he arrange for the marriage? That was crazy.

So it had to be that Max and I had asked him to take us to the County Clerk and to a chapel, but that made no sense either. None of it made sense unless the driver was after something else.

I immediately grabbed my purse and rummaged in it to find my wallet. Going through it, I found my ID and all my credit cards. All my cash was still there. But that didn't mean he didn't copy my information.

I went online, logging into my bank to see if there were any weird purchases. Everything looked normal, but not wanting to take any chances, I called the bank and talked to their customer service about my concern that my account had been compromised. He told me he'd cancel my debit card and send me a new one. Then he recommended that I call my credit card companies to cancel the cards and have new ones sent. That was such a pain in the ass, but it had to be done.

I needed to let Max know. I wanted to call him, but that was just because I wanted to hear his voice. I reminded myself that it wasn't a good idea to keep longing for him. So instead, I sent him a quick text telling him I was concerned that my bank information had been stolen and I wanted to check to make sure his hadn't either. Quick and to the point.

Then I remembered his dyslexia and I wondered if maybe I should call instead. And then I had to think about what if he did call me back or text me back asking why I thought my information was stolen? Should I tell him that the hotel denied sending a car to pick us up? All of this was just too weird. The only thing that made sense was that the driver was telling the truth and whoever I talked to at the hotel either didn't know or didn't want to tell me because I wasn't the guest. That wasn't what she said, but then again, she knew who I was related to, so perhaps it was safer for her to deny sending a car than to tell me to mind my own business.

I tossed my phone on my desk and rubbed my hands over my face. I was driving myself crazy with all this. It didn't really matter who sent the car or who the driver was. It didn't change the fact that I was married to Max, and as soon as possible, he was going to file to annul our marriage.

CHAPTER NINE

Max

I downloaded the documents for an annulment, of which there were many, and went through them. Eventually, I gave up. My excuse was that I was still tired from jet lag and settling back into my routine. Several days later, the documents were still incomplete on my computer. Reading always took effort, but legal documents were some of the most difficult reading. For one, the print was usually small, and two, legalese always seemed like a bunch of words strung together without much consideration on whether or not they made sense to someone who wasn't a lawyer. Besides, what was the hurry to fill out the documents? I wouldn't be able to file them until after Thanksgiving, anyway.

I refocused on my business. It reminded me that I needed to talk to Sam and let him know I was coming out after Thanksgiving. I scheduled a video call for the two of us.

When his face came on the screen, I was relieved to see it wasn't filled with depression.

"How are things out there in California?" I asked him.

"Looking up."

I could tell he wanted to be excited about whatever gains he'd made with Kate but was also being cautious. He knew Kate was like a skittish cat, and any little thing might send her running. In Kate's case, she might scratch him first and then run off.

"I want her to come to Thanksgiving."

I arched a brow. It seemed like that should be good news, and yet I could still hear the uncertainty in his voice.

"Wouldn't throwing her into a family gathering across the country be a little too much, too soon?"

"Five years ago, I planned to spend my life with this woman, and she'd never met you, Vivie, or Mom and Dad. Plus, except for her brother, she doesn't really have a family. At least not like ours. I want her to know what that's like to have a close-knit, loving family."

I smirked. "It sounds like you don't think you're enough and you need to have your family seal the deal."

"Fuck you, Max." But he said it with humor.

I laughed. "So aside from Project Win Kate Back, how are things going on the business front?"

The quick glance away told me that he hadn't thought much of the whole reason he'd gone out there in the first place, to find and build a club. *This is why relationships are a problem. They distract one from the things they need to focus on.*

"It's coming along. You know I had to give up on the club we bought because it was too close to Kate's."

You see what I mean? We had bought a club, but now because it upset Kate, we couldn't build there anymore. I knew it wouldn't go to waste. We'd find a way to make use of it, but it set us back.

"Do you have other locations?" I asked.

"I've got the realtor lining some up."

I got the feeling he was just saying what I wanted to hear. "I'm planning to come out with you after Thanksgiving and see how things are going."

His eyes narrowed and darkened. "You don't trust me?"

I narrowed my eyes at him. "Is there some reason that I, as your partner, shouldn't see what's going on?"

He stared at me through the video conference as if he was trying to figure out whether I had ulterior motives. I did my best to maintain a serious expression so he wouldn't figure out why I really needed to come west. Of course, there would be no way for him to know that it was to get an annulment. He didn't even know I'd been in Las Vegas for an extra two days. I'd planned to tell him, but after everything that happened with Amelia, and now this crazy marriage, I figured I'd go back to the old plan and wait until we finished the club in Los Angeles before starting one in Las Vegas. I recognized the irony in that I was letting a woman dictate my business actions.

"I don't have any problem with your coming in and checking up on me."

I rolled my eyes. "All the other clubs we've done together side-by-side. I'd just like to be a part of it."

I hadn't set out to guilt trip him, but when his expression morphed from annoyance to guilt, it was a nice side effect.

"Yeah, okay. I get it."

We discussed other business items and then hung up. As happy as I was that I was going to go to Las Vegas with no one knowing what I was doing, it didn't mean I didn't feel guilty too. Sam and I were close, and I hated keeping this information from him, even though he'd probably laugh his ass off and then offer support. I suppose it was embarrassment or my pride that had me wanting to keep my dealings with Amelia secret, but that came with guilt as well. It made it seem like Amelia was unworthy of recognition, which wasn't the case. Had I not woken up married, I probably would've told Sam about meeting her when I told him about staying the extra days in Las Vegas. It wasn't my tryst with Amelia that I wanted to keep a secret. It was the fact that I became a cliché. I was one of those numb nuts who got wasted and married in Las Vegas.

I finished my work for the day and then headed over to my parents' house for dinner since Vivie had arrived home. Vivie was like a spark plug, always firing, but in a fun, jovial way. Maybe a better description was that she was like bubbles. Effervescent.

73

When I walked into the house, she launched herself into my arms. "Sam, my favorite brother, I'm so happy to see you."

I set her down with a glare.

She smirked up at me. "Oops. You're Max, aren't you?"

"Well, at least I know where I stand now."

This was a long-running gag she had with both me and Sam. As kids, we really looked alike, but as men, we had subtle differences that anyone who knew us would use to distinguish us. So, Vivie knew exactly who I was.

"Do you suppose you'll ever stop being annoying as hell?" I said playfully.

She pressed her finger to her chin and slanted her gaze upward as if she were thinking. Finally, she looked at me with a grin. "Not where you and Sam are concerned."

I laughed and pulled her in for another hug, giving her a kiss on the cheek. "Welcome home, Vivie."

At dinner, I heard all about Vivie's travels and answered what questions I could about Sam's work out in California. I didn't mention Kate or the possibility that she would come for Thanksgiving. That was Sam's news to share. But with thanksgiving a week away, he needed to do it soon.

After dinner, I headed home and made arrangements to go to California with Sam, and then I figured from California, I'd get a ticket to Las Vegas. Then I got a drink from my liquor cabinet and went and sat on the couch, turning on the TV. There was a sports recap show that I let run in the background as I picked up my phone to call Amelia. I needed to let her know about my plans after Thanksgiving. That was the reason I told myself I was calling. But the truth was, it was an excuse. Ever since the last time I spoke to her on the phone, I'd been wanting to call her back. Not to talk about the annulment, but to talk about anything and everything, whatever.

It was well past nine here, which put it past six in the evening out there. Hopefully, she was done with her workday.

She picked up on the second ring, and I wondered if that meant she was excited to see my name pop up on the screen. *Don't go there, Max.*

"Max. How are you?"

I settled back into my couch, hoping I wouldn't be such a doofus on the phone this time and would be able to talk with her. "I'm good. My sister arrived home for Thanksgiving today. It was fun to see her and hear about all her after college travels."

I couldn't be sure that Amelia cared one way or the other about my family, but I didn't want this call just to be about the annulment, so I led with something else. Something more personal. A little bell in my head clanged in a warning, but I took a sip of my bourbon to shut it up.

"A world traveler? Wow. Did she go to all the usual places or some of the more exotic ones?"

"Little bit of both. It actually sounded like a lot of fun, but I could tell my parents are eager for her to either go to graduate school or get a job."

Amelia laughed.

"On the other hand, you should see her Instagram feed. Maybe you could give her some pointers on how she could turn that into some sort of influencer cash."

There was a pause on the other end. It was long enough to make me realize what I had said. I'd essentially suggested that Amelia meet my sister.

The bell clanged louder, but I couldn't figure out what words to say to take it back.

"What's her Instagram name?"

I gave her Vivie's name. A few seconds later, she said, "Wow, she's had some adventures."

"That she has. Have you traveled much?" I asked.

"Not like that. My father's well-traveled, but he never took me or James with him. I went to Mexico on spring break out of high school, and Hawaii after college. Most of the traveling I do now is for work."

That reminded me of her new big clients. "How's the celebrity restaurant client doing? And the vineyard?"

"Both are doing very well, thank you."

I grinned, feeling happy and proud of her. "That's fantastic."

"How about you? How's your business in Las Vegas?"

I knew she was talking about the club Sam and I were planning, but what I immediately thought of was the annulment.

"Speaking of business items, I downloaded those papers from the Nevada website."

"Oh."

I swore that the tenor in her voice had gone from happy to disappointed. Fuck. Then again, it was probably wishful thinking on my part.

"I haven't filled them out yet. All this gobbledygook makes it look like I need to deliver them directly," I said.

"If you want, when you come out here, I can go through them with you." There was a tentativeness in her voice, but I couldn't be sure if she was worried about implying that I needed help to read the document because of my dyslexia or a disappointment that I was determined to fill out the documents at all.

My first instinct was to go with the latter and think she didn't want me to file the documents. Jesus Fuck. I wasn't sure I wanted to file the documents. That made no sense. I knew this woman for two days. Why would I even contemplate wanting to stay married to a woman I didn't know? I wondered if Sam's brain was scrambled like this. It would make sense why he was acting like a maniac ever since Kate had walked back into his life. These crazy thoughts and emotions were just another reason relationships should be avoided. A person couldn't live like this.

"It wouldn't hurt to have another pair of eyes on it to make sure I've understood everything. I suppose I could hire a lawyer, but I'd rather not do that."

"Yes. I understand." Her voice still sounded as if she didn't like what I was saying. I wanted this call to go well, but I could quickly feel it slipping away.

"I'll be flying out to California with my brother after Thanksgiving to check on plans for our Los Angeles club." Because I didn't want her to think I was sharing my schedule so that I could meet with her to get the annulment, I continued on. "I have this feeling that my brother hasn't done anything since the last time I was there. His mind and his heart are totally elsewhere."

"Oh? Where's that?"

"He ran into his ex when he got out there. But she's not just any ex-girlfriend. She was the one he had hoped to marry."

As much as I didn't feel I should share Sam's business, since it was unlikely Amelia would ever meet him or any of my family, I figured it wouldn't hurt to tell her.

"So, he has a second chance?"

"That's what he's hoping for. To be honest, he acts like his very life depends on it. I don't get it, but Sam has always been like that."

"Like what?"

"He's much more open with his feelings. But Kate isn't making it easy for him, and I'm worried she's going to break him."

"Oh, that's sad."

"She has some justification for not trusting him. But Sam is in it for the long haul, and if she ever sees that in him and how much he loves her, hopefully, she'll give him a chance." While I wasn't interested in forever after, I knew Sam was, and I hoped he'd get it.

"Well, I hope she does. True love is nice, don't you think?"

I scraped my hand over my face. I'd wanted to talk to Amelia, but not about love. "I suppose. For Sam, anyway."

"But not for you?"

"Not for me."

She was silent on the other end for a minute, and I wondered what she was thinking.

"It sounds like there's a story in that but one that you don't want to tell, so I won't ask."

"I appreciate that." I should've let the topic drop right there, but my curiosity got the best of me. "What about you? Is there a true love in your future?"

She sighed. "I don't know. Maybe someday. That's not the focus of my life right now. I'm not looking for a man. "

"So when you tried to steal my car at the airport, you weren't trying to find yourself a husband?"

She let out a loud laugh, which I was glad to hear, and at the same time, it ouched a little. Like I wouldn't be a man she would want as a husband. *Good God, Max. It's good that she doesn't want you as a husband.*

"If I remember correctly, you were the one who undressed me with those green eyes of yours and then asked me to give you a tour."

I laughed. "I meant a tour of the city. But I was very happy to have a tour of your body too."

"So I discovered."

I took another sip of my bourbon and settled deeper into my couch, happy that the conversation was going somewhere that was easy for us—sex. "So, if I were to tour your body now? What would I find? What are you wearing?"

She laughed. "I'm afraid you'll be disappointed. I'm in exercise shorts and a tank top. I just got back from the gym."

I don't know why that would disappoint me. I could easily visualize her long, bare legs and her tits filling out a tank top.

"Sounds sexy."

She snorted. "What about you? What are you wearing?"

"Slacks and a shirt. Not very sexy either. But my dick wants to get loose thinking about you in shorts." Maybe I shouldn't do this. Maybe I should say goodnight. But I couldn't bring myself to stop.

"Poor thing. What will you do?"

Her responses told me she was with me on this. Or at least this far. How far would she let me go?

"I'll have to take matters into my own hand, I suppose."

Her breath hitched, and I wished she were here so I could see her hazel eyes cross over to green as they did in the heat of passion.

"Will you think of me?"

I shifted, undoing my pants and shoving them down to free my cock that was bulging at her words. "Yes."

This time, she let out a breath.

"Do you like the idea of my thinking of you?" With my dick free, I stroked once and then released him.

"Yes."

"Why?"

I could imagine a blush on her cheeks at my naughty question. "Every woman wants to be a man's fantasy."

She was definitely mine.

"What will you fantasize about?"

All of it, I thought. Her sucking me off. Me fucking her from behind, her fucking me, sixty-nine . . . all of it. I stroked my cock again and rubbed my precum over the tip.

"Everything. What about you, Amelia? Do you pleasure yourself?"

There was a pause. Finally, she said, "Yes."

"How about now? Does it make you wet to talk like this?"

"Yes. You know it does."

"I don't know. You have to tell me. What do you fantasize about?" I was so fucking hot now. Since I wasn't a man to have relationships, I'd never had the opportunity for phone sex. I wouldn't have guessed it would light me up so much.

"Everything," she repeated my answer back to me.

I finished my drink, setting it down. Then I lay back on the couch, putting the phone on speaker so I could close my eyes and listen to her while I took care of my raging hard-on.

"Would it shock you to know that I'm stroking my cock right now, thinking about you?"

She let out a moan. "No. Really?"

"Yes. I'm hard as a rock, Amelia."

"Will you make yourself come? Can I listen?"

"Yes." My need ratcheted up. It wouldn't be long before I blew my load all over my stomach. I released my dick and unbuttoned my shirt. I'd rather have cum on my stomach than my shirt.

The line was quiet for a minute.

"I need to hear your voice, Amelia. Tell me what you want to do to me or what you want me to do to you."

"I want to suck your dick, Max. It's so thick and hard. Mmm."

Oh, fuck. Oh, fuck. "Yes . . . you like sucking my dick."

"Yes. The tip is so soft, and you taste good. I like to run my tongue up and down your dick. Suck your balls."

I imaged her lips on my cock, and it felt do fucking good. As I careened to the edge, I groaned. "I'm going to come, Amelia."

"I wish I could drink it up."

Jesus, how I wished that too. I released my dick even though it screamed at me not to stop. "Are you touching yourself, Amelia?"

She was quiet. I couldn't decide whether she was embarrassed to say yes or didn't want me to know she wasn't joining in.

"Take your clothes off, sweetheart, and lie on your bed. We're going to do this together."

"Hold on." The line was quiet except for some movement in the background. "Okay. I'm back. Will you make yourself come now? I want to hear you."

"I'll do you better than that. I'll let you watch." I switched to video and angled my phone to my dick. The warning bells dinged louder. Showing my dick over a video call was a classic no-no, but I was too lost in desire to heed the warning.

"Oh, God. He's so beautiful."

I nearly laughed. Dicks weren't beautiful. At the same time, my chest filled with warmth to hear her reaction to mine.

"Tell me again what you want to do?" I started stroking my dick.

"I want to lick and suck it until your eyes roll back in your head."

My hips rocked as I fucked my hand. "Yes . . . fuck yes." I wanted to see her face, her tits, her body, but to do that, I'd have to turn the phone around. There'd be time for that.

"I want to drag my tongue around the rim of your cock and then take it deep into my mouth."

"Yes . . . oh, fuck . . ." I was like a horny teenager jerking off to his first experience of porn. "Yes . . . Amelia . . . I'm going to come . . . drink it up, baby, all of it."

"Mmm . . . give it to me, Max."

My hand slid down while my hips jerked up. Cum splashed out, landing on my stomach and even on my phone. "Yes . . . yes . . ." I continued to stroke until the last bit of cum dripped down my dick and over my hand. Jesus fuck, that was good. Not as good as the real thing, but still, really good.

I turned the phone and peered into it, seeing her lovely face on the other end. Her cheeks were flushed. I couldn't see all of her, but I saw enough to know she'd done as I'd asked. She was naked in bed.

"Look what you did to me." I showed her the cum on my stomach.

"I wish I were there to lick it up."

God, my dick twitched. He'd just emptied his load and her words had him wanting to come to life again. "I'd like that too. More than that, I'd like to return the favor and eat that sweet pussy of yours."

CHAPTER TEN

Amelia

I wasn't a prude, but I'd never had phone sex before. It was interesting how Max could be so reserved regarding his feelings, and yet so open about his sexual interests. I suppose that was because sex didn't require emotions.

"Are you wet?" he asked me.

I was sopping. "Yes."

"Can I see?" He asked it gently, like he knew I wasn't so sure about this. I was a social media manager. I knew that things like this could get out and ruin people. But I'd just watched cum shoot out from his dick, so I supposed I didn't have to worry about him and revenge porn.

I adjusted my phone so he could see my pussy.

"God, I wish I could taste it."

I wished that too.

"Touch yourself, baby."

Sweetheart and now baby. That was just part of the intimacy, right? Not a term of endearment.

I slid my hand down my belly, then used my finger to rub my clit.

"Do you have a vibrator?"

Not yet. But I'd already thought about getting one. "No."

"Too bad."

"It wouldn't be as good."

"Damn right, it wouldn't."

I continued to massage my clit, my body beginning to rock.

"I'm sucking your clit now and my fingers are fucking you. Does it feel good?" he asked.

"Yes." My legs fell open wider as pleasure built.

"You're so wet and pink. I want to drink you up."

"Oh!" I was teetering on the edge.

"Come, Amelia. Let me see your sweet pussy come."

His words tipped me over the edge. My orgasm rocked through me.

"Yes. Make it last." He urged me on.

Finally, the pleasure subsided and embarrassment took its place. I couldn't believe I did that.

"Amelia?"

"Yes." I hadn't been able to turn the phone back to my face. Right now, he had a view of my ceiling.

"Are you okay?"

"Yes."

He laughed. "Will you come back on the screen?"

I picked the phone up and gave him a sheepish smile.

"You're not embarrassed, are you?"

"A little."

"Don't be. Look." His screen turned, and he showed his dick which was hard again. "You did that." He brought the camera back so I could see him. "Watching you turned me on."

I smiled. "You're so easy, Max."

He grinned. We stared at each other for a moment, and then he said, "I'll let you go. Have a good evening, Amelia."

"You too."

The screen went black, and I lay back in bed, still shocked at what I'd done. I remembered in high school my best friend telling me that a sure way to know that you really like a guy was how hard you worked to interpret every little thing he said, wondering if it meant anything or not. There had been a few guys I'd had crushes on in high school and college, but I hadn't understood her statement until now. During the course of the call with Max, for every little thing he said, I was trying to decipher what it meant. Was he just calling to tell me about the annulment? Did he call to have phone sex? What did *sweetheart* and *baby* mean? Did he still want the annulment?

Of course he did. That was crazy wishful thinking, which highlighted the fact that I was in deep trouble. Even so, I was eager for his visit after Thanksgiving. As much fun as phone sex was, it wasn't nearly as satisfying as if he were here.

I slapped my forehead with the palm of my hand. "You can't go there, Amelia. Don't be a dumb schoolgirl."

Aside from the crazy thoughts and emotions going through me, having an orgasm made the rest of the night nice. I was relaxed. It made me think of the sleepy sex we'd had before discovering we were married.

I was eating some dinner while watching a baking show when my phone rang again. Looking at the caller ID, I saw it was my brother. I'd hoped it was Max again. Good lord, I had it bad.

"Hey, James," I said when I answered. "What's up?"

"Dad's back in town and he wants us to have Thanksgiving dinner together."

I sat with that for a minute. It wasn't that we never had holidays together, but over the last few years, it was hit or miss, and I preferred the misses. Having dinner with my father was always torture. The whole time, I was on edge, walking on eggshells, making sure I didn't say or do anything that would give him fodder for the fire to use against me. I knew that sounded terrible, and it wasn't like my father was out to ruin me. But he could be mean and petty just because he wanted to be. If he were a woman, he'd be called a bitch.

I had a six-figure business, and yet he often asked me when I was going to get a real job. He downplayed how I was making my living even though I was successful doing something I was good at and passionate about.

"I imagine he's going to call you at some point, but it was clear to me that he wasn't inviting us over. He was *demanding* our attendance."

Just great. "I might have the flu that day."

"You know that won't stop him. He'll just send one of his goons over to grab you out of bed and haul you over."

He wasn't wrong. James called my dad's men goons, whereas I called them henchmen. My father would call them security, but it was clear that they were no normal security team. I suspected most of them were ex-mercenaries. I didn't know where he found them, but it wasn't from a reputable security agency like Saint Security.

"I'll go to Bora Bora instead."

James laughed. "I'd go with you if I thought that would work. You know him, Amelia. He won't stop until he gets what he wants. We learned a long time ago that it was easier to give in than to fight him."

He was right. We treated it like ripping a bandage off. It was painful but best done quickly.

I decided that I would grit my teeth and get through Thanksgiving knowing that afterward, I would be able to see Max. It wasn't a good idea to use Max as something to look forward to, or to soothe me after time with my father, but I wasn't going to worry about that now. When it came to my father, I would use whatever I could to help me through it, including another large glass of wine, which I poured once I got off the phone with James.

For the next few days, I went through life as normal. Except for the frequent thoughts and dreams I had of Max, my life had resumed its normal routine. I figured eventually, the thoughts and dreams would go away, so I didn't worry about them too much.

On the Tuesday before Thanksgiving, my phone rang just as I was closing the house and getting ready to call it a night. It was only nine o'clock, but I decided I would read in bed and go to sleep early. Holidays were busy times for my clients, which meant a lot of work for me and my clients. At the same time, I wanted me and my staff to have time off as well, so we worked hard to be able to take Wednesday afternoon and Thanksgiving off. Of course, I would've been happy to work rather than see my father, but James was right, my father wouldn't stand for it.

I'd just gotten into bed when my phone went off, the ring tone playing New York, New York. Yes, it was another bad sign that I've given Max his own ringtone.

But the little thrill that zipped through my body from his call made it impossible to worry about how much I was falling for Max.

"It's late back there. Shouldn't you be in bed?" I said when I picked up.

"Who says I'm not?" The deep tenor in his voice, laced with sensuality, sent a sizzle through me, straight down to my core.

"How about you? Am I calling too late?" he asked.

"Not at all. I just climbed into bed to read a book."

"You're in bed." He said it like he was pleased by it. "Then I called at the right time."

Okay, so this call was going to be about sex. I was okay with that. Despite my feelings, I couldn't want any more than that.

"The right time for what?"

"Crossword puzzles."

I laughed.

"What is a six-letter word for sensual pleasure?"

"Hmm . . . not sex . . . not come . . . orgasm?"

"You're good."

I smiled, but it was bittersweet. Max was proving to be just the sort of man I would have liked to have a relationship with if only the timing weren't so bad. That and he lived across the country.

Late-night phone sex over the last few nights was great, but not enough to alleviate the tension I felt as I walked into my father's house on Thanksgiving. Other people from dysfunctional families might have shown up with a few drinks under their belt to cope, but I didn't dare have a drink when I visited my dad. I needed all my wits about me when I was around him. For my dad, everything was transactional, and he'd find a way to use any little tidbit of information he obtained to his advantage. Even when it involved his kids. I didn't want to give him anything that he could exploit. In particular, my accidental marriage to Max.

When I was escorted into the living room, I was glad to see that James was already there. He held a glass with clear liquid which could've been vodka but was probably water. He knew as well as I did that it was important to stay sober and on our toes around Dad.

My dad sat in a wingback chair looking like he was the king on his throne. He checked his watch. "You just made it."

If I were braver, I would've responded with something snarky about not wanting to keep His Majesty waiting. But I wasn't brave enough to put him on my bad side, which was why I arrived right on time, which he was pointing out by checking the time.

"Happy Thanksgiving, Amelia." James came to me, giving me a hug and a kiss on the cheek. He whispered into my ear, "The sooner we eat, the sooner we can leave."

I smiled. "Happy Thanksgiving, James." I turned to look at my dad. "You too, Dad."

My father grunted out a Happy Thanksgiving to me.

Luckily, we were saved from small talk by being called to dinner. Once we were seated and the traditional Thanksgiving turkey was served, my dad asked, "Have you talked to your mother lately, Amelia?"

I chewed my first bite of turkey slowly as I tried to figure out why my father would be asking about our mother. When she'd left eight years ago, he'd pretty much cut her out of his life, and she did her best to cut us out of hers as well. While she wouldn't have earned mother of the year, she wasn't a bad mother either, so it was a surprise that she never reached out to me and James, especially after we were out of the home. I told myself that she worried that by being in touch with us, somehow, our dad would be able to get to her. James's take on it was a little bit different. He felt that she had only been biding her time until I graduated from high school and then escaped not just from Dad, but from us as well. He believed she had us only out of duty to my father. When he first told me that, I didn't want to believe it, but I think deep down, I knew it was true. It was difficult to believe that neither of our parents wanted to be parents. Sometimes, it was work to tell myself that their indifference to us was a reflection on them, not on me or James. He and I were worthy to have loving parents. We just hadn't been blessed with them.

"No. You know, we don't talk to her, and she makes no attempt to talk to us," I said.

He shrugged nonchalantly as he cut his turkey. But he didn't fool me. His question meant something.

"I just thought maybe you had some news to share with her or something. Something a daughter would want to talk to her mother about."

I looked across the table at James, wondering what my father was talking about. James looked at me and shrugged. Apparently, he was clueless too.

"No."

My father picked up his wine, taking a sip, his eyes studying me over the rim. I wanted to squirm at his scrutiny. I turned my attention back to my food, hating that I was letting him know he made me uncomfortable.

"Are you sure about that?"

By flinching and turning away, I had given away my unease, which he took advantage of. What could he be asking me about?

Max flitted through my brain, and I stiffened. Oh, God, did my father find out about Max? I needed to pull myself together. I had to shore up my strength and keep my façade firmly in place. My father's knowing about Max would be the worst.

I shook my head. "There's nothing except for I secured a client in Los Angeles and I'm on the verge of signing a vineyard in Northern California." Normally, I didn't let my father know about my clients either, worrying he might find a way to exploit that relationship as well.

"Speaking of news, Dad, we've secured Lars Masterson for that project he has in East Las Vegas."

I sent James a silent thank you.

My father's gaze stayed on me for a beat and then he turned to my brother. "That's great, Son. But what about the Kragen deal?"

Inwardly, I shook my head at my father's response. He always expected more and better from James, with very little regard for his achievements.

"I'm meeting with him next week."

My father nodded, taking a bite of his mashed potatoes.

When he swallowed, he turned his attention to me again. "Didn't you have a big client meeting just before I left town?"

My father never took an interest in my business, so this was getting really uncomfortable. And, considering the big client he thought I had was actually a date with Max, I began to think my father did know about Max. But how much? My father knew a lot of people in Las Vegas. He had eyes everywhere watching everyone's every move so he could use it to his advantage. I knew that and still, I hadn't been as discreet as I should've been when I saw Max.

"That deal is still in the exploratory phase," I said, taking a sip of wine when I really wanted to take a gulp. But a gulp would show that I was hiding something.

"Well, I hope it works out for you. It could be a really good move in your financial future."

I wish I could know for sure whether he was talking about Max or if I was being paranoid.

As soon as James and I could escape, we did. James walked me out to my car.

"What was all that Dad was asking you about talking to Mom or news?"

"I don't know for sure, but I'm a little worried that he knows about my date with Max."

James's brow furrowed as he looked like he was trying to decipher why my father would care. "I guess he's from a prominent family and is looking to build a business out here. It still doesn't explain why you'd call Mom."

My gut roiled because I agreed with him. The only reason my father might think I'd call my mom was if I had gotten married.

But if that were the case, my father would have surely said something. He might be manipulative, but he was very rarely subtle.

As I thought about the evening during my drive home, it became clear that I needed to get this annulment as soon as possible. I needed to get Max out of my father's crosshairs.

CHAPTER ELEVEN

Max

On Tuesday before Thanksgiving, Sam called me to let me know what he'd lined up for us to look at after the holiday. If I played it right, I could fly out and spend a few days with Sam, make a stopover in Las Vegas on the way home to submit annulment papers, and then return to New York and no one would know I was married.

In the meantime, I had to get through Thanksgiving with the family. I was sure it would be as festive as usual, but I wondered how Kate would fit in.

"Mom is pretty excited to finally meet Kate. She's going overboard to make sure everything is just right," I told Sam. "We're all guessing that since she's coming, you two have reconciled."

"I can't say we're fully reconciled. But I'm feeling really good that we're getting there. In fact, I'm hoping by the time Thanksgiving is over, we will be well on our way to being mister and misses, just like we planned. The only thing I have to decide is do I give her back the ring that I gave her before, or would that be too much of a reminder of our past? Maybe I need to get a new ring representing our new start."

Holy cow. "Marriage? Wow. Don't you think it's a little too soon? It's only been, what, two months, maybe?"

"Too soon? I've been waiting five years."

God, I hoped she didn't break his heart.

Sam and Kate took a red-eye flight out and arrived Wednesday morning. We were all excited to meet Kate, especially Vivie, who ran outside to greet them when they arrived. I was more patient, waiting in the foyer.

Sam and I hugged, and then I hugged Kate. She looked nervous, and I hoped that all of us would be able to put her at ease. My family was about as nice as a family could be.

"Mom and Dad didn't want to overwhelm you by being obnoxious like Vivie and me, waiting impatiently for your arrival. They're in the sunroom where there's coffee and breakfast."

"That gives you another two minutes to calm your nerves," Sam said, rubbing Kate's back.

Mr. Gabriel, my parents' butler, entered the foyer. "Shall I take the bags up to your room, Mr. Clarke?"

Vivie and led the way to the sunroom. When we entered, our parents were mid-embrace.

"Oh, God. When are you guys ever going to learn to get a room?" Vivie moaned. To be honest, I agreed. I loved that my parents were still madly in love, but I didn't like seeing it on display. It was weird to think of them that way.

"Welcome to our home," my mother said, giving Kate a hug.

"How was the trip?" my father asked.

"It was fine. It's very nice of you to have me for Thanksgiving, Mr. and Mrs. Clarke."

My mother waved her hand. "Please, call me Juliana."

"And I'm Drew."

"You're probably exhausted, but we have coffee, juice, and breakfast if you'd like," my mother said. I'd already sat down to eat, as did Vivie.

"Pancakes?" Sam asked.

My parents rolled their eyes.

"Of course, there are pancakes." My mother gave Kate an amused look. "As if I wouldn't have pancakes for Sam. I swear, if he could get away with it, it's all he'd eat."

After breakfast, Sam and Kate rested, and then he took her on a tour of New York. I hung out at my parents' home, helping with Thanksgiving prep. That evening, Vivie and I decided to watch a movie in the home theater. We invited Sam and Kate to join us.

Sam entered the theater and took a seat next to me.

"Where's Kate?" Vivie asked.

"She's jetlagged, so she's gone to bed early."

"She seems different," I said, handing the bowl of popcorn to Sam.

"She's just nervous about being around the family."

"She's nervous around us? We're a family of cream puffs." Vivie laughed.

"I know. But she's had some experiences in the past that make her wary of people."

"Well, she's here, so that's a good sign." At least I hoped it was. Kate seemed more subdued than I remembered, and Sam was bending over backward to make sure she was okay. It seemed like a lot of work. Shouldn't love be easier? I thought of Amelia. Everything between us was easy. The conversation, as well as the sex.

The next day, I was up early to help my parents execute the festivities. They always gave their servants Thanksgiving and the days following off. It meant more work for us, but it had become a family ritual to cook and decorate for the holiday.

I helped my dad put the leaves in the dining room table. "Why do we need more leaves? We fit fine at breakfast yesterday."

"Sandra and Chelsea are coming," my father said as he pulled the table, opening the space for the leaf.

"Oh, shit," I muttered. "I thought they were in Boston now."

"They are, but she's in New York for business. As you know, they don't have anyone else, so your mom invited them for Thanksgiving."

"Does Sam know?"

My dad looked up at me. "Uh . . . I don't know." He frowned. "I hope so."

Jesus. If he didn't know, that meant Kate didn't know. How would Kate respond to Sam's ex and her daughter showing up for Thanksgiving dinner?

When I entered the kitchen, Sandra and Chelsea were talking with my mom. I looked over at Vivie, who was rolling out pie dough. She shrugged like she knew I was asking about Sam and Kate.

"Have you seen Sam?" I asked, trying to sound casual.

"We saw him when we came in," Chelsea, Sandra's five year-old-daughter, said, eating a cookie from a batch my mom made yesterday.

I looked over at my mother. She shrugged too. That had to mean that Sam hadn't known Sandra would be here. He was probably upstairs trying to explain it to Kate now. I wondered how she'd take it.

"Vivie, can you let Sam know that these potatoes won't peel themselves?" my mother asked my sister.

"Sure thing." Vivie exited the kitchen. My mom led Chelsea to a room off the kitchen. A hundred plus years ago when the home was built, the room was for live-in servants, but since my parents' help didn't live-in, Mom used it as a craft room. She'd set up Thanksgiving crafts for Chelsea.

"Oh, my God." Vivie rushed back in.

"What?" I asked.

She looped her arm through mine. "Come help me." She dragged me out of the kitchen into the dining room, leaving Sandra alone.

"What's going on, Vivie?"

"I didn't want Sandra to overhear, but Kate and Sam are fighting in the foyer. She's leaving."

"Because of Sandra?"

"Who's leaving?" my father asked, entering the dining room with a box of Thanksgiving decorations.

"Kate. She's not happy that Sandra is here," Vivie said.

"Surely, she knows she and Sam are done," my father said.

Vivie arched a brow. "I know I wouldn't like it if I was with a guy who spent Thanksgiving with his ex."

"Can I help?" Sandra entered the dining room.

"Yes. Maybe you can deal with these. I'm going to find Juliana," my father said.

Vivie and I looked at each other, feeling awkward about the whole thing. It was a reminder to me of how messy relationships could be.

We helped Sandra with the decorations, then Sandra went to check on Chelsea. When I entered the kitchen, Mom was busy with the turkey. I looked out in the sunroom where Sam was murderously peeling potatoes.

She shook her head. That couldn't be good.

Later, Sam brought the peeled potatoes into the kitchen, getting ready to cut and boil them.

"You want some help?" I asked.

Sam shook his head. He wasn't ready to talk so I left him alone.

Sam wasn't able to make it to Thanksgiving. It killed me that Kate left. I hated how despondent Sam looked. I never, ever wanted to feel like he looked like he felt.

After dinner, I brought a bottle of scotch up to his room.

"I've got a bottle of scotch," I said through the closed door.

"Door's open."

I entered his room and handed him the bottle and a glass. "I wasn't sure you would want to use this, but I brought it."

Sam ignored the glass, pulling the lid off the bottle and taking a long swig.

"Are you sure you don't want to talk?" I asked.

"Nope."

"I'll leave you to it, then." I left, wishing there were something I could do to help my brother.

. . .

The next morning, Sam showed up for breakfast. The entire family, including Sandra and Chelsea, were there. He looked like shit, but at least he was going through the motions of life.

He poured himself a cup of coffee and snagged a pancake. Around the table, people were glancing back and forth at each other. We didn't know what to say.

"Max, I have a flight scheduled back to California this afternoon. Why don't you join me and we can get started on all the club details today?"

I looked at our parents, wondering if they had any thoughts on Sam's plan. I'd arranged to go to California, but not today. My parents shrugged.

"Yeah, okay," I said.

Sam scarfed down his pancake, took his plate into the kitchen, and then went upstairs.

"Do you think he'll be okay?" my mom asked.

"This is my fault, isn't it?" Sandra was the most uncomfortable of all of us. "If I'd known—"

"It's not your fault," my mother said.

But it sort of was, I thought. Sandra lied to my brother, and as a result, he'd left Kate five years ago.

"I'll go check on him." I went upstairs, entering his room. "What if I went back and started working on things, and you stayed here for a little while?" He didn't need to go back to California right away. He could take time to deal with his emotions.

Sam arched a brow at me. "Pulling the twin switch isn't going to change anything."

I smiled remembering how we used to trade places. He'd once pretended to be me to take a test for me. "I wasn't talking about switching. Well, maybe I was, but not me being you and you being me. I was thinking I could take over the Los Angeles project and you could do the Las Vegas one." That would solve two problems. If I took over Los Angeles, I wouldn't have to worry about being distracted by Amelia.

"I'm good. Once we get back to work, it's all going to be okay."

I wasn't so sure, but I had to trust that Sam knew what he was doing. I left him to pack my bag. We arrived in California late Friday night, heading straight back to Sam's house and going to bed.

The next morning, when I woke up, the house was empty. As I looked out over the beach, I saw that Sam was taking a walk. I went to the kitchen and made coffee. It had just finished brewing when Sam returned. Not saying anything, he got a cup of coffee, then grabbed his tablet and went out onto the terrace.

I was about to join him when there was a knock on the door. "I'll get it."

I opened the door and was immediately grabbed and pushed into the house, slammed against the wall.

"You fucking sonofabitch."

It took me a moment for my brain to catch up to what was happening.

"What the fuck is wrong with you, Sam?"

Before I could tell him that I was Max, Sam pulled the man off me. "What the fuck is wrong with you, Ethan? You come into my house and attack my brother?"

He blinked, looking between me and Sam.

"If you have a beef with me, talk to me, not my brother. Second, I don't know why you think you have a beef with me. Your sister is the one who left." Sam pushed Ethan again. "Were you part of the plan too?"

"What are you talking about?" Ethan said, pushing his hands away.

I was curious too.

"The lets-get-back-at-Sam plan. Didn't Kate tell you? It worked like a charm. Now if you don't mind, get the fuck out of my house before I call the cops and have you arrested for assaulting my brother and trespassing."

Ethan's eyes narrowed. He stepped forward, getting into Sam's face. "I'm here to find out why you're not doing right by my sister. You broke her heart five years ago to do the right thing, but now that she's the one that's pregnant, you want nothing to do with it?"

What the hell?

"I said get the fuck out of my house." Sam looked ready to toss Ethan out of the house. Did he know about the pregnancy or had he not heard what Ethan said?

"Wait, what?" I stepped into the mix. "Are you saying Kate is pregnant?"

Sam looked at me and then to Ethan.

Ethan smirked. "Like you don't know. I really wanted to kick your ass when you came back to town, but I'd hoped you would be the one person who could reach her, to help her open her heart up. But all you did was abandon her again."

"I did no such thing. I don't know what she's telling you. She's the one who left."

He gave Sam a shove and then headed to the door. "It's probably better if you don't come around. You're clearly not in your daughter's life, so why would we expect you to be in this baby's too?"

What?

When the door slammed behind him, he turned to me. "What the hell was he saying?"

I wasn't sure. "I'm pretty sure he just said that Kate is pregnant." What did he mean by not being in his daughter's life? Did he think Chelsea was Sam's? Hadn't Sam cleared that up with Kate?

Sam grabbed his keys from the bowl by the door.

"Where are you going, Sam?"

"I'm going to talk to Kate."

"I'll come with you. I'll drive."

"I don't need a chauffeur or a chaperone."

"You do need a chauffeur. You're pissed. Let me drive you."

On the drive to Kate's club, the Sea Siren, Sam fidgeted impatiently. "You drive like an old lady, do you know that?"

I slanted my gaze at him. "I'm ten miles over the speed limit. If I get a ticket, it will only slow us down."

The Sea Siren wasn't open, but when we arrived, there were a couple of cars in the parking lot indicating that staff was there.

Sam rushed out of the car, trying to open the door, but it was locked. He pounded on the door. "Open up, Kate."

I got out of the car and leaned against it. "Maybe don't go barging in like her brother did. We don't want her calling the cops."

Someone let him in. A few minutes later, he came out, still fuming. He got in the car and I drove us back to his house.

"What happened?" I finally asked after several minutes of driving.

"I can't believe she was fucking with me the whole time."

"You think she was toying with you?"

"What else should I think?" Sam looked at me and his expression broke my heart. "She wasn't going to tell me about the baby."

"She said that?" I was beginning to hate Kate.

"Not in those words, but what else am I to think?"

When we got back to his place, I let Sam stew. It was clear that we weren't going to get much work done, so I went to the beach.

"Sam?"

I turned to see his neighbor walking to me carrying a baby.

"It's Max, Mrs. St. Martin."

"Oh, I'm sorry. Please call me Harper. How is Sam?"

"Not good." I shouldn't tell Sam's business, but I was worried about him.

She held her baby close as the wind picked up. "I think the world of Kate, but she's letting fear keep her from a sure thing."

I nodded. Sam was a sure thing, but I suppose considering how he'd left five years ago, Kate was once bitten, twice shy.

"We should do something."

I arched a brow. "Like what?"

She thought for a moment. "Take Sam for a walk on the beach tomorrow." She gave me a time. "I'll have Kate here."

"I'm not sure either will be okay with that."

She gave me a stern look. "They need to air their grievances and share their feelings. I know. I've been in their spot. Will you do it?"

I nodded even before thinking better of it. I didn't think this was a good idea, but I did agree that something needed to be done. I wanted Sam to be happy, and Kate was the one he wanted. I was glad my happiness didn't rely on a woman.

. . .

99

I was right. Sam wasn't happy when Harper and I put him and Kate together. They talked for a moment before Sam returned.

"Don't ever play matchmaker again," he growled at me, getting a glass of scotch.

"She didn't respond well?"

"I'm done." He downed the scotch.

"Listen, Kate did wrong by running off and not listening and trusting you, and by not telling you about the baby, but all this started five years ago when you walked out on her for Sandra." He needed to fight harder.

"What else was I supposed to do? I did exactly what our dad did. I did the right thing by her." I poured more scotch.

"How come you weren't angry at her?" I asked him.

"Who? Sandra? I was. I was pissed." He took the bottle and a glass to the couch, settling in for a long binge.

"Not when she showed up with the baby. When she told you about the baby, you weren't pissed like you are now at Kate. Instead, you insisted that you and her and the baby would be a family. But now, not only are you pissed at Kate for not telling you she's pregnant, but I don't think you have once offered to do the right thing, have you?"

He swallowed his scotch. "I told her that I was going to be a part of this baby's life. All of it. I'm not going to be some every-other-weekend dad."

"That's not what you told Sandra. If I were Kate and I was analyzing this, I'd think you never really loved me. At least not as much as Sandra."

"She'd be wrong."

"I know, but from her point of view, you dropped everyone and everything to be with Sandra, who waited until Chelsea was born to tell you, but you didn't act like you are now with Kate."

He glared at me. "It's not the same. You know that."

"All the more reason to wonder why you won't step up for Kate. As far as I can tell, right now, you're doing the thing that she's been doing for the last few months. You're trying to kill your feelings for her. How is that working?"

He didn't respond.

"The way I see it, Sam, this is your tipping point. Right now, Kate is right there, ready for you to take hold of your future together. But if you miss it, you're going to lose her for good."

"That's assuming Kate even wants me."

"Sam, what do you really want?"

"I want her!" He turned away like he wished he hadn't said that.

"Then you have to try again because if you don't, you will look back at this moment and regret it, probably even worse regret than having left five years ago. You know as well as I do that this is the make-or-break moment for you and Kate."

He set the glass and scotch bottle on the coffee table and stalked toward the front door.

"Are you going to see Kate?"

He shook his head. "Kate is the last person I plan to see."

I sighed. It looked like the happily ever after my brother was after wasn't coming. Thank fuck I didn't want a committed relationship. That made me think of Amelia. Not of the annulment we needed to get, but of spending time with her. *Don't think that, Max.* I didn't want any part of what Sam was going through now.

I stayed a couple of days with Sam. I saw the properties and told him whichever he wanted would work. When I left, I think he was relieved not to have me hovering around.

I had my own issues to deal with, starting with getting my marriage to Amelia annulled. It was a little weird to have our late-night phone trysts and at the same time be getting ready to end our marriage. But it was just sex. It had always been just sex. And now I had to make sure that it stayed that way. In fact, as I disembarked from the plane in Las Vegas and ordered a car to take me to the hotel, I determined that this visit would be platonic and professional. We would take care of the paperwork, and then I would file for the annulment and serve her paperwork as required by Nevada law. Then tomorrow, I would hightail it out of Las Vegas until I had a court date. The Nevada website said it could take up to three months to get a court date, which seemed to me to be plenty of time to move on from a woman. When we went to court, our time together would just be a sweet memory.

While I was in the car heading to the airport's hotel, I texted Amelia to let her know where I was and that she could drop by anytime. Initially, I thought I would go to her house, and we'd do the paperwork then and I would go to the courthouse to file them and leave. But Amelia insisted that she could meet me at the hotel. I got the feeling she didn't want me at her house. It was weird how that bothered me. But I told myself in the end, it was a good thing. She was on the same page about this relationship as I was. We needed to get this annulment and then go on with our lives like it had never happened. After all, that was the definition of an annulment, right? To make the marriage disappear.

When I got to my hotel suite, I hit the minibar and then kicked back and relaxed until Amelia arrived. I was well into my second drink when there was a knock on the door. Going to it, I peered through the peephole and saw a blast of wild red hair. I flexed and then fisted my fingers as I fought the wave of lust that came over me.

I opened the door, seeing Amelia, and a second wave of need crashed through me. It was like a fucking tidal wave. A tsunami of need that went straight to my dick. Our gazes met and held as she stepped into my room. As the door shut, we stood there like idiots, staring at each other. In the recesses of my brain, a voice was telling me to step away from Amelia. It was reminding me that we were just here to fill out paperwork.

But Jesus fuck, every cell in my body wanted her. I stared down at her, wondering if she was feeling the same. Her hazel eyes sparked with a flame, her cheeks were flushed, and her breath hitched. Yes, she was feeling it too.

"Our phone calls have been nice." My voice was hoarse as I sought to confirm that she wanted what I wanted.

"Yes." Her voice was breathless.

"But not quite like the real thing."

She gave a small shake of her head. "Not even close."

Unable to stand the tension, to fight off the need any longer, I wrapped my arm around her, tugging her against me, fusing my lips to hers as I walked us both back until I had her pressed against the wall. Heaven help me, but I was lost in this woman.

CHAPTER TWELVE

Amelia

I was surprised by how my heart had thumped hard in my chest when Max opened the door and I saw him again in person. But then again, ever since I met him, he'd had a strange effect on me.

While we'd been engaging in phone sex, we hadn't spoken since before Thanksgiving. Mostly, he sent me short texts letting me know when he'd be here. I wondered if he planned to simply fill out the papers and file them.

But then his green eyes darkened and desire radiated off him. Thank God, because I was halfway to throwing myself into his arms.

He pulled me to him even as he pressed me against the wall.

"What do you do to me?" he murmured against my lips.

I wanted to ask the same thing, except now, his mouth was consuming mine, his tongue dancing with mine.

His hands were all over me, then sliding the skirt of my dress up. His fingers dipped under my panties and found me wet and aching.

"Max."

"Fuck. I'm mad for you."

I undid his belt buckle and pants. He pushed my panties down and then lifted me, pressing me against the wall as I wrapped my legs around him.

He looked at me with the same mixture of confusion and need that I felt. Then he thrust in, hard and deep. My breath escaped on a whoosh.

He groaned. Or maybe it was me. I couldn't tell anymore where I ended and he began. All there was were sensation and heat and drive and increasing need. He pistoned in and out of me wildly. My pussy was on fire, the friction burning it up.

"Fuck . . . now, Amelia . . . come now." He buried his face in my neck as his movements became erratic, frenetic.

And then I was there. I hit the edge, and with a driving thrust, he sent me soaring. Pleasure rushed through me to every cell.

"Max!" God, it felt so good.

He grunted and drove in, grinding against me, doing it again and again as his orgasm overtook him.

When he stopped, we remained plastered against the wall, heaving in large breaths.

I clung to Max as best I could since I didn't think my legs would be able to support me.

"I feel like I should apologize." Max's arm held onto me while his other hand pressed to the wall as if he needed help staying upright as well.

"What for?"

He lifted his head, looking at me. "I was a little rough. I got carried away. I hope I didn't hurt you."

"Not at all. I was swept right up with you." That was what it felt like. The attraction drew me to him, the chemistry sizzling hot, and I was helpless to resist it. To be honest, it made things confusing. I didn't have the time for a relationship, and certainly not one with someone who lived three thousand miles away. And yet, I didn't want to let him go. For a moment, I wondered if he'd move out here, not just for me, but for the club he planned to build. But then my father flashed in my head and I knew it didn't matter. I needed to protect Max from him at all costs.

He stepped away, straightening out my skirt and then pulling up his pants. "Hi."

I laughed. "Hi, yourself. I liked that greeting."

He flashed a grin. "Why don't you come in? Can I fix you a drink?"

Disappointment swirled in my gut. Now, we were on to the business part of our meeting. "Sure."

I followed him to the living area of the suite and sat in one of the plush white couches with the view of Las Vegas.

"How was your Thanksgiving?" he asked as he pulled a small bottle of wine out from the mini fridge.

"Stressful. My father had been out of town, and I sort of hoped he would've stayed out of town. I would've rather had Thanksgiving just with my brother." Once the words were out of my mouth, I wondered why I was sharing so much. He didn't need to know about my dysfunctional family. I should have just gone with the standard "fine" answer. "How about you?"

He let out a laugh as he picked up two glasses of wine and brought one over to me. He sat down next to me. "It was quite eventful. Not the usual Clarke family holiday."

I kicked my heels off and tucked my feet underneath me, turning to face him. I wanted to know all about him and his family. I wanted to do anything except the task we were here to do, filling out annulment papers. I was in a bad way for him.

"What happened?" I asked.

Max swirled his wine in his glass and then took a sip. "My brother brought Kate home to meet the family."

"She's the one he was trying to reconcile with?"

He nodded. "To be honest, I was sort of surprised she came. She's been working really hard to keep him from penetrating that locked up heart of hers. The fact that she came suggested that Sam was getting through to her."

"Sometimes, feelings happen whether you want them to or not." I knew that firsthand as I sat here longing for something more with Max.

He gave a nod and half a shrug. "All seemed to be going well until his ex and her daughter showed up."

My eyes widened. "His ex? I thought Kate was his ex?"

Max shook his head and then nodded. "Well, yes, Kate was his ex, but he had an ex before Kate. That first ex was one of the reasons Kate became his second ex." He looked at me, his eyes shining with sincerity. "He didn't cheat. Sam is a good and decent man. In fact, that part of him, the need to do the right thing, was what ultimately ended his relationship with Kate." He shook his head. "It's a long, convoluted story. Suffice it to say, Kate didn't take it very well when Sandra showed up for Thanksgiving dinner."

I studied him, trying to figure out why an ex would be invited to Thanksgiving dinner. "Did she just show up?"

He shook his head again. "I know it all sounds melodramatic, like my family lives in a soap opera, but it's really not. Sandra had a brand-new baby and her family basically abandoned her. So, she went to Sam, suggesting it was his. Sam and my parents took her in. She and her daughter recently moved to Boston, so I don't think Sam considered that she would be there."

Understanding dawned. "So, Kate hadn't been warned."

He nodded. "Exactly. And Kate, for as smart and interesting she is, she has a lot of trust issues. In some ways, I don't blame her. I know what Sam did five years ago really hurt her. But I wish she could see how much he loves her. How much he regretted what he did. How committed he is to her now."

"So does that mean they're done?" I sipped the wine. I didn't wish heartache on anyone, but I had to admit I was glad to hear even perfect families had their issues.

"I think so, but this time, I don't think it's on Kate's end. When we got back to California, Kate's brother Ethan showed up and started to kick my ass thinking I was Sam. He was angry that Sam wasn't doing the right thing by his sister."

I arched a brow. "When a man is told to do the right thing, that usually means she's—"

"Pregnant. But she hadn't told Sam. Sam believes she wasn't going to tell him. And that was it for him. He realized she wasn't ever going to trust him again."

"What about the baby?"

"He's not going to do the right thing because he's obligated. Sam is going to love that kid. Like I said, I can understand why Kate is hard headed and not wanting to trust, but at the same time, trust goes both ways, right? My brother was busting his balls to prove to her that he was the man she wanted, and in the end, she's the one who betrayed him. It's too bad, really, because I haven't seen Sam so happy in a long time." He took a sip of his wine and then shook his head. "You don't want to hear all about my family drama."

"I like hearing about your family. They're definitely better people than my dad."

"Well, he has a lovely daughter."

We were quiet for a moment, and the silence started to turn awkward. Was now the time he was going to pull out his laptop and we were going to fill out the annulment papers together?

He looked at his watch and then at me. "I suppose it's a little early for dinner, but I didn't have lunch. Any chance you're hungry and want to go out to eat?"

I absolutely wanted to do that. What I didn't want to do is go out and be seen with Max in case my father had his henchmen watching over me.

I let out a sigh. "I'm so comfortable here. The view is great, and I like the secluded privacy. Perhaps we can get room service."

His green eyes studied me, and I wished I knew what he was looking for. Maybe I should tell him about my father and how I didn't want Max to get dragged into any scheme my father would cook up.

He gave a quick nod. "Actually, that sounds nice. What would you like to eat?"

"Is there a menu?"

He rose from the couch and went to the table where the phone sat. On top was a binder which he picked up and brought back. He sat next to me, leaning in close, so close I could smell the sexy scent of him. My heart rolled in my chest with longing.

He flipped to the menu and began scanning. "Do you suppose salmon is good in Nevada? Isn't this a desert state? How would they get fresh salmon?"

"They fly it in, probably."

"Well, then I'm going to have the salmon. How about you?"

I scanned the menu but didn't really read it. "I'll have the salmon too."

He turned to the wine list. "Do you have a wine preference?"

I shook my head. "I'm sure you know more about wine than I do."

He turned his head to look at me. "But surely, you're learning. You are trying to get a vineyard as a client, right?"

I nodded. "Yes, but my focus has mostly been on learning their wines."

"Are any of them on this list?"

I scanned the list and found a red from the vineyard I was very close to signing as a client. I pointed to it. "But red doesn't go with fish, does it?"

"We'll get a white and a red. We're staying in, so it doesn't matter if we get a little sloshed."

I laughed. "It's not like we can get into any more trouble than we already have from drinking too much."

His lips twitched upward slightly at the joke but then faltered. I kicked myself for reminding the both of us why we were here.

"How about dessert?" I said to get us off the topic of our drunken marriage and upcoming annulment.

He turned to a page with a long list of desserts. "What's your fancy?"

"How about that molten lava cake? I love gooey, sticky chocolate."

He looked at me again, and this time, I saw fire in his eyes. "You like sticky, huh?"

This time, the fire was inside me, blazing through my bloodstream. "I do. I like it with a lot of whipped cream, too."

"Well, then. I'd better order some."

He stared at me for a long moment, and I got the feeling he wanted to say something. Finally, he gave a quick smile and stood to go order the food. When he walked away, I realized that I hoped he was about to tell me that he wanted to continue a relationship with me. Oh, sure, we would still have to go through with the annulment. But that didn't mean we had to end. He hadn't said anything. I kicked myself for not being able to manage this crazy yearning.

By the time our meal arrived, the sun was just finishing its ascent and the lights of Las Vegas were coming on.

He glanced out the window as the city lit up. "I guess you're used to all this, aren't you?"

I put my napkin in my lap. "I guess I am. Surely, they have lights in New York City."

"Not like this. It sort of makes me think of Christmas."

I looked out the window at the view. All I saw were blinking lights shouting *come lose your money here*. Or *come watch our dancing girls here*.

"Do you like Christmas?" I asked.

He turned his attention to me, his expression turning into a boyish grin. "Absolutely. I love the lights. I love the music. I love the scents. I love the snow—"

"And the presents?"

He laughed. "Those are nice too, but Christmas has always been special with my family."

Max made it sound like his family was like a Norman Rockwell painting during the holidays.

He tilted his head to the side. "I take it that Christmas isn't the same for you."

I shrugged, flaking off a piece of my salmon. "I like it just fine if it's just me and my brother, James." I sighed, not sure I should say any more and at the same time feeling compelled to make him understand. "I don't think my father has a single cell that contains empathy, generosity, or any of the things that go along with family and the holidays. He's all about him, and if you're not careful, anything you say or do will be used against you if it suits him."

Max reached across the table, putting his hand over mine. I turned it over, and he laced his fingers with mine. My heart skipped a beat, and the longing rushed through me again. There was something here. Something between me and Max. More and more, even though I knew it was fruitless, I wanted it to keep going.

"I'm sorry that your father's like that. You deserve more. Better."

I smiled at him. "Thank you, Max. I think that too, but sometimes, it's nice to hear other people think so too. Sometimes, people are judged by their family, you know?"

"I suppose I have it the opposite of you. My family has a good reputation, and so people naturally assume I'm going to be like them. I try to be, but I'm not sure I've achieved the level of openness and generosity that my parents have."

"I think you're selling yourself short."

He stared at me again in the same way he had on the couch. Like there was something he wanted to say. But then he released my hand and turned his attention back to his food.

When I finished my food and my second glass of wine, I was stuffed.

Max looked over the table at me, his green eyes glinting with wickedness. "How about dessert?"

All my girly parts fired up to full throttle. I stood. "Let me."

I walked over to the bar area where our server had left the tray of food. I picked up one of the lava cakes with whipped cream. Because it had been sitting, the whipped cream was liquefied, but that was okay.

I walked over to the table, setting the cake on it and looking down at Max. "Lava cakes are messy. Maybe you should take your clothes off."

He stood and tugged me close to him. "I will if you will."

"I will. You first."

He stripped, and I marveled at his sexy body. I wanted to spread chocolate and whipped cream over every inch of him and lick it off. I started by brushing chocolate onto his lips and then licking and kissing it off. He groaned, and when I stepped away, his dick, which had already been filling, was now at full staff. I longed to straddle him and take him inside my body, but I ignored my need, focusing on worshiping this man's perfect body.

Dipping my fingers in the chocolate and whipped cream, I ran them down his chest, following with my mouth, licking the sweetness off his warm skin.

I watched his eyes as I scooped up more of the dessert. They were hot with desire. Desire for me.

I lowered down to my knees, looking up at him. "Mmm."

He groaned. "I might just come from watching you kneeled in front of me."

"Not until I get a taste." I ran the chocolate along the length of his dick, swirling it around his tip.

"Jesus fuck, Amelia." His head fell back.

I took him in hand and then slid him deep into my mouth. I was going to consume every inch of this man. I was going to get my fill. As much as I wanted more, I knew it was impossible, so I needed to make memories that would last a lifetime.

CHAPTER THIRTEEN

Max

I wasn't supposed to be fucking Amelia again. I told myself I wouldn't. But here I was, surrendering to her sexy, hot mouth. And later, I would be inside her tight pussy again. How could I not be? This woman was smart and sweet and funny, and I wanted more of her.

I was supposed to be filling out annulment papers but couldn't bring myself to broach the subject. When she joked about our drunken marriage, I thought she was bringing it up. At the very least, she gave me an opening. But I didn't take it. I didn't want to take it. This was what I wanted. Spending time with her and talking and touching. She was a drug, and I was now hooked.

Her lips sucked on my dick, and she made "mmm" sounds that vibrated along my shaft. I watched my dick as it disappeared into her pretty pink mouth. Jesus, it was sexy.

I threaded my fingers through her wild hair and moved my hips with her. I was in a fucking fantasy. I wanted this moment to go on and on, but it was too exciting, too erotic. I flew like a shooting star toward oblivion.

"Fuck!" I yelled out as I bucked forward and exploded into her mouth. She continued to suck and lick my cock until I worried that I wouldn't have any more to give her. But I didn't have to fuck her to please her.

She looked up at me with a smug, satisfied grin. She ran her tongue around her lips, licking off my cum and chocolate. My dick twitched, and I knew that it wouldn't be long before I'd be able to get inside her. But in the meantime, it was my turn for dessert.

I stripped her and set her on the table. I coated both hands with the chocolate and covered her tits. I leaned over, sucking her nipple. Good Christ, she tasted divine. Chocolate covered Amelia was my new favorite dessert.

I smoothed the chocolate over her belly, licking the goodness off her silky skin. Finally, I reached her pussy. I covered it in chocolate and then devoured her. She moaned and arched and urged me on. My dick was now at full tilt, wanting to be inside her. But I waited, using my tongue to drive her up and up until she cried out and her pussy juice coated my mouth. Yes, chocolate covered Amelia was my favorite dessert.

I straightened and gripped her hips. "I need to fuck you."

"Yes." Her hands settled over mine. I jerked forward, thrusting in until I was as deep as I could possibly go. What was it about this woman that made me need her so desperately? That no amount of sex seemed to quench my thirst for her?

A part of me wanted to slow things down. Take my time. Offer tenderness. But I was so filled with desire that I couldn't rein it in. I fucked her like a madman.

"Max!" She arched, and her pussy clamped down on my dick so hard, I saw stars as she took me flying with her. We moved and moved until the waves of pleasure fell to a ripple and then subsided.

I looked at the mess we'd made. Sex juices and chocolate and whipped cream were smeared over our chests and bellies. I'd had sex with many women in my life, but there was something about Amelia that was different. Whether we were going hard and fast like maniacs, or slow and smooth on a sleepy morning, or playful like now, it seemed like it was always the best orgasm I'd ever had. What I didn't want to look too closely at was the way that it felt more than just physical. When my dick was inside her, it wasn't just two bodies joined together. It felt like our souls were merged as well. That had to mean something, but I didn't want to know what.

She laughed as she lifted her head and looked at the same mess I had been eyeing. "Well, that was fun."

I let out a laugh, loving how open this woman was. I held out my hand to her. "How about we take a shower?"

Her hazel eyes gleamed. "Can I wash you?"

I groaned as sweet erotic sensations picked up again. "Only if you let me wash you."

It goes without saying that I fucked her in the shower and then later that night against the window with the lights of Vegas as a backdrop behind her.

When she finished, we stared at each other. I was pretty sure she was thinking the same thing I was. How was this going to end? We could ignore the reality of our situation for only so long.

She looked down. "I need to go soon."

I nodded and stepped away. I picked up the robe that she'd been wearing when we came out of the shower to hand it to her.

"I can just get dressed." She scooped up her clothes that lay on the floor by the table. I set the robe aside and picked up the one I'd worn and slipped it back on. This was my cue to get my laptop and my portable printer so we could finally do what we were supposed to do, fill out the annulment papers. I could file them and serve her tomorrow before I left.

I watched her for a moment. The lights were off in the suite, so the moonlight and glow from the city below shone through the window, casting her in a beautiful, ethereal light. My heart clenched tight in my test chest.

"Why don't you stay the night?"

Her head jerked to me, surprise shining on her face. And maybe hope, although perhaps I was projecting that.

"Unless you have an early meeting or something."

She shook her head. "I don't have any meetings until the afternoon."

Something deep inside me propelled me toward her. I put my hands on her bare arms. "Then stay with me tonight. We can deal with . . . things . . . tomorrow."

I studied her, thinking she was going to say no. A part of me hoped she would. I hoped that she was strong enough to break this crazy tether between us because it was clear that I couldn't.

She nodded and leaned forward against my chest, looking up at me with her pretty hazel eyes. "Okay."

I took her hand and grabbed the extra bottle of wine we'd ordered and escorted her to the bedroom. There was no doubt I was going to have sex with her again, but I was also going to talk with her. Not about annulments or what was going on between us. We'd talk about anything and everything but that. I wanted to spend as much time as I could with her. Get my fill. When the annulment was done, she'd be out of my life. So I had between now and then to savor this magnificent woman.

It felt like I had only just fallen asleep when my phone on the bedside table started ringing. I reached my hand out, grabbing the phone and tilting the screen toward me as I turned my head just enough to look at it. It was just after five in the morning. The call was from the manager at the club in the Hamptons.

Fuck. This couldn't be good. I looked over at Amelia sleeping soundly. I wanted to curl up behind her and hold her until she woke. Instead, I slid out of bed, poking the answer button

"Hello?" I stepped out of the bedroom and into the living area.

"Sorry to bother you, Boss, but we have a couple of the detectives here asking us about drug sales out of the club."

I raked my hand through my hair, not quite awake. "What?"

"They believe there are drugs being sold from the club."

Motherfucker.

"This seems like something that you or Sam should come and deal with. I know Sam's out in California, so I called you."

My deception just caught up to me. I hadn't told anybody I was coming to Las Vegas, so everyone thought I was back in New York by now. Shit. Fuck. It was at least a six-hour flight to New York. It would take another couple of hours to charter a plane and get to the airport.

"Are they there? Can you put one on the line?" It wasn't wise to talk to the police without my lawyer, but I knew I would need to do something until I could get there or could get a lawyer there.

"Who am I talking to?" I asked.

"This is Detective Daniels," she responded. "We'd like to question you and your staff about drugs being sold from the club. "

"I can assure you that the club isn't involved in any such thing."

"Nonetheless, we need to talk with you."

"I'm out of town right now, but I can be out there tomorrow. I'm going to tell all my staff not to talk to you unless, of course, you have a warrant or you're arresting someone. If you're going to insist on talking to them now, you're going to have to wait until I can get a lawyer out there. Or you can come back tomorrow, and I will be there."

I could hear muffled talking, and I presumed she was talking with her partner. "We'll be here tomorrow. If you're not here—"

"I'll be there."

I hung up, hurrying back into the bedroom. I tossed my clothes in the bag except for the ones I was going to wear. Then I went into the shower, taking a quick one and then getting dressed. I didn't bother with shaving.

As I exited the bathroom, I saw Amelia still sleeping in bed. I so badly wanted to climb back in and curl up around her. I carried my bag into the living area and found my laptop case. I pulled out a piece of paper and a pen and started to scribble a note, but my handwriting was much like a doctor's, so I quickly pulled out the portable printer, turning it on and slipping in a piece of paper. Then from my phone, I typed a message and printed it onto the paper.

I hated leaving like this, but it wasn't because we hadn't filled out the annulment paperwork like we planned to do. I hated leaving her side. For a moment, I wondered if she'd be annoyed that we hadn't filled out the paperwork. Well, if she was, I'd just make arrangements to come back again. Or maybe she could fill it out, and hopefully, being drunk would pass as a reason for not being of sound mind when we got married.

I folded the paper in half and set it on the bedside table so that it was upright like a tent, so I could be sure she'd find it. I desperately wanted to lean over and kiss her goodbye, but I didn't want to wake her. So, with one final look at Amelia, I walked out of the bedroom, grabbing my laptop case and my bag, and left the suite.

On the ride to the airport, I was able to book a charter flight, and an hour and a half later, the plane's wheels left the ground. I was returning to New York still a married man.

CHAPTER FOURTEEN

Amelia

I woke the next morning feeling warm and relaxed. Immediately, memories of the night before with Max flooded my brain. Images of soft touches and hard thrusts sent tingles through my body. I reached my hand out to the other side of the bed, but it found emptiness. I turned my head and saw that Max was already up. Checking my watch, I discovered it was seven. It was early, but then I remembered it was three hours ahead in New York, so Max was likely working.

I wanted to get up and go to him, enticing him back to bed for a repeat of last night. I suspected he'd be game for it, but I didn't move. As much as I wanted him, if I went to him, we'd need to finish the business we hadn't gotten to the night before. I wasn't ready to deal with it.

I turned over onto my other side. A piece of paper was tented on the side table. I picked it up, lying on my back as I held it open to read the typed text.

Amelia,

I'm sorry I'm not there with you as you wake up this morning. I received a call of an emergency in New York, so I had to leave. I didn't want to wake you because you were sleeping so peacefully, and I know I kept you up most the night.

My body flashed with heat at the memory of all the things he did to me last night.

I know we have unfinished business. I hope you're not annoyed that it's not completed. I'll be in touch about it soon.

In the meantime, you're welcome to stay in the suite for as long as you'd like. Order room service breakfast. It's all covered.

Talk to you soon,

Max.

I dropped my hands on the bed beside me and stared up at the ceiling, trying to decipher every word in the letter. Did he really just want me to sleep? Or did he not want to deal with me this morning? If he didn't want to deal with me, did that mean he didn't want to fill out the annulment papers? It seemed like if he was ready to be done with this affair, he would've stayed and finished the paperwork. So the emergency must've been real.

He expressed concern that I'd be annoyed that we hadn't completed the enrollment papers. Was that projection because he was annoyed we didn't get them done? I covered my face with my hands and groaned. *Amelia, you're making yourself crazy.*

Deciding to push it all away, I rose from bed and took a shower. I didn't order breakfast, but I did get a cup of coffee and sat at the table to enjoy the view before I headed home.

Once home, I busied myself with work. Christmas was a little more than a few weeks away. The holidays were a busy time for businesses, so I and my staff were busy as well. Just like Thanksgiving, we needed to work ahead if we wanted time off at Christmas. Not only did we need to cover the few days around Christmas, but we also needed to prepare for the new year. It was a good thing to be busy because it was a distraction from thinking about Max.

As the next few days ticked by and he didn't call or text, my mind once again worked to decipher what his note and subsequent silence meant. Was he too busy with his emergency to contact me? I didn't know what the emergency was, but if it involved family, of course, he would be too busy to call the woman he was having an affair with, even if she was technically his wife.

Maybe he was trying to quit me cold turkey. His life was in New York, and we were going to get an annulment, so there was no reason to draw this affair out. Or I could be reading everything all wrong. I shouldn't have been trying to read anything at all. I needed to wait until Max called me.

On Friday, I received a call from the vineyard I was hoping to sign as a client, inviting me up for the weekend, and to a meeting on Monday morning to hash out details. When I completed the call, I rose from my chair, doing my happy dance. For a moment, I wondered if leaving town was a good idea because Max could call and indicate that he was flying back to Nevada to take care of the annulment. But government offices weren't open on the weekend, so it wasn't like we would be able to file until next week, anyway.

I chastised myself for considering pushing off this trip to California to sit around and wait for a man. This was exactly the reason I wasn't in a relationship in the first place. Business had to come first.

I booked my flight to San Francisco and then a little puddle jumper from there up to wine country. The more I thought about it, the more I realized I needed time away. Time away from thinking about Max, as well as time away from Las Vegas.

Saturday morning, I woke early, preparing to leave for the airport. My nerves were a jumble in my stomach. Nervousness before meeting the client wasn't unusual, but this time, I almost felt sick.

I made it to the airport in time, and the flight from Las Vegas to San Francisco was uneventful. The flight from San Francisco to wine country was a little bumpier, but that was to be expected in smaller planes. Still, it didn't help my stomach any. When I got off the plane, a woman greeted me as I headed toward the small terminal building.

"Ms. Dunsmore?"

I nodded and held out my hand. "Yes, I'm Amelia Dunsmore."

She gave my hand a quick sturdy shake. "I'm Lara Winthrop. It's nice to meet you. Thank you for coming."

"Winthrop?" Winthrop was the name of the winery.

She smiled. "It's a family business. My dad is running it, but I plan to take over someday. It was my idea that we hire a social media expert. We don't want to get left behind."

She wasn't the person I'd been dealing with, but clearly, she was important. And because she was here personally greeting me, I felt important as well.

I nodded. "I'm here to help make sure that you don't."

She drove me in her sleek little Audi out into the countryside, once covered with trees but now covered with vines. The Winthrop winery was exactly like one might expect. It had hundred-year-old Italian architecture surrounded by gardens and natural beauty.

"I'll give you a tour of the winery and the vineyards a little bit later. Our main house is a little bit further up the road, and we have a guest-house there for you to stay while you're here."

As she drove us toward the main house, she recounted the history of the vineyard, starting from the Italian immigrant who had brought a few grape vines with him from Tuscany. The Winthrop family bought it just over fifty years ago, and it had stayed in the family ever since. Of course, I knew all this because I did my research. But I listened because there was so much more to be gained by the client giving me information than reading it on the Internet. In her tone, I heard pride in her family and excitement to be the next generation preparing to take it over.

She dropped me off at the guesthouse and gave me time to settle in before we were off on a tour of the winery and the vineyard. I used my phone to take pictures and write notes as marketing ideas came to me.

That evening, I was invited to the main house for dinner. Her parents were there, along with Lara, the foreman, Mr. Serrano, and a business manager, Mr. Laszlo, who had been the one I'd been talking to until Lara picked me up this morning.

The family was friendly, yet formal. I wondered if that was because I was here or if they were always like that. When I was a little girl, before my mom left, dinners were what I imagined state dinners at the White House were like. We had to dress up, and we were served by people wearing white coats. My mom had been a fan of historical dramas, and I think she wanted to live like the aristocrats did over a century ago.

"Lara isn't going to have to start dancing in videos, is she?" Mrs. Winthrop asked once our plates were served.

I understood where the question was coming from. Social media was always changing, but sometimes, some of the trends were odd to people older than me.

"Not unless she wants to," I said.

Lara laughed, but her mother frowned.

I cleared my throat. "One of the most successful social media influencers of today got his start talking about wine on the Internet. But I can tell you he never danced."

"What does it involve?" her mother asked, and I could see she was distressed that this newfangled social media thing was going to hurt the winery's reputation.

"Social media is like other forms of marketing, except it's more immediate and accessible to your market. It allows your market to learn more about you and even engage with you. We could create campaigns around the process of the wine being created, from caring for the vines, all the way to the bottle hitting the table of the consumer. This can be done with a series of photos or short videos. Another idea would be to feature each wine with a meal pairing. What would be the best wine to have with salmon, for example? There's really a lot of different things we could do."

I studied the table to gauge their responsiveness. Most of them were nodding. Mrs. Winthrop still didn't look convinced.

"With the holidays coming, there could be campaigns on the best wines to give as a gift or when you're invited to a holiday party. There could be a campaign designed to teach people how to taste and understand the subtleties of wine. They can become armchair sommeliers."

Mrs. Winthrop frowned. "Armchair?"

"A play on the term 'armchair detective'. The person who stays at home and helps solve mysteries. In this case, it would be people at home becoming wine experts by learning from you and your wines."

"I think all those ideas are fantastic." Lara smiled at me, I suspected to give me encouragement.

"I have to concur," Mr. Laszlo said. He was a little bit older than me by fifteen years or so. But he wasn't so much older than he didn't understand the power of social media.

Mr. Winthrop reached out and patted his daughter's hand. "You're going to be taking over the vineyard someday, so I'm open to all these new ideas of marketing. But I share your mother's concern that we don't want to end up looking like fools."

I had to be careful how I responded to this. Sometimes, telling the client that their competitors were already maximizing social media could backfire. It made them feel behind the eight ball, and sometimes, they responded by backing away. On the other hand, knowing competitors were using social media could also help tip them to the side of this new marketing option. It told them that they wouldn't be alone and that if they didn't join in, they could be left behind.

"Coldspring's vineyard launched social media campaigns about six months ago." I mentioned the winery up the road from them. That was probably the closest competitor.

Mr. Winthrop's brow furrowed. "Really? Old man Santorini is on social media?"

I nodded. "I reviewed it, and I've tasted their wines. Yours are better, and I know your social media can be better too." I didn't know the first thing about wines, but I wasn't lying when I said that the Winthrop's wine was better, at least to my inexperienced palate. I wondered what Max would think. He seemed to know something about wine.

"We have set up time tomorrow for more tours, and then Monday morning, we can hear your full presentation," Mr. Laszlo said.

"Yes. Let's not talk business. Let's enjoy dinner," Lara said.

Her mother nodded but still didn't look happy. "I don't know why you're so focused on business instead of getting married and having children," she said to Lara.

Lara rolled her eyes. "My mother still thinks a woman's place is in the kitchen."

"I do not." Her mother's eyes flashed with pain. "But I know life is fuller with a family. If you put it off, life will pass you by and it will be too late."

"You just want grandchildren."

"I'm not going to deny that." Mrs. Winthrop looked at her husband. "Is it too much to want grandchildren?"

"Not at all, dear."

Lara pursed her lips at her parents. "I'm focused on learning the business and making sure it endures. I can't nurture a relationship or raise children and do what I need to do for the family business at the same time. At least, not right now."

I nodded in agreement.

"I take it you're not married either?" Mrs. Winthrop asked me.

"No. I'm focused on my business as well. I have nearly a dozen staff who rely on it to support themselves, so I need to do what I can to grow the business." I felt it was important to let them know that I wasn't a little one-woman show.

"I don't understand women these days. Why don't they want to get married and have families?"

"We never said we didn't want that, Mother. We just don't want it now. I'm only twenty-nine. I have time."

I hoped they didn't ask my age. I was younger, but I didn't want them to worry that I was too young to trust their social marketing to.

"Now ladies, let's enjoy dinner." Mr. Winthrop gave Lara and his wife a look. I imagined this wasn't the first time he'd had to step in on the discussion of marriage and family.

Later that evening, I chilled in the guest house, checking emails and sending reports to staff about the meeting so far. I frequently looked at my phone for texts or messages from Max, but there were none.

The next morning, my nerves wreaked havoc on my stomach again, but by the time the day got going, it settled down. Today, the tour was longer and more in-depth, giving me insight into the process of winemaking and introducing me to many of the people involved.

In Mr. Winthrop's library, I looked through old records and pictures depicting the vineyard's history. I spent the rest of the evening adding what I'd learned on my tours to the presentation.

When I woke Monday morning, I should have felt good that I was going to close the deal today. But the first thing I did when I got out of bed was head to the bathroom and get sick. What the heck was wrong with me? I pressed my palm to my forehead. It didn't feel warm. Doing my best to ignore it, I took a shower and got dressed. By the time I was at the main house in the library where my presentation was scheduled to happen, my stomach had settled down.

I went through my presentation for all the same people who'd been at the dinner table Saturday night. I finished with a campaign that we could start running as soon as they signed on the dotted line. It focused on the fact that the Winthrop vineyard and winery started as a family-run business and was still a family-run business. What better way to bring joy and festivity to families during the holidays than from a family-made wine? Maybe it was a little cheesy, but holidays and families went together like peanut butter and jelly, and consumers loved the idea of supporting families, not large conglomerates.

While Mrs. Winthrop was still skeptical, she supported Lara, and then Mr. Winthrop and Lara signed on the dotted line. It was all I could do to contain my excitement. Of course, I thanked them for their business, but I didn't jump on the table and do my happy dance like I wanted to do.

When Lara drove me back to the small county airport, she said, "My parents did research on you. They got concerned when they learned you were an influencer in high school and college. I think they were afraid that was what you were going to try and sell them. But clearly, you know your stuff."

"I'm glad I was able to convey that to them."

"I really appreciate your coming here and spending all this time with us and getting my parents on board. I'm having a case of wine sent to you in thanks."

I smiled. "Thank you, but that's not necessary. Having your business is all I need."

She glanced at me briefly with a grin. "I know you're going to help us become a premier winery in Northern California, maybe all of California. Maybe the whole United States."

I laughed. "It's good to have goals."

At the airport, I said goodbye to Lara and made the return trip to Las Vegas. It was late afternoon when I finally walked into my townhome. I dropped my bag and my purse by the door and flopped on the couch feeling exhausted. I checked my phone for the umpteenth time. No missed call or voicemail and no text from Max. This was good, I told myself. I'd just signed a big client, and I needed to focus on that. Max's lack of communication would make that easy.

As I rested, a kernel of guilt grew. Maybe I should call or text Max. He'd left quickly because of an emergency. I should call to make sure he was okay. We weren't on the track to happily ever after, but we had a connection. A friendship. A friend would check on him.

Then again, maybe I should leave it alone. Perhaps silence was his way of cutting ties. We still had that situation of a drunken marriage to deal with but could file the papers. I'd always heard that being drunk wasn't an excuse to get an annulment in Las Vegas, but considering that neither Max nor I could remember anything about getting the license or getting hitched, maybe it would work.

But I wasn't going to do it right now. Right now, I was exhausted. I needed to rest. I would look into it tomorrow.

CHAPTER FIFTEEN

Max

The day after arriving back in New York, I was out in the Hamptons dealing with the police and the fact that someone was selling drugs out of the club. I'd hoped that a single talk with the police would resolve the situation and the issue would be put to rest, but that wasn't the case. I needed to stay on site to deal with the club as well as the police. Thankfully, my family had a house in the Hamptons so I had a place to stay.

I'd involved our attorney in the problem, but I hadn't yet called Sam to let him know what was going on. I also hadn't called Amelia after my abrupt departure. I told myself the absence and lack of communication were necessary. It proved that while I enjoyed being around her, we weren't anything more than two people who had great sex. How could it be anything more? Everything about us was an accident, from her nearly taking my car at the airport to our somehow ending up married. Lives weren't built on accidents.

The problem I had was that deep down, my soul kept calling my brain a liar. Working on a problem like drugs in the club didn't distract me or lessen the desire to want to call or see Amelia. Even in the middle of talking with detectives, she would come to mind. There was no rhyme or reason as to why I'd think of her. It wasn't like something the detective said triggered a memory. It was as if she was always there on the edge of my mind. It was starting to drive me mad.

Monday evening, I was having a drink sitting in the sunroom of the Hampton home looking out over the dark Atlantic Ocean. Normally, I liked to sit outside, but it was early December in New York, making it too cold.

I should have been thinking about calling Sam to let him know what was going on at the club. But I didn't want to add any more to his grief. I hadn't heard from him since I left him angry and hurt from Kate's actions. But if I put it off too long, he'd be angry at me for not keeping him in the loop.

At this moment, though, my not calling had nothing to do with him and instead everything to do with Amelia, whom I couldn't stop thinking about. I'd left without saying goodbye except for the note, which felt woefully inadequate. But she hadn't called or texted me either. What did that mean? Was she just going on with her life, thinking our affair was over? Was she angry at me for leaving the way I did? The fact that these and other questions constantly flooded through my mind proved that forgetting her wasn't going to be easy. I really needed to get in touch with her about the annulment, but talking to her would only prolong the yearning I had for her. Yearning I shouldn't have for her.

My phone rang, and I grabbed for it like it was a fucking lifeline. My heartbeat sped up and hope filled my chest. I looked at the caller ID.

Sam.

The disappointment was swift and acute. I began to wonder if I would ever stop feeling like this about Amelia.

I poked the answer button. "Sam."

"I'm getting married."

My brain must've been addled, either from the constant thinking of Amelia . . . or maybe it was that I was on my second glass of scotch. "What?"

"I'm getting married. I'm getting married and having a kid." Sam's voice was the happiest I'd ever heard him. My brother was giddy with joy.

I was happy and envious at the same time. I told myself it was practicality, and not jealousy, that had me saying, "Don't you think it's a little soon? You said you were going to get married at Thanksgiving, and that didn't go over very well."

"I know you're looking out for me because you love me, Max, but I'm not going to let you put a damper on my happiness."

I took a sip of my drink, giving me a moment to think about how I wanted to respond. My brother was a grown ass man who knew Kate and knew her issues with trust and how badly she could hurt him. But he wanted to go forward and create the life with her that he had planned five years ago.

I had no business taking that away from him. "Well, then I'm happy for you. What happened? When I left, it seemed like you were the one who wasn't going to reconcile with her."

"I won't deny that I was angry, but she showed up a couple of days ago and we talked. I was finally able to tell her all about Sandra and Chelsea, and she shared her fears with me. I asked her to believe in me, and if she ever had a moment when she felt scared, to tell me about it instead of getting angry and running away."

"And she agreed?"

"Yes."

"And you're getting married?" I could totally see Sam running full steam ahead into life with Kate, but I wondered, as much as she loved Sam, whether she needed more time to commit to something like marriage.

"Well, first I'm going to ask her to move in with me. And if that goes well, maybe by Christmas, I'll give her a ring."

I did the mental math, figuring we were only about two and a half weeks from Christmas.

"You're not worried she'll think it's too much, too soon?" As much as I wanted to support him, if I could spare him heartache, I wanted to.

"Maybe. But I trust her to tell me if I need to put on the brakes. I waited five fucking years for this, Max. It's all I can do not to ask for it all right now. I know she needs time, so I'm trying to give it to her."

I laughed. "A week to move in together, and another week or so to get engaged?"

He laughed. "You know, for me, that's like an eternity."

"I'm happy for you, Sam. I really am."

"Thanks, bro. You know, you have something to offer a woman as well. Maybe you should think about finding someone for more than an occasional orgasm."

His words surprised me because I was pretty sure he thought I was a monk. "You know me. I like to play things safe."

"If we played it safe, Max, we'd be working for Dad and Uncle Daniel. Or maybe for Aunt Bri. Life's too short not to live it full-throttle. I've learned that from my experience with Kate."

I supposed he had a point. But living through life full-throttle made it too easy to go off the rails and crash and burn. I'd done that more than once and didn't want to do it again.

"I know you had some shady girlfriends in the past, but you're older and wiser now. I know there's someone out there who will love you the way you deserve. They won't give a fuck that you see Ds backward or whatever the hell it is you do."

I thought of Amelia and how I told her about my dyslexia. She hadn't looked at me like I was an idiot. When she suggested that we could do the annulment paperwork together, I was certain she was doing it because she knew of the dyslexia, but it didn't feel like pity or that she felt I was incapable.

"How did you know, Sam?"

"Know what? That we would be kickass club owners?"

"No. That Kate was the one."

"I think I knew the minute I saw her. It was like destiny."

I practically choked on my scotch. "You're laying it on a bit thick, don't you think?"

"Not at all. I hadn't wanted to go to the Halloween party. She told me she hadn't wanted to go either. If either of us had not shown up that night, we would've never met."

"You also wouldn't have spent the last five years like a mope."

"Maybe not, but I wouldn't have experienced the happiness I felt back then. The happiness I feel now. I'm with the woman I love and we're having a child. And it was all by chance, by accident, that we were at the party. And because I went, I met a woman who changed my life."

It didn't escape me how he used the word 'accident'. I'd thought it earlier in relation to how Amelia and I had met.

"I saw Kate, and it was like right then and there, my heart tied itself to her. I know it sounds stupid. Of course, at the time, I thought it was just lust. I'm sure she did too. We only planned to have a hookup. But then that one night turned into a weekend, and not long after that, we were living together. Every time one of us made a move to end what we thought was just a little fling, we couldn't. We always ended up back in the same orbit. And finally, we stopped fighting it. Maybe that's how you know who's the one. It's that even though your mind is telling you it's just a fling, you can't stop thinking about or being with that other person."

Every word coming out of Sam's mouth was doing weird things inside my chest. They were resonating with something inside me, something that I'd been fighting to admit. Oh, sure, I knew I was falling for Amelia, but now I realized that I wasn't. The truth was, I'd already fallen. I was in love with her. Jesus fuck. What was I going to do now?

I made a noncommittal sound to know I heard him, unable to verbalize a response.

"But I know you're probably worried about what's going on businesswise out here. We didn't get a chance to look at the properties, but I feel confident on one of them. I'll send you a video and specs for you to check out."

"If that's the one you think is best, I'm okay with that. Do you have ideas on what to do with the property out by the beach?"

"I haven't settled on that yet. I think if we demolish the building, the property value will go up. It's worth more vacant than with that shack. But I haven't thought beyond that."

"That sounds fine to me too."

There was a pause on the other end of the line. "Are you okay, Max? You're not usually so agreeable."

I rubbed my temple because all this confusion about Amelia was starting to give me a headache.

Of course, I couldn't tell him that. "We've had a problem at the Hampton club. I've been out here for the last few days, dealing with it."

"What?"

"Drugs are being sold there."

"What the fuck? How long has this been going on?"

I winced, knowing he felt like I should have called him sooner. "I can't tell you when it started. I know the cops have been watching the place for a couple of months, at least."

"You didn't tell me? What the hell, Max?"

Now I was getting a headache for a whole new reason. "I only just heard about it last week. I came out here, and I've been dealing with it the last couple of days."

"And I ask again, why didn't you tell me?"

"Because when I left you, Sam, you weren't in a good headspace. I didn't want to add to that. If I felt it was necessary to loop you in sooner, I would have, but I think it's all going to be okay. It's no one on our staff—"

"Of course it isn't. Everyone who works there, we've vetted and have worked with."

"Yes, well, none of the staff is directly involved in the drug sales, but it looks like it's possible that Allison's cousin is our drug dealer." Allison was an assistant manager and one of the people on the short-list who could relocate to California to run the club out there.

"Allison? There's no way she would allow something like that to happen at the club."

"The police are trying to figure out if maybe she's getting a cut—"

"That's bullshit, Max, and you know it. You're not throwing her under the bus, are you?"

"No. But neither do I need the police giving the club a bad reputation, or worse, closing us down."

"We have to stand by our people—"

"I am, Sam. Shut up for a minute and let me tell you what I think is going on. I think Allison is either being blackmailed or threatened. The police were ready to bring her in for an interrogation, but I convinced them to let me talk to her wearing a wire. And before you start busting my balls again about wearing a wire, I don't like deceiving her, but surely, it's better than having her brought to a police station, interrogated, and having her cousin think she's snitching on him, don't you think?"

"Fuck."

"That was my thought too. I'll be wearing the wire. I have no doubt that whatever she says will prove that she's not a volunteer participant."

Sam was quiet on the other end for a moment. "You still should've told me."

"I'm telling you now."

"I can fly out to New York—"

"It's not necessary. Really. Stay in California. Make love to the woman of your dreams and move forward on the club we want to build there. Everything's going to be fine here."

"Okay. You know, I was thinking that if we were able to get the L.A. club project moving, we might be able to speed up starting on the Las Vegas club."

I thought of Amelia and what could happen if I relocated to Las Vegas. It wasn't supposed to be a permanent relocation, but neither was Sam's move to Los Angeles supposed to be permanent, as it looked like it would be.

"Let's take it one step at a time."

"Okay. Keep me posted on what's going on out there in the Hamptons," Sam said.

"Will do. Do you think you'll be home for Christmas?"

"I don't know. I think Kate is going to want to be with her brother and sister-in-law and their kids. Plus, I want to be with her alone, in our own place, when I ask her to marry me."

"Well, you explain that to Mom. I don't want to be there when she starts weeping."

Sam laughed. "Those will be tears of joy, Brother."

When I got off the phone, I finished the scotch and headed to my bedroom. It was just after ten, but I decided to go to bed. I wanted a good night's sleep since tomorrow was the day I was going to have to talk with Allison while wearing a wire. I hoped that if it turned out that her cousin was using her, the police would be able to protect her from whatever she happened to tell me or them. Her cousin wasn't known to be violent, but when drugs were involved, it seemed like anything could happen.

I fell asleep worrying about Allison, but somewhere in the middle of the night, I was back in Las Vegas. I was in the Desert Oasis, but it wasn't the rundown heap that it was today. It was remodeled in the style of the Golden Age of Hollywood. There were pictures of glamorous movie stars from the 30s, 40s, and 50s. Holograms of icons such as Marilyn Monroe and James Dean danced with customers. The club was filled with laughter and music. The place was the new go-to location in Las Vegas being written up, not just in Vegas or Nevada tourism articles, but in travel sections of newspapers and magazines all over the country. I watched it all from the corner of the club.

"I couldn't see your vision or picture something that wasn't going to seem redundant or kitschy, but you've really created something amazing here, Max."

I looked to my left where Amelia was standing next to me, praising my efforts. She lifted her left hand, straightening my tie. The lights from the club glinted off the ring she wore on her left hand. It wasn't the ring that she had woken up with the day we discovered we were married. It was a platinum and diamond ring.

I woke with a start. The dream was unsettling, but not because it suggested a future with Amelia. What was unsettling was how much I wanted it to be true.

CHAPTER SIXTEEN

Amelia

A week later, when I was still waking up with the dry heaves, I knew something had to be wrong. I'd had nerves before, but never the level of stress that made me sick every day. Maybe I'd developed an ulcer. I hoped that was what it was and not something more serious. Whatever was going on, it was time that I found out and did something about it. I had an afternoon free and was able to make a doctor's appointment.

While I always thought I was someone who could manage stress, as I sat in the waiting room, my mind wandered to all sorts of potential ailments. It could be something serious, in which case, what would I do with my business? I had great people working for me, but no one was trained or appointed to take over in the event that something happened to me. I decided that figuring that out was going to the top of my to-do list once I finished this doctor's appointment.

The nurse called me in, taking my weight, my blood pressure, and temperature, and then told me the doctor would be in shortly as she left the room.

A few moments later, the doctor, a middle-aged woman with

bright eyes and a friendly smile, entered. She reached out her hand. "I'm Dr. Vale."

I shook her hand. "Amelia Dunsmore." The fact that my doctor had to introduce herself to me was a reminder that it had been a long time since I'd been to the doctor, except, of course, for my gynecologist.

She sat down in the chair next to the computer, reviewing my notes. "What seems to be the problem?"

"For the last week or ten days or so, I've been feeling queasy. I thought it was nerves because I had a big business deal. But that's over and done with. I feel like I'm worse today than I was when I first started feeling it."

"Do you have any pain?"

I shook my head. "No. Just queasy. Almost like I'm seasick or what I imagine being seasick must feel like."

She nodded and typed in a few notes. "Is this something that you feel continuous through the day or at certain times, say, after eating?"

I thought about that for a moment.

"It's worse when I first get up. Sometimes, it lasts as long as to lunch time, but it's almost always gone in the evening."

She lifted her head, looking at me as she asked, "Have you had any changes in your diet or maybe medications?"

"No. I don't take any medication, except for birth control." Thank God for that because on more than one occasion, Max and I had sex without a condom.

"Is there any chance you might be pregnant?"

"Nope."

She arched a brow. "You don't have a boyfriend, or you haven't had sex in the last two months or so?"

"I don't have a boyfriend." Technically, that was true. Max wasn't my boyfriend. He was a short-term lover whom I just happened to be married to.

"But have you had sex?"

"Three times. But I'm on the pill." I'd already said that, but maybe she missed it.

"Did he use a condom?"

"Yes." That wasn't a lie, either. He did use a condom. Usually.

"Every time?" she asked.

"Maybe not every time, but like I said, I'm on the pill." The unsettling feeling in my stomach grew, only this time it wasn't the nausea.

She turned to the computer and started typing. Surely, she didn't think I was pregnant. After a moment, she rose and looked at me. "Let's go ahead and take a urine sample. Let's at least rule out pregnancy. From there, we can look at a couple of other options and do blood work as well."

"Will that tell me if I have an ulcer?" Please, let it be an ulcer.

"It could be one of many things. But let's start with the most obvious—"

"Most obvious? My being pregnant isn't the most obvious."

She smiled. Inwardly, she was likely rolling her eyes. "Diagnosing an ailment is all about eliminating possibilities. Let's eliminate pregnancy and go from there."

I felt like a petulant teenager as I grumbled, "Okay, fine." I took the cup with my name and birthdate on it and went to the bathroom, giving her sample and leaving the cup for the lab to pick up. I returned to the room, sitting on the exam table, waiting until the doctor returned.

It seemed like forever when she came back into the room. I watched her but couldn't read her expression.

"Do you have a gynecologist?" she asked.

Panic whipped through me. "Yes, why? Do I have ovarian cancer or something?"

Her lips twitched as if she thought what I said was funny, but she schooled them back into place. "No, you don't have cancer. You're pregnant."

What? No. "How is that possible? Are you sure it was my pee you used?"

Her expression morphed into concern. "Is being pregnant a problem? You seem very agitated about this."

"I just don't see how it's possible."

"Well, you're on a low-dose pill. There's a lot of things that can impact the effectiveness. Certain herbal supplements—"

"I don't take those."

"Some medications—"

"I don't take those either." I was perfectly healthy.

"And if it isn't used properly—"

"What do you mean, properly? I take a pill with a glass of water every day."

"But do you take them at the same time every day? For example, was there any time that you missed it and you ended up taking it the next day?"

I thought about the few times that I'd spent the night with Max and hadn't taken my pill at the usual time in the evening.

"Sometimes, in that case, we recommend that you take both doses at the same time if you've missed one."

"So just a few hours off and I'm no longer protected from pregnancy?"

She nodded. "There are some women out there who take their pills exactly as prescribed, and they still get pregnant. There's really no sure way to prevent pregnancy except abstinence. If you're having sex, even with birth control, there's always going to be a risk of pregnancy."

I didn't remember reading that on the box that came with my pills.

"Now, if you need support or guidance, I can help you arrange that."

Oh, my God. I was pregnant. I pressed my hand to my belly. It didn't feel real. "I'm financially stable."

"That's good. But it takes more than money to raise a child. There are other options if you don't feel emotionally ready."

I stared at her in confusion. "Options?" What was she suggesting?

"Well, there's adoption or—"

I shook my head. "I'm going to keep my baby." I was shocked and scared to death, but there was no doubt in my mind that I wanted this child. It was strange how certain I was about that. It was the only thing I was sure of at this moment. I didn't know how I would tell Max or how he would respond when I did. I remembered how he told me his brother had done the right thing by a woman, and I imagined Max would too. But that didn't mean he'd be happy about it or wouldn't develop a resentment toward me. My memory flashed to a moment when we woke up married and he acted like I'd done it on purpose. Like I'd tricked him into it.

She told me to start taking prenatal vitamins, eat right, and avoid alcohol. Feeling like I was in a fog, I left her office. When I arrived home, I tried to distract myself by checking in with work. But the magnitude of what I'd learned at the doctor's office pushed me out of shock and into reality. I was going to be a mother. Despite my current marital status, I was going to be a single mother. Max would likely provide financial support, and I suspect he'd want to be involved in the baby's life, but what he and I had together wasn't happily ever after. We liked each other and had great sex, but we weren't in love.

Oh, who was I kidding? Despite my best attempts to keep things casual between us, I'd fallen head over heels for the guy. Who could blame me? He was sweet and kind. He was smart and successful. And most importantly of all was how much he cared about his family. I heard the love in his voice when he talked about them. I saw the concern in his eyes as he talked about his brother's difficult relation-ship. I envied him his close family. Sure, I had James, but I didn't have loving parents. Mine were self-centered and selfish. How I would love to be part of a family like Max had.

But even if Max had fallen for me, he wouldn't be getting as good a deal as I would. I had no doubt that my father would constantly look for ways to take advantage of my relationship with Max. It would only be a matter of time before Max grew tired and resentful of my father's intrusion, which would put a strain between us.

For a moment, I thought about moving to New York. My business was portable, and by being in the same city as Max, it would be easier to co-parent the child together. Even better, I would be able to raise it away from my father.

But moving to New York would take me away from James, leaving him here to deal with my father by himself. Further, I suspected New York City was much more expensive than Las Vegas. While my business did well, my budget would tighten living in New York.

All these thoughts rattled around in my head, making me nuts. It reminded me that I had important decisions and plans to make. I needed to train someone in my business who could handle things while I was having the baby or when the baby was sick. I had to review my health insurance documents to make sure it covered prenatal care and well-baby visits. Although I believed Max was a decent guy, I had to protect my parental rights, so I would need to talk to a lawyer about establishing legal custody of the baby.

Feeling overwhelmed by it all, I went to my living room and lay down on the couch. I closed my eyes as fatigue overwhelmed me.

My phone went off, startling me awake. I picked it up, noting the time was nearly eight thirty at night. I'd been asleep for several hours. As I hit the answer button, I realized the ring tone was *New York, New York*. Max was calling.

"Hello?"

"Hi, Amelia. It's Max."

Warmth spread through my body at the sound of his voice. But then I remembered the news I needed to tell him and the warmth turned to worry. Not only had we accidentally gotten married, but we'd also accidentally gotten pregnant. How would he respond?

"Amelia?"

"Yes, I'm here. Hi, Max."

"Are you okay?"

"Yes, of course." I used my thumb and forefinger to wipe the sleep from my eyes.

"Are you sure?"

"I'm sure. How are you?" I remembered that he had left because of an emergency. "Is everything alright with you?"

"It is now. I wanted to apologize for running off the way I did last week and not calling or texting."

My heartbeat sped up as it took his words to mean something more than they probably did. He was apologizing for not calling me, but not because we were in a relationship. It was because we had unfinished business.

"You said there was an emergency, so I figured you had your hands full with that. I hope everything's okay."

"Yes. I had an issue with one of the clubs, but it's mostly resolved now."

"Well, that's good."

He let out a soft laugh. "I had to wear a police wire the other day."

My heart leapt in my chest, but this time, it was in fear. "What? Isn't that dangerous?"

"In this case, I don't think so. I learned that drugs were being sold out of the Hamptons club and it was possible that one of our employees was part of it. But neither Sam nor I believed that was possible, at least not voluntarily. So, I convinced the detectives to let me be the one to talk to her to find out the real story, but they wanted me to wear a wire."

"Wow. So what happened?"

"It was just as I suspected. Her cousin was threatening her, so she was turning her back on his dealing drugs out of the Club. It pisses me off that she would put me and Sam at risk like that, but I'm also bothered that she didn't feel like she could come talk to us. I always felt like we were approachable and supportive to all our staff."

"I'm sure you are. But maybe her cousin was threatening her about telling you as well. And sometimes it's hard to know how people will take unexpected information, even if you believe them to be a good and decent person." I definitely knew that firsthand. I had very important news to tell Max, but hell if I could find the words to say them. Perhaps as the call went on, I'd find the nerve and the words.

"I suppose you're right. How are things with you? Have you signed the vineyard yet?"

I smiled, loving how he remembered aspects of my life. Again, my heart wanted to believe it meant something. But all it really meant was that Max was a nice man.

"I did. I spent the weekend there and then gave my presentation, walking away with a signed contract."

"That's fantastic."

"Not only did I get the contract, but she said she was going to send me a case of wine." Of course, I wouldn't be able to drink it for the next nine months.

"That's great, Amelia. I'm sure you deserve both. Listen, by running out the way I did, we didn't finish taking care of the paperwork."

It was stupid how disappointed I was that he wanted to talk about the annulment. "I was thinking I could file the paperwork. I'm still not sure that being drunk is enough to say we were incapacitated, but since we can't remember getting the license or getting married, I figured I could try."

"I still need to sign something, right?"

"First, I'd have to serve you. I could hire a courier to get it to you." I wanted to seem helpful even as I hoped he'd come to Las Vegas. Or maybe I could go to New York. I could find out just how expensive it would be to live there.

He was quiet for a moment. "No. I can fly out. It will have to be right before Christmas. Or if you're busy, I can wait."

"I'm available before Christmas." It was ridiculous how excited I was by the idea of seeing him sooner rather than later.

"I can fly out on the twenty-third. I'll have to fly back on Christmas Eve because my family is expecting me for Christmas. Looks like my brother is going to be spending it with Kate in California, which will be the first Christmas we aren't all together. It's important to my mom that I be home."

"So, things worked out for him?"

"It sounds like it. He plans to propose on Christmas Eve or Christmas."

I pictured a man who looked like Max down on his knee. "Wow. That's fast. But very romantic."

"He seems certain, so I'm going to have to trust that he knows what he's doing. He's been in love with her for a long time, so I'm hopeful that things will work out."

"I hope so too." There was a lull in the conversation. This was the time I should tell him about the baby, but the words didn't leave my mouth. I'd wait until I saw him the following week. It would be better to tell him in person anyway, right?

"I'll let you go. It was nice talking to you, Amelia."

He was hanging up? No innuendo? No phone sex? Tears rushed to my eyes, making me feel stupid.

I was jealous that Max's brother and his girlfriend were finding their happily ever after. Fairytales were for silly schoolgirls, but who didn't want to find a pure and passionate, everlasting love? Ever since meeting Max, my desire for true love had grown exponentially. Despite my best attempts to keep emotions out of it, I'd fallen hard for him. How ironic that I was married to him and having his baby, but none of it was real.

CHAPTER SEVENTEEN

Max

The line went dead, and inwardly, I kicked myself for bringing up the annulment. The minute I had, the atmosphere of the call changed. Dammit.

Hearing her voice had been like a balm on my weary soul. The worry and stress from dealing with law enforcement and a drug dealer working out of the club took its toll. I was tired and frustrated and more than a little concerned for Allison. Sitting in the enclosed porch of the Hampton house and having a few drinks only did so much to reduce the strain and tension of the situation. I needed a respite. I needed Amelia.

I called her under the guise of the annulment papers, so I shouldn't have been so annoyed with myself for bringing it up. Ending our marriage had become the excuse to be able to talk to her, to see her.

I loved hearing the excitement in her voice at getting the vineyard client. I was proud of her, although I didn't say that because really I had no reason to be proud. At best, Amelia and I were friends with benefits. Sure, I'd fallen for her, but she and I could never be more than what we were now.

I thought about Sam and Kate and how it appeared they were finally going to have the life they had planned together five years ago. I was happy for him. Maybe even a little jealous. It was the envy and the unrelenting yearning for Amelia that were the worst. In fact, it pissed me off. I didn't want to be in love. I didn't want my heart to be susceptible to a woman who could break it.

I remembered how I continued to push Sam to pursue Kate when she was so resistant and he'd wanted to give up. Life came easily to Sam. Technically, it had come easily for me too, except for the dyslexia that made reading difficult and resulted in ridicule from other students as I was growing up. But Sam breezed through life and had never had to work hard, really hard, to achieve his goal. Every time he gave up on Kate, I'd encouraged him to continue on. Mostly, it was because I knew how much he loved her and how his happiness was wrapped up in her. But I suppose a part of me wanted him to have to truly earn something. Perhaps that was my envy at work as well.

But now I understood why he wanted to give up on Kate. Handing your heart over to someone who could stomp on it was no easy feat. I'd vowed that I would never do it again after my last two disastrous attempts. It didn't matter how much I loved talking to Amelia. It didn't matter how much I longed to see her. It didn't matter how much I wished I could have with Amelia what Sam had with Kate. It wasn't going to happen. I wouldn't let it happen. It should be easy to move on since we lived on opposite sides of the country. We both had careers to focus on to distract ourselves. I imagined she was doing just that. But here I was, sitting in the dark, drinking and thinking of her.

I downed the last of my whiskey after switching to it because I finished the scotch yesterday. I savored the burn sliding down my throat, waiting for it to numb the crazy emotions I was feeling. Of course, it didn't work. Alcohol never worked to fix an emotional problem.

I rose and went inside, rinsing my glass and putting it in the dishwasher. Tomorrow would be my last day here in the Hamptons. I had done my duty for the community, the detectives, and for the club. I'd worn a wire and interviewed Allison. At first, she remained stoic, denying any knowledge of her cousin's activities. I was sure the police weren't happy with me, but I told her flat out that she was on the verge of being fired and possibly arrested. At that moment, she crumbled, weeping as the stress of her situation overcame her.

It turned out that her cousin's drug activities were helping support Allison's mother and younger brother. The cousin had told her that if she didn't look the other way while he did business in the club, her mother would be left destitute since she was currently out of work, and her teenage brother would be arrested for selling drugs, something she hadn't known he was doing. I wanted to point out that if her brother got in trouble, the cousin would too since he was the one who enlisted her brother. But at that point, it didn't matter. She'd been afraid for her family. I'd do anything for my family, so I couldn't blame her.

I didn't have time to confer with Sam, but I figured he'd be on board with the decision I made, which was to assist Allison and her family as much as we could. Allison would stay employed, but she'd need to regain our trust. Once she did, we would talk to her about relocating with her family to California where she could run the club there as we'd tentatively planned.

The woman practically dropped to her knees to thank me. It was a reminder to me of how lucky I had been growing up. My parents were successful financially and gave an abundance of love and support to me and Sam and Vivie. I believed that given a second chance, Allison could pull her life together, so I was willing to help her.

Tomorrow, I would stop by the club again and make sure everything was back to normal and then head back to Manhattan. I would spend the next couple of days checking in with the other clubs as well as preparing for Christmas and my quick trip out to Las Vegas.

It was right around midnight when I finally went to bed. I was mentally exhausted even with the alcohol sloshing around in my brain. Sleep swallowed me whole when my head hit the pillow.

Amelia showed up right on cue. She sauntered into my dream, the one place I could be true to me and my feelings.

"You look tense," she said, stripping off her robe as she walked toward me, naked, my dick at full salute as I lay on the bed.

"Do I?" I stroked my dick, loving how her eyes flared with heat as she watched me touch myself.

"I can help you with that."

"I'd love it if you did."

She straddled my legs, leaned over, and sucked my cock deep into her mouth.

"Jesus fuck." My hips bucked up as I cried out at the wash of pleasure flooding my body.

"Mmm." Her moan vibrated through my body. When I popped out of her mouth, I nearly grabbed her, begging her not to stop. But she moved up my body, positioning that sweet, tight pussy over my cock. Her eyes were seductive as she lowered down.

"So fucking good." I gripped her thighs as she settled over me. My dick had never been so happy than when it was buried inside Amelia. "Ride me."

She smiled, tossing her head so that her wild hair flowed down her back. My hands went to her tits, squeezing and pinching as she rocked over me.

"Are you getting enough friction, baby?" I wanted to come, but more than that, I wanted her to be enjoying the ride as well.

She leaned forward, resting her hands on my chest. "Yes." She rode faster, her tits bouncing, her cheeks flushed as she chased her pleasure. I could live right here forever with Amelia blissed out, riding my cock.

She cried out, and her pussy tightened around me.

"Fuck." I levered up in bed, shooting cum all over my sheets and chest. I collapsed back, letting the orgasm and the dream fade away. Once Amelia and I got our annulment, dreams would be all I had. I hoped they didn't fade over time. Orgasms from dreaming about Amelia were so much better than with a woman, except, of course, Amelia herself.

. . .

Back in Manhattan, my life returned to normal except for the nightly visits Amelia made to my dreams. As the days until my trip to Las Vegas ticked closer, my eagerness and excitement to see her grew even as I actively tried to tamp them down.

Today, I visited the clubs in the city, making sure there were no drug deals and checking that we were ready for the holidays. When I finished, I headed over to my parents' house for dinner. We were all excited for Sam's reconciliation with Kate, even as my mom was sad that he was going to miss Christmas with the family in New York.

"We can hardly blame him for not wanting to bring Kate here for Christmas," Vivie said from her seat at the dinner table. "Thanksgiving didn't go so well."

"That's an understatement," I said.

"The important thing is they are together now. It's usually the case that the harder you have to work for something, the sweeter the reward." My mom looked at my dad with a sappy smile. My father returned it, extending his hand, which she took and squeezed.

I rolled my eyes.

"Oh, please." Vivie shook her head. "You guys never fight. Everything between you has always been easy."

"That isn't true," my dad said. "In fact, your our story isn't that different from Sam and Kate's."

"Yeah, Sam and I were five or six when we finally met Dad." Even so, I sort of agreed with Vivie. Once my mom and dad's orbits had collided again, it seemed like we came together as a family quickly.

"I know. You've said it before. I just find it hard to believe that once Mom came back to New York, the two of you weren't back in your happily ever after mode." Vivie chased a cherry tomato from her salad around the plate with her fork.

"It took some time. And definitely some work," my father said.

My mother nodded. "Having an attraction, or even loving someone, doesn't automatically make for a good relationship. Your dad and I had to come to terms with our past. We'd had misconceptions about what happened when we parted. We had to learn to trust each other again, which meant starting over. In fact, I might even describe it as starting from a negative position because going into it, I'd been angry at your dad."

My dad squeezed her hand again. "And I'd been angry at your mom. You have to really open up your heart and be willing to risk getting hurt to get what your mom and I have."

Vivie scoffed. "We all know Sam walks around with an open heart on his sleeve."

I nodded in agreement as I sipped my wine. "But Kate doesn't. We can't blame her, considering what Sam did five years ago. But that wasn't all she had to endure emotionally. Apparently, her grandfather had disowned her, and while she had a brother to help her, she's stubborn enough that she was going to fight her way through the world, and that made her harder."

Vivie slanted her gaze at me. "How do you know so much?"

"I was in California a lot as Sam and Kate were going through all their shit."

"Well, it sounds like Kate has come around. And they're having a baby. I hate that they won't be here for Christmas, but Sam promised that they would come for a visit soon." My mom sighed, clearly feeling happy for Sam, Kate, and the baby, while also sad that she wouldn't see them on Christmas.

"Yeah, you just have to make sure Sandra and Chelsea aren't here at the same time," Vivie warned, finally stabbing the tomato and popping it in her mouth.

After dinner, Vivie asked me if I wanted to go down to the theater room and watch a movie with her. It was something we regularly did, so I agreed.

I made the popcorn and met Vivi in the theater. She was sitting in one of the reclining chairs and I took a seat next to her.

She reached over and grabbed a handful of popcorn. "Do you think Sam and Kate are going to be like Mom and Dad? I mean, do you think they're going to make it?"

I shrugged. "I hope so. I haven't seen them together since they reconciled. When I left last time, he was the one who was done with her. But I hope so."

Vivie opened a can of spiked seltzer while I twisted the top of my beer off.

"What about you? I never see you dating anyone," she said, sipping her drink.

"I date on occasion."

She smirked at me. "That's not dating, Max. You're such a player, and nobody even knows it."

I shrugged. "There's something to be said for discretion." I thought about how I'd been having an affair with Amelia, who happened to be my wife, and no one in my family knew it. A tinge of guilt settled deep in my belly, but it wasn't enough for me to confess.

"You don't want to fall in love, do you?"

I furrowed my brows as I looked at my sister. "Why would you say that?"

She wiped condensation off her seltzer can. "I don't get the feeling you're playing the field until the right woman catches your fancy. I think you're with a woman when the urge strikes you, and the rest of the time, you want to be alone. Why is that?"

I leaned over, bumping my shoulder against hers. "Since when did you become a psychologist?"

"I'm not. But that doesn't mean I don't know my brothers."

"What about you, little sis? I don't see you pulling out the bridal magazines."

She laughed. "I'm only twenty-two. I think Mom and Dad would have a cardiac arrest if I tried to settle down now."

"Still, you could be dating. There should be some handsome, smart guy sitting in this seat instead of your big brother."

She shrugged. "I was dating someone, but I don't know . . ."

I turned my upper body to face her as worry grew. "What happened? Did he hurt you?"

"Once. But mostly, it was just weird and creepy." She looked at me with serious eyes. "Don't tell Mom and Dad."

"I'll tell anyone I need to tell to keep you safe."

She shook her head vehemently. "It's not a problem now. It just made me question my choice in men, you know?"

151

I nodded. "As long as you're safe."

She nodded and grabbed another scoop of popcorn. "If I met the right guy, I would commit in a heartbeat, though. Wouldn't you love to have something like Mom and Dad have? Before Sam and Kate imploded, you could just tell that there was a lot of love between them. I would love something like that. Wouldn't you?"

"Yeah, I would." The words were out of my mouth before I could think better of them.

"Really? I thought we decided you were a confirmed bachelor."

I took a sip of my beer, unable to articulate what was going on in my head. There was no denying that I was in love with Amelia and that I was dying to see her again. Or that those two facts scared me shitless. But Vivie was right. Seeing my parents' happiness, and Sam's, I couldn't help but want that level of joy in my life. Was Amelia the one who could do that for me?

There was no doubt that the happiest I'd been over the last few weeks had been with her. And it hadn't been hard, like my mom said love needed to be. Amelia and I talked and laughed, and the sex was tremendous. Maybe it was time I gave a relationship a try. I would still sign the annulment papers, but maybe we could still give a relationship a try. I could talk to Sam about starting on the Las Vegas club sooner. He'd already brought it up.

As Vivie pressed the button to start the movie, I sat in my chair, staring at the screen but not seeing the actors. Instead, I was thinking about what I could say to Amelia when I went to Las Vegas in a few days to convince her that we were more than just an affair.

CHAPTER EIGHTEEN

Amelia

It was strange how I was much more excited about seeing Max than about celebrating Christmas. Granted, Christmas wasn't a joyful time of year for me like it was for most people, but since James and I had left home, we had found ways to make it more joyful than it had been growing up. Over the last few years, I would get a tree, and he would come over, and we'd drink spiked warm apple cider while we decorated it.

This year, my cider wasn't spiked, although I didn't tell James that. I hadn't told anyone about the baby. Not even Max. I had an equal amount of anxiety and excitement about seeing Max, wondering what he would do when I told him about the baby. The last several nights, I had dreams of our being a family. Every morning, I woke up chastising myself because I knew fairytales weren't true. But that didn't stop the wish that it could be true. As the day of Max's arrival drew closer, though, more and more, I wondered if it could be true. Maybe we weren't ready to be married and have the picket fence, but when we were together, we always got along. Even if he didn't love me like I loved him, he had to at least like me or he wouldn't have spent all that time with me. Maybe we could build on that. Maybe he would develop deeper feelings for me.

Of course, if we were going to be a family, I wanted it to be because he loved me and not because he felt obligated due to the baby. That left me with the question of figuring out how I would know if he was with me out of love or obligation. And once again, I was driving myself crazy with questions and thoughts. Questions that might be answered today when Max arrived.

Because of the sensitivity of what I needed to talk to him about, I invited him over to my townhouse. It didn't seem like telling him about the baby was something I should do in a hotel.

I checked my watch, noting I had a half-hour before Max would arrive. It was late in the afternoon, and I'd done everything I needed to prepare for his visit. My home was clean. The ingredients for dinner were prepped. The lights were sparkling on the tree.

At the knock at the door, my stomach did a somersault, but it wasn't from the baby. It was excitement at seeing Max again. I went to the door, jerking it open. My smile was beaming, ready to see the man I loved and to tell him we were having a baby.

"Hello, Amelia."

My smile dropped. "Dad. What are you doing here?" Panic began to boil up. I couldn't risk my father knowing about Max. Inwardly, I cursed. I should have arranged to meet Max at the hotel like we did last time. These were the types of mistakes one made when they let their emotions get the best of them.

He arched a brow. "Are you going to let me in?"

I didn't want to let him in, but I couldn't think of a good excuse that wouldn't make him suspicious. Maybe I could see why he was here and get him out ASAP.

I opened the door to let him in, but I stayed near it so I could open it again to escort him out. "What brings you by?"

"Can't a father stop by and check on his daughter?"

I crossed my arms over my chest. "You've never dropped by before."

"Yes, well, I realized that I haven't been a very attentive father."

That was an understatement. The only time he paid attention to either James or me was when he needed something.

"James and you are living your own lives. I don't know what's going on in them except for what I hear through the grapevine."

In my father's world, the grapevine wasn't simple gossip. His grapevine was the eyes and ears he paid or coerced to keep him in the know in Las Vegas. My heart sped up as the panic grew. Had his people discovered my relationship with Max? Or the baby?

"Have you dropped by James's place too?" I hoped my voice sounded steady and calm even though inside, my nerves were shaking.

My father shrugged. "I do happen to see him more because he works for the company. He is very dedicated. He has no life outside of the office." His eyes watched me, like he was assessing my reaction.

I did my best not to squirm under the scrutiny. "I'm dedicated to my career as well. I don't have anything to share."

His gaze went to the box of wine from Lara sitting under the table next to the door where I kept my purse. "I understand you were out of town not that long ago. It looks like you closed that deal you were looking at getting."

I studied him, wishing I could read his mind. I couldn't help the feeling that he was a cat and I was the mouse that he was toying with. "I did. Between that and the holidays, my team and I have been really busy. I haven't had a lot of time for anything else."

He gave me an expression that was a mixture of hurt and disappointment. "It pains me that you don't feel you can tell me what's going on in your life."

"I just told you the biggest news. My life isn't that interesting." It had never been interesting to him, so it was nerve-racking that he was taking an interest now. "So, you're all caught up. Maybe on Christmas afternoon, I can stop over and visit again." I had to get him out of my house. Max would be here soon.

He shoved his hands in his pockets and stared at me, the fake pain and disappointment morphing into the piercing stare of a cat before it pounced. "How come you haven't told me about Max Clarke?"

The proverbial other shoe dropped. "Who?"

My father got a feral gleam in his eyes. "You don't really think you can do anything in this town without my knowing about it, do you?"

Shit. It was just as I feared. Why hadn't I been more careful? Why didn't I say no to that second date with Max? But even as I thought it, my hand went over to my belly and my heart rolled in my chest. I couldn't regret my time with Max or this baby.

"I happened to meet him and gave him a tour of the city. We had dinner. That was it." I don't know why I thought he'd buy that. He knew the truth. I could see it in his face. The remnant of my father's fake concern for me was now gone.

He stared at me with the hard eyes of the ruthless man he was. "You and he seemed to get along well. He's a good match. So why are you trying to pretend you're not married?"

It was never a good idea to let my father know when he had surprised me or somehow gotten to me, but I couldn't stop my jaw from dropping.

My father laughed like he was in on a joke that I knew nothing about "Who do you think made it happen?"

I went completely cold inside as my father's words sank into my brain. Now I knew why Max and I couldn't remember that night. My mind quickly scanned what I'd learned about that night. The hotel hadn't sent the driver. My father had. Max and I both felt more inebriated after the champagne in the limo, which meant only one thing. My father had drugged it or the glasses we consumed the bubbly from.

My father was capable of unscrupulous deeds, but I would never in a million years have thought he would've done something like drug us and force us to get married.

"How could you? Why would you?" I couldn't stop my eyes from welling with tears that my own father would do something so heinous. But I did my damnedest to not let them fall.

He shrugged like it was no big deal. "Like I said, you two looked like you were getting along, and he'd be a good match. Imagine all the things I could do with a man like Max Clarke in the family."

"It's always about you, isn't it?"

"To be honest, Amelia, I don't know what you're griping about. The guy is good-looking, he's rich, and he's nice to you. How can that be so bad?"

My father wasn't wrong about any of that. The truth was that I had fallen for Max. And if I were ever going to get married, he'd be the man I'd want. "It doesn't matter that Max is all those things. What matters is that you took away our choice. We don't want to be married. We're going to get the marriage annulled."

His brows drew together. "If you two really wanted an annulment, you would have filed already." He laughed again. "Both of you have resisted it. Why do you think that is? You love him. And I bet he feels the same. Come on, Amelia. This is good for you."

"For you, you mean." But was he right? Had we unconsciously not filed for the annulment so far because of our feelings? I pushed that away. The whole reason he was coming tonight was for the papers. While I planned to tell him about my feelings and the baby and my hope to pursue a relationship, I had no illusion that we'd stay married. Marriage, if it happened for us, would be in the future. It would be our choice, not because my father set it up.

"We're ending the marriage."

My father scowled, giving him a sinister appearance. "You will not annul the marriage. It took a lot of finagling and money to get you two married. You're going to stick to the plan. Now if you want to divorce him and get a settlement and alimony, we can consider that."

I could only stare at my father in horror. Even if I did that, how did he think he'd get the money from me? Oh, who was I kidding? He'd find some way. He hadn't come this far with his plan without having figured out how he'd get a settlement and alimony.

He reached out, grabbing my arm. His fingers dug in, making me wince. "Do you hear me, Amelia? We stick to the plan."

The situation was so putrid that the contents of my stomach rose up. I pulled away from my father's grip and rushed to the bathroom, dropping to my knees in front of the toilet and emptying out my stomach. I should've known my father was behind our marriage. But I couldn't imagine he was the type of man to drug people and pay whoever he had to pay to get us married. I'd underestimated him. In that moment, I knew I would have to move to New York. There was no way I was going to raise my child in Las Vegas, the same city my father lived in.

I rinsed my mouth out and brushed my teeth. I looked at myself in the mirror and almost didn't recognize myself. The horror of what my father had done had made the blood drain from my face. I gently pinched my cheeks to put color in them.

When I came out of the bathroom, my father was gone. I sank to the couch, trying to figure out what I should do. Of course, I wasn't going to follow through on my father's plan. I didn't want or need Max's money. And I certainly wasn't going to give my father access to it or to Max's clout.

I checked my watch. It was still a few minutes before Max would arrive. I thanked God he hadn't shown up while my father was here. My father's revelations made it even more important that Max and I follow through on the annulment. I went to my office and got my laptop, bringing it to the living room. I set it on the coffee table and pulled up the annulment forms I needed from the State of Nevada's website.

My heart tore in two as I realized that I had to let Max go. I couldn't ask for a relationship knowing what my father planned for him.

Filling out the forms was difficult as my eyes were filled with tears, but it had to be done. When I finished, I printed them out. I retrieved them from the printer in my office and brought them back to the living room. Checking my watch again, I saw that Max was ten minutes late. For a moment, I worried that he might have overheard the conversation. I shook that thought away. That was just my fear talking. If Max had overheard, he'd have confronted my father. Right?

CHAPTER NINETEEN

Max

"You will not annul the marriage. It took a lot of finagling and money to get you two married. You are going to stick to the plan. Now if you want to divorce him and get a settlement and alimony, we can consider that. Do you hear me, Amelia? We stick to the plan."

I was a fucking idiot. There was a reason I'd stayed away from relationships, but my dick had clouded my judgment. No, not my dick, my heart. Right now, standing outside Amelia's front door, said heart was blown to smithereens. I'd fallen for Amelia's sweetness and humor, her intelligence, and her dedication to her business. But it was all a fucking lie.

After hearing her and her father talk about their plan to get my money, I left without letting her know I was there. What was the point? I'd come to see if maybe she felt the way I did and whether we had the possibility of pursuing a relationship. But she didn't feel anything for me except that I was dumb enough to fall for her scam.

I used my phone app to order another car to take me back to the airport. Luckily, one was close by, and in a few minutes, I was in the backseat telling myself that I'd dodged a bullet. What if I hadn't heard her and her father talking and I had been able to make my pitch? Clearly, she would have accepted it. How far would things between us have gone before I realized it was all a lie? Would we be married for real? Would we have kids?

My chest hurt and my stomach felt sick. When had the scam started? Had she targeted me at the airport when she tried to take my car? I couldn't figure out how it was possible that she knew I'd be there. My initial plans had been to fly home to New York that day. So, more likely, after spending a day and a night together, she saw an opportunity. She made comments about her father not being a good man, but clearly, they were a lot alike as she had roped him into her little scheme.

I remembered waking up the morning we discovered we were married, and there'd been a moment when I'd thought she had set the whole thing up. She was an Academy Award-winning-level actress because I'd dismissed that idea based on her reaction. She was even going along with the annulment, but now I could see the speed bumps she'd put in the way to avoid ending the marriage. She'd claimed being drunk wasn't reason enough to prove incapacitation to get an annulment. Her thinking must've been that I would want to avoid a divorce, or maybe it was just to give her more time to make me fall for her, and like a fucking idiot, I did. I fell for her hook, line, and sinker. And now I was stuck with a wife who would make sure that she got money from me.

As I arrived back at the airport, I wondered how she would've played it had I followed through and completed the annulment paperwork. Maybe she knew her plan was working, that I was dragging my feet because of my growing feelings for her. Jesus, I was stupid.

I couldn't find a flight leaving Las Vegas to New York soon enough, so I splurged and arranged for a charter. It was nearly nine p.m. when the plane's wheels left the ground heading east. I had the time it was going to take to get to the East Coast to get my shit together. Maybe it was time that I hired a lawyer to deal with this annulment. Clearly, I needed to do something to protect my assets. It wasn't just my personal money I needed to protect, but my business with Sam. How could I have been so fucking stupid?

It was six a.m. on Christmas Eve when I landed in New York. I ordered a car and had it take me to my apartment where I closed myself in, grabbing a bottle of scotch and taking it to the living room, where I drank directly from the bottle. I might've drunk the whole thing, except if I died of alcohol poisoning, Amelia and her father would probably try to claim some inheritance.

Feeling fairly well sloshed, I set the bottle on the coffee table and then spread out on the couch to sleep. My parents expected me for dinner and to stay the night for Christmas, so I needed to rest. I didn't know how I was going to hide all this from them, but I sure as shit was going to try.

I woke to my phone ringing. My hand shot out to the coffee table, knocking over the scotch bottle as I picked up my phone. My first thought was Amelia. *Oh, that's right, Amelia used me and broke my heart.*

Looking at the caller ID, it was my mother.

"Hello?" I winced at the sound of my voice. It was the sound of a man who'd been drowning his sorrows in scotch.

"Max? Are you okay, sweetheart?"

I was a grown ass man, but the sound of my mother's loving voice filled my chest with emotion. I was six years old again, having fallen, and she was there to comfort me. My eyes blurred with tears, and I cursed that I had allowed Amelia to bring me to this.

I cleared my throat. "Yeah, Mom. I'm fine."

"You don't sound fine."

I levered up, swinging my feet onto the floor and using my thumb and forefinger to dig the booze and sleep out of my eyes. "I was just resting for a minute. What's up?"

"We were expecting that you would be here by now. Dinner's going to be ready in a little less than an hour. Are you going to be able to make it?"

I looked at my watch, noting that it was five thirty. Shit. I slept all day. "Yeah. I'm on my way out the door."

"Are you sure you're okay?"

"Yes, Mom, I'm fine. I'll be there in thirty." I ended the call before she could continue to ask me if I was okay. At six years old, I was open to telling her all my troubles, but I didn't want to tell her about Amelia and falling for her scam. I was humiliated enough with just me knowing.

I stripped and took the quickest shower in history, then dressed in black jeans and a red shirt. It was about as festive as I was going to get.

Since I'd already been packed for my trip to Las Vegas, I grabbed that bag to stay with my parents for the night. I grabbed another bag, stuffing all the presents I had ordered and paid to have wrapped into it. Then I ordered another car to take me over to my parents' house.

During the ride over, I checked my phone like the idiot I was to see if Amelia had called or texted. After all, I'd ditched our date. I'd stood her up. But there were no messages from her, which only validated what I had learned yesterday. Any normal woman would have tried to reach out to me to make sure I was okay or find out why I hadn't shown up. But she hadn't. Did she realize that I discovered her scam?

Panic fluttered in my belly. If that was the case, she would be going on the defensive, doing what she could to make sure she'd still win the game. I didn't know what that would look like, but I suspected it would be bad. Perhaps she'd plant a TMZ report that I had abandoned her. Maybe she would reveal that I'd gotten drunk-married or that because of my dyslexia, I'd been unable to understand the documents. Maybe she would file divorce papers and ask for a shit-ton of money in a divorce settlement and a piece of Sam's and my business.

Fuck. There was no way I would be able to keep what happened a secret. I'd be the laughingstock of the family. But there was nothing I could do about it now. It was Christmas Eve, and tomorrow was Christmas. Anyone I could enlist for help, such as lawyers or the courts, were closed.

As I entered my parents' house on Christmas Eve, I did my damnedest to push my troubles away. I plastered on a jolly smile and hoped to hell that I could pull off a scam of my own. A scam that made my parents and my sister believe I was happy.

I knew I wasn't succeeding in the goal by the way my mother

would look at me or watch me, but at least she didn't say anything during dinner. After dinner, I busied myself with assisting in the dinner cleanup since my parents always gave their help time off during the holidays. Then afterward, I immediately roped Vivie into watching a movie with me.

"Can we watch the original *Miracle on 34th Street?*" Vivie asked when I proposed the idea. "I know everybody thinks *It's a Wonderful Life* is the best Christmas movie, but I love Miracle. Unless you want to watch *The Polar Express* or *Elf.*"

"You choose." The truth was, I wasn't likely to watch any of the movie. I just needed an excuse so that my mom wouldn't corner me and ask me what was wrong.

Vivie and I settled into the basement theater with a large bowl of popcorn. I had my usual beer, and she had her usual hard seltzer.

"You okay, Max?"

Jesus fuck. Not her too. "Sure."

She tilted her head and studied me. "Is all that business about the drug dealing in the Hamptons club settled?"

I grabbed popcorn, stuffing it into my mouth so I didn't have to talk. I nodded. "uh-huh."

"It seems to have taken a toll on you."

Thank you, Vivie. She gave me an excuse for my mood.

I shrugged as I swallowed my popcorn. "It was stressful. I'm still a little worried about Allison and what her cousin might do, but as far as the police are concerned, neither the club nor me and Sam are suspects."

She nodded. "That's good. Speaking of Sam, do you think he's really going to ask Kate to marry him?"

Even better, we were moving on to a subject that didn't involve me. "Of course, he is. You know Sam. He goes with his gut. Follows his heart." For once, I had done the same, and it had turned out to be a disaster. Lesson learned.

We ended up watching *Miracle on 34th Street,* which I enjoyed because the female protagonists and the little girl were cynical about the world. But by the end, they believed in love and Santa and miracles. That wouldn't be me. We also watched *Elf*, which was funny, but it, too, ended with a message about love and belief. Didn't Hollywood know that fairy tales weren't true?

Despite the fact that Vivie and I were adults now, Christmas morning was the same as it had been every year since we were kids. Vivie and I woke to find our stockings hanging at the end of our bed. As kids, we'd been allowed to open our stockings right away without them so they could sleep in later. We weren't allowed to wake them up until there was some semblance of daylight, so for many years Sam and I,, and then later Vivie when she got older, would hang out by the Christmas tree until the sun started to rise.

I'd woken early this morning, but not from the excitement of Christmas. Amelia had invaded my dreams and I woke up pissed off. I took a shower to wash away the dream, and hopefully, some of the anger.

When I came out, I dumped my stocking on the bed and found the usual—candy, a toothbrush and toothpaste, and an orange, which Sam and I thought our parents stuffed in the stockings so it would take up space. We would've much rather had more candy. Sometimes, we'd find little wrapped presents as well, like toy cars or an action figure. I didn't get toys anymore. This time, there were razors and a new tie.

When I went downstairs, I found Vivie lying on the couch reading a book. "You're up, sleepyhead."

I checked my watch. "I'm still up before Mom and Dad."

But it wasn't long after that my parents came down and we opened presents. Afterward, we all went to the kitchen to make Christmas breakfast.

"Since Sam isn't here, I thought we might have French toast instead of pancakes for breakfast," my mother said, surprising me. I knew she was sad that Sam wasn't here, and yet at the same time, I could see that she was accepting that her children were grown. I suppose someday, Vivie would be married and having Christmas with her family as well. I'd be the lone kid at home every Christmas morning. Part of that sounded pathetic.

While Mom made French toast, Dad made the bacon, I made coffee, and Vivie squeezed fresh orange juice.

When we sat down for breakfast, Dad came out with a bottle of champagne. "Christmas morning mimosas." He popped the cork and added champagne to our freshly squeezed orange juice. He sat at the head of the table, holding up his glass.

"Every day since your mother came back into my life, I am so thankful. Even after over twenty years, there are times I go to bed afraid that it's a dream and that I'll wake up alone. But then I wake up and here you all are—"

"Except Sam," Vivie said. "That means Max and I are your favorites now, right?"

We all laughed.

"The point is, I'm a very lucky man. I have a beautiful wife and I have children of whom I couldn't be any prouder."

My mom lifted her napkin to her eyes to wipe away her tears.

"Sometimes, you guys are so sappy." Vivie rolled her eyes.

I clinked my glass with my parents and my sister, trying to decide whether what my parents had was one in a million. But then I thought of my Uncle Daniel and Aunt Bri. They seemed blissfully happy. So did my Uncle Zach and Aunt Eleni. Sam and Kate were well on their way to wedded bliss as well. All the Clarke men had found their one true love. All of them except me. As I drank my mimosa, I vowed it would never be me.

Later that day, Sam called to wish us Merry Christmas and announce that he and Kate were now engaged and planning to get married on New Year's Eve. My mother and father exchanged a look that suggested they worried it was too soon, but they didn't say anything. They were letting him live his life.

He asked me to be his best man, which of course I was honored to be. Vivie was asked to be a bridesmaid. But then they told us the wedding was going to be in Las Vegas. I never wanted to step foot in Las Vegas again. I remembered learning that once the annulment papers were filed and served, if someone didn't show up, the annulment would automatically be granted. That meant I never had to go to Las Vegas again. And when Sam started talking about a Las Vegas club, I'd find another city. Atlanta, maybe.

Unfortunately, I couldn't avoid going to Las Vegas for his wedding. There was nothing I could say to try and talk them out of the location without giving away my stupidity.

Later that night, I was glad to be back at my own place where I didn't have to work to pretend to be happy. I'd always loved Christmas, but this year, it had really been the shits.

The next day, I went to work, even though many of the office staff were still off for the holiday. The clubs would be open, so we had to run with a minimal office staff.

It would have been nice to get lost in work and forget Amelia, but I couldn't afford to. I had to figure out how to protect myself financially. I had failed to protect myself emotionally, but I was sure as shit going to make sure that neither Amelia nor her father got ahold of any of my money or assets. In fact, I made a list of things that I could do. The first was to sign over my half of the business partnership to Sam. There was no reason he should suffer because I was an idiot.

I was going through lawyer possibilities, trying to decide whether I wanted to get a lawyer in New York or hire one in Nevada, when my phone beeped that I had a text. I looked down and saw it was from Amelia. My instinct was to delete it and block her. But I needed to know what her next move in her little scheme would be. I opened the text.

The papers are filed. I need to serve you. Shall I send them by courier?

I sat back, studying the text. What did she mean by paperwork? The annulment paperwork or a divorce, in which case she would ask for money? I supposed it didn't matter at this point since she'd already filed them.

. . .

I texted back.

I'll be in Vegas on New Year's Eve. We can meet then.

I had an urge to ask her whether she was really so coldhearted, if every minute that we had spent together had been a lie? But she'd humiliated me enough, so I wasn't going to put myself in a position that she could do so again.

I tossed my phone on my desk, pressing both of my palms on the desktop and taking deep breaths to settle my nerves. In less than a week, this would all be done, if I was lucky. I would take care of the papers, and on January first, focus on putting Amelia and our marriage behind me.

CHAPTER TWENTY

Amelia

When Max didn't show up as planned just before Christmas, there could be only two reasons that he didn't call or text to let me know he wouldn't be coming. The first was that he was in an accident or something happened that was preventing him from reaching out to me. When I called his office in New York, I was told he wasn't available, indicating he hadn't been in an accident or otherwise detained.

The second possible reason that he was a no-show was that he'd overheard my father talking about his deranged scheme and decided he needed to get away as fast as he could. I could only imagine the anger he felt. My father had drugged us and forced us to get married like an evil villain in a superhero movie. I couldn't blame Max for taking off and cutting all contact.

It occurred to me that Max's actions also meant that he thought that I was a part of my dad's scheme too. If he thought I was a victim of my father's actions, wouldn't he have shown up? At the very least, he could've confronted me. So the only real answer was that he had overheard my father, and he decided I was complicit too.

I wanted to defend myself and at the same time, I knew that

severing all connections with Max was the best thing I could do for him. Completing the annulment and never talking to him again were the only way to keep him safe from my father. My father might try to ruin Max's reputation with lies and gossip about what happened, but I had to believe the Clarke family was big enough to squash my father's attempts.

It occurred to me that what my father had done was illegal. Maybe I should call the police, but until I talked to Max, I had to keep our agreement that no one was to know about our marriage.

Angry and heartbroken at what my father had done, I had to get away. I was able to find a rental near Death Valley and drove down on Christmas Eve. There was no way I was going to celebrate Christmas with my father. I felt bad about leaving my brother alone with Dad, but then just as I settled into my rental in the beautiful desolation of the desert, James called to apologize for skipping out on Christmas. He and a friend decided to head up to Lake Tahoe to ski. I had no idea whether the ski slopes were open on Christmas, but even if they weren't, being in the snow-covered mountains on Christmas was way better than being with my father. I texted back my apology that I had run away too, only I'd gone to the desert.

After that, I turned off my phone. I turned off the world for two days. My life didn't improve in that time. I had still lost Max. My father was still going to make my life a misery. But for two days, I put all that on hold.

The day after Christmas, I rose and left the desert early in the morning, returning to Las Vegas just before eight. I stopped home to pick up the papers I'd filled out the night Max was supposed to come over, and I drove down to the county clerk's office to file them. Once I left the clerk's office, I texted Max to let him know the papers were filed and that I needed to serve him. His response was that he would be in Las Vegas on New Year's Eve. He didn't ask how I was. There wasn't the usual lightness or innuendo in his communications like we had before. Then again, my text to him didn't have the same tone as it had before, either.

I wanted to call him to find out for sure whether he'd overheard my father and if he thought I was to blame for our situation. In the end, the answer didn't really matter because regardless of the answer, I had to let Max go.

For the next few days, I buried myself in my work, creating the best social media marketing campaigns I could for all my clients. I began making lists of new clients I could pitch to. Now more than ever, I needed to get lost in my work to distract me from the pain of losing Max.

But at night in my dreams, I couldn't hide from him. He entered my dreams, but now there was a distance. He was with me, but not with me. Sometimes, I'd wake up and wonder what would've happened had I told him that I'd fallen for him. Would he have broken off with me right then because he didn't want a relationship? Or would the truth about my feelings hurt him more when he discovered what my father had done?

When I wasn't working or sleeping with Max haunting my dreams, I was crying. Sometimes, it was an angry cry toward my father. Other times, it was soul searing. I'd had the most precious gift with Max, and my father took it away.

On New Year's Eve, I arrived at the hotel at the time that Max told me to come. I knew he was at his brother's wedding and didn't want to intrude, so I texted him from the lobby that I was here.

A few minutes later, I saw him striding toward me. My heart expanded in my chest to see him. It wasn't that he was amazingly handsome in his tux that had my emotions overflowing. It was the yearning in my heart for the man whose expression confirmed that he thought I was complicit in our marriage. His eyes were dark. He looked at me like I was the lowest form of life. My heart cracked even more.

"Amelia."

"Max." I studied him, wanting to find the man I'd fallen for.

He looked away. "I need to get back to my brother's wedding."

I nodded. "I can follow you." Clearly, he didn't want to be away from the reception for too long. He held out his hand, indicating that I should proceed him. As we reached the ballroom, he took my arm and led me to a corner.

"Do you have the papers?"

I looked at him again, not wanting to give him the papers. Not wanting to let him go. But even if he wasn't angry at me, I couldn't keep him. Not with my father viewing Max as a dollar sign.

I nodded and reached into my purse. I pulled out the envelope with the papers and handed it to him. He opened the package, slipping the papers out. His jaw tightened. His gaze turned away toward a couple on the dance floor. I knew it had to be his brother. He had the same blond hair and physique. The difference was his brother was incandescently happy, as was the woman in his arms.

Max sighed and turned his attention to the papers. He signed them with a flourish, like he was happy to be rid of me.

My hands trembled as I took them back. "Your brother looks happy."

"He is."

I inserted the papers into the envelope and looked up at him. "I'll deal with these on Monday."

He nodded. "The sooner, the better."

I flinched at how vehemently he wanted all this to be over. For us to be over.

I should tell him about the baby, but I couldn't find the words. Besides, now clearly wasn't the time or place. Not at his brother's wedding reception. I'd have to find another time.

"Bye, Max."

"Bye, Amelia."

My legs felt like jelly and my stomach churned as I exited the ballroom. What I wanted to do was turn around and throw myself at Max. I wanted to tell him that my father was a vile, greedy man, but I had nothing to do with his marriage scheme. I wanted to tell him that I loved him. I wanted to tell him we were having a baby. But I didn't turn. I kept walking.

When I reached the lobby, I couldn't take another step. I sank into one of the chairs for guests.

I rubbed my temples, feeling confused. Deep down, I knew the best thing I could do for Max was to leave this place and never make contact with him again. But in doing that, he wouldn't know about the baby and the baby would never know its father. That didn't sit right with me.

At the same time, telling him about the baby probably wouldn't go over well. Then again, maybe it would be the opportunity for me to explain everything, to tell him what my father had done, not just to him but to me too. And most importantly, to tell him I loved him.

But now wasn't the time. Not at his brother's wedding. I'd already determined that I had to leave Las Vegas and get away from my father. Maybe if I moved to New York, I could seek Max out then and tell him about the baby.

Would he be willing to meet with me if I contacted him there? During the brief encounter that we had tonight, he made it clear that he could barely tolerate being around me. The only reason he agreed to it was because it was necessary to end our marriage.

I blew out a breath. Maybe I could tell him when we went to court for the final annulment. That is, if he came to court. The law said that if Max didn't show up to the court date, the annulment would be granted as a matter of course. He knew that. From the moment he signed the papers, his obligation to terminate our marriage had ended.

Around me, bells rang out from the casino. People talked and laughed. Some shouted in joy at winning while others yelled at losing. Life was going on. But I couldn't go on. Not with so much left unsaid. Not without telling him about the baby.

I stood and made my way back toward the ballroom. Music and laughter emanated from inside. I wished I could be part of a family that expressed so much joy. But I wasn't a part of them. That meant I couldn't walk in and demand to talk to Max. Instead, I found another chair and sat to wait until the wedding reception was over and he exited the room.

I didn't have to wait long before a man who looked just like Max exited the ballroom carrying his wife. The two of them looked like the happiest people in the world. The complete opposite of me.

Max's brother set his bride down, tugged her close, and gave her searing kiss, which she returned.

"How about we go consummate this marriage?" Sam said to his new wife.

"I'd say it's about damn time."

They grinned, all their joy radiating around them. He took her hand, leading her up the hall, presumably to the elevators. As he walked by me, his eyes caught mine and he cocked his head to the side. He looped his wife's arm in his as he changed direction and approached me.

Panic slid up my spine because I knew Max would not want this.

"I saw you earlier with my brother. I didn't realize he was bringing a plus one," Sam said.

I stood and shook the hand that he extended.

"I'm not his plus one." I was his wife and the mother of his child. Of course, I couldn't say that, so I went with the same excuse I'd been using all along. "I'm a social media marketing manager. I was consulting with Mr. Clarke."

Sam's expression turned quizzical. "Really? He never said anything." He looked at his wife, grinning. "Then again, I've been preoccupied."

"Congratulations on your wedding," I said.

"Thank you," they said in unison.

Sam studied me for a moment longer and then said, "Well, if you'd like to join the party, you're welcome to. But right now, my wife and I have a honeymoon to celebrate."

I smiled and nodded. "Of course. Congratulations again."

The door from the ballroom opened, and Max strode out. He stopped short when he saw me, his gaze going from me to Sam and back again. I couldn't read his expression, but it wasn't good. Anger? Panic?

He strode up to us. "What's going on here? I thought the two of you would be naked by now." It was clear he'd worked to make his tone light even though his green eyes bore darkly down on me.

"We're heading that way. I didn't know you've been consulting with a social media manager. When I'm back from my honeymoon, I'm going to want to hear more about that." Sam's tone was light, but his expression suggested he thought something was going on with Max. I wondered why Max hadn't told him or any of his family. Yes, it was embarrassing to end up accidentally married in Las Vegas. But everything he'd said about his family made them seem like they'd be supportive.

Max's jaw tightened. "It was something I was looking into, but I don't think it's going to work out."

I felt the words like a punch to the gut. Sam and Kate jerked, their eyes widening as they looked at me and then to Max. Max had essentially told them that he wasn't going to do business with me right in front of me. To everyone else, that would have been rude. But Max was seething, and that was probably the nicest way he could manage to say it without revealing the true nature of our relationship.

I turned to Sam and Kate again. "It was lovely to meet you. Congratulations again. I can see you two are going to be very happy."

Sam wrapped his arm around Kate, leaning over and giving her a quick kiss. "At last, eh, babe?"

"At last," she said. Whatever reservation she'd had before was clearly gone. They'd come through the difficult times and were now on the road to their happily ever after. For a moment, I wondered if Max and I could manage that, but I quickly dismissed it. Sam and Kate had loved each other before, and this was their second chance. While I loved Max, we were never technically in a relationship.

Sam and Kate walked away. Max watched them for a moment and then he turned his dark green eyes on me, his hands on his hips. "Why the hell are you still here?"

"I'm sorry, but I need to talk to you."

He looked toward the ballroom door, presumably to make sure nobody he knew could hear us. He leaned closer to me. "I know what you did, Amelia. I don't know what pisses me off more, that you were capable of doing such a terrible thing or that I was so stupid as to be taken in."

I shook my head and reached my hand out to touch him, but he backed away like I had a communicable disease. "It wasn't me, Max. My father . . . I told you how he was—"

"I heard you, Amelia. I know you and your father are out to take my money, but you can rest assured that I will ruin the both of you before that will happen."

I saw the vehemence, the truth of his words, in his eyes.

My heart was thundering in my chest. The urge to run was acute, but I couldn't leave until he knew about the baby. "I have something I need to tell you."

He pointed his finger at me. "There's nothing you can say that I want to hear." He turned to walk away.

"I'm pregnant."

CHAPTER TWENTY-ONE

Max

What the fuck did she just say? I whirled around on her. "What?"

Her eyes were both pleading and sad, but I knew this woman. I knew her guile. She was a grifter, and she and her father were out to take my money. For a moment, when Amelia left with the papers, I wondered if I was wrong about her or maybe they recognized that I wasn't a man to fuck with since she hadn't asked for any money. But if she said what I think she said, I realized that the real plan wasn't in getting money in a divorce. With a child, they had eighteen years to soak me for money.

"I'm pregnant."

Just what I thought she said. Anger and shock and self-recrimination vied for attention. It made me speechless.

The door to the ballroom opened, and Vivie walked out with our cousin Lyra. She looked over at me, tilting her head in question. I turned away because I didn't want her to see how intense my conversation with Amelia was.

"Blackjack or roulette?" our cousin Lyra asked Vivie. Vivie's eyes narrowed at me, and I could see she wanted to find out what was going on, but Lyra tugged her up the hall toward the casino.

When they disappeared, I took Amelia by the elbow and tugged her in the opposite direction. I would've taken her up to my hotel suite, but it was next to my parents' and Vivie's. I didn't need them seeing Amelia go in or out of my room.

At the end of the hall, I found an open door to a medium-sized conference room. I walked in, pulling Amelia with me.

I stared at her with so much anger swirling through me that I couldn't form a coherent sentence.

She swallowed. "I wanted to tell you about the baby when you were coming out just before Christmas—"

"Is that when you are going to let me know of this elaborate scam you pulled on me? Do I have a big L on my head for loser? Did you choose me because I could be easily duped?"

She shook her head, tears streaming down her cheeks. I vowed I wouldn't be swayed by her tears. They were an act. I'd learned my lesson.

"No, Max. I was duped too."

I scoffed. "Yeah, right. Like your father would drug you and force you to get married."

She nodded vehemently. "I told you, my father isn't a good person."

It was inconceivable to me that even a bad father would do such a thing to his own daughter. I didn't buy it. She was here trying to salvage the scam.

"You don't know my father. He's capable of anything." She looked down. "I wouldn't have guessed it either until he came to my apartment and told me. I was horrified. I . . . I'd wanted to tell you about the baby and that I loved you, but when he told me what he'd done, I knew I was bad for you."

I loved you. Something stirred deep in my heart, wanting desperately to believe her. But I'd been here before. Twice before, with women who didn't respect me.

"Which is it, Amelia? You love me and are having my baby, or you're bad for me? From my point of view, it's the latter."

"That's why I stayed today. To tell you about the baby. But being around me is bad because my father is a ruthless, greedy man. I don't want him to hurt you."

I laughed derisively. "He didn't. You did."

She jerked.

I was done with this charade. "How much money do you want?" Maybe I could appease them both so they'd leave me the fuck alone.

Her gaze shot up to mine. "I don't want any money."

"That's bullshit. I might have believed that if you'd gone through with the annulment, but now you're telling me you're pregnant. How do I know that's even true?"

"If you want to get a pregnancy test, I'll take it."

"It won't prove that it's mine." I knew the words coming out of my mouth were clichéd. Wasn't that what every man said when he discovered he'd knocked up a woman? But I felt justified in them. She had seduced me, and then she and her father had drugged me and married me off. It wasn't unreasonable to think they would pawn a child off on me too.

Her head snapped back as if I'd slapped her. Her eyes narrowed, and she was either offended or pissed that her plan wasn't working. She stared at me for a long moment, and then it looked like all the air left her.

She sank into a chair by the long table. "If you want a paternity test, I will get one." She gazed up at me, and while she still looked defeated, there was determination in her eyes. "And if you don't want anything to do with the baby, that's okay too. I just felt you had the right to know."

"I'm not falling for all this bullshit, Amelia. What the fuck do you and your father want from me? How much money will it take to make all this go away?"

She gasped and her hand covered her stomach. "I'm not making this baby go away."

Jesus fuck. That wasn't what I meant. I leaned over, setting my hand on the table and pointing my other finger at her. "I'm not telling you to get rid of the baby. I want to know how to get rid of you and your father. If this baby is mine, I'm going to be a father. In fact, considering what you and your father did to me, I can probably get sole custody. I'll raise the child while you and your father rot in prison for fraud and whatever other crimes you committed while drugging me."

Her face drained of color. Her eyes were wide with shock. "You can't take my baby."

Filled with righteous indignation, I straightened, tugging my coat and buttoning it, finally feeling like I had my power back. "Just watch me."

I started to walk away but then realized my business with her still wasn't done. I turned back and strode toward her, holding out my hand. She looked at it, and she lifted hers almost like she thought I was asking for her hand.

"Give me the annulment papers. I'm going to file them myself because I don't trust you."

Her hands shook as she reached into her purse, pulling out the envelope and handing it to me.

"I'm going to file these, and when the court date comes, I'm not going to show up. Maybe you think I can't read, but I can, and I know from the annulment website that if I don't show up, by default, the judge will grant the annulment. And if I hear from you or your father, you can bet that I will do everything in my power to take you down and put you in jail."

It was a threat I would keep even though it meant I would be opening myself up to ridicule for having been taken in by her and her father. But I'd do what I had to do to protect my family and the child Amelia was carrying.

With that, I turned and left the room. I made it only a few steps up the hall before my legs felt like they were going to give out. I leaned against the wall, bending over slightly with my hands on my thighs as I took deep breaths. To be honest, I was a little shocked at some of the words that came out of my mouth. But I was tired of being the butt of people's jokes. I was sick of people thinking that I was stupid, even though Amelia and her father proved that I was.

Realizing that Amelia would emerge from the conference room at any minute and not wanting her to see me like this, I straightened and headed up the hall, making a beeline for the elevator.

I'd never felt so angry, so sick, so disappointed in my life. For a short moment in time, I'd let myself think that Amelia could be the one for me. That I could have what Sam and Kate had. What my parents had.

This time, I would face the truth. My siblings could expand the family and give my parents grandchildren. My heart was officially closed.

CHAPTER TWENTY-TWO

Amelia

My entire body shook as I sat in the conference room alone. I understood Max's anger, but I was hurt that he would think I was part of my father's scheme. I was shocked and horrified by the threat he made to take the baby from me and send me to jail. I would've never thought Max would be capable of something so cruel.

But then it occurred to me that I didn't really know him. It felt like I did because every time we were together, it was perfect. But I could count the number of times we'd actually been together in the same location on one hand. We talked on the phone several times, but in reality, over the last few weeks, we'd only seen or talked to each other less than a dozen times. How ridiculous, then, that I would feel I was in love with him. I thought I knew him, but the man I saw today wasn't the man I had come to know. He wouldn't listen to me. He not only didn't trust me, but he also thought I was out to get him.

I managed to stand on wobbly legs. The exchange with Max had left me shaken. As hurt as I was that he wouldn't listen to my side of the story, I knew the true person to blame was my father. My anger bloomed into rage, making me want to seek my father out and find a way to hurt him as badly as he'd hurt me.

I thought about what Max had said about my father's actions being illegal. As I left the conference room and through the hotel toward the exit, I thought about going to the police. Would they believe me? And if they did, was there anything they could do about it? I didn't know who the driver of the car that picked Max and I up after dinner had been. Whatever they used to drug us was out of our systems for sure. Could I prove that the paperwork was forged or signed under duress? Would the fact that Max and I had thought we'd gotten drunk and married, instead of suspecting we'd been drugged, work against us?

I wanted more than anything to bring my father down, but I wasn't confident that I could without evidence. If I went after him and failed, who knew what the ramifications for me would be? My father had the power, influence, and resources to retaliate in a way that I wouldn't be able to recover from. If it were only me, I still might do it, but I had my baby to think about.

I pulled out my phone, using the app to order a car, glad I'd made the decision to take a rideshare instead of driving. I wasn't in the right headspace to get behind the wheel.

As the driver headed toward my home, I sat in the backseat feeling so utterly alone. Already, I missed Max's support and sweetness. I grieved that I would never have it again. Instead, I would need to find a way to protect myself and the baby from him.

"Are you alright back there, Miss?"

I lifted my eyes to look at my driver through his rearview mirror. It was only by seeing my face in the mirror that I realized I was crying.

I gave him a wan smile. "Not really."

"The address that I'm taking you to, is there somebody there who will be able to help you?"

I shook my head.

"Maybe there is somewhere else I can take you. Maybe to a family member or a friend?"

I started to shake my head, but then I thought of James. It had always been James and me against the world. If there was a time that I absolutely needed him, it was now. It would be dangerous for him to help me because even though he was part of my father's business, he wasn't safe from my father's ire or from getting thrown out of the family business. But the driver was right that I needed to talk to somebody, and James was the only person in my life who cared about me.

I gave the driver James's address. He seemed relieved as he made a right-hand turn toward the section of town that James lived in.

I probably should've called him to let them know I was coming, but I knew once I started talking, I would probably completely break down, and I didn't want to do it in the car. I was freaking my driver out enough.

My brother lived in a condo community that was more like an all-inclusive resort than a residential area. Anything and everything he could possibly want or need was available in the community. It was the type of place where a rich bachelor might live, but my brother wasn't a partier or a playboy. I think he lived here mostly out of convenience.

I arrived at his condo, backing up to a man-made lake. I knocked on the door and only then wondered if maybe I was wrong and he was entertaining guests for New Year's Eve. He opened the door wearing a pair of sweatpants and a T-shirt, looking like he had just come back from the gym.

He smiled, but then immediately, his smile faltered. "What's wrong?"

"Everything." With that, the floodgates opened, and I wept so intensely that I could barely breathe.

"Oh, shit, Amelia." He reached out, taking my hand and tugging me into his condo. He led me to his living room and set me on the couch. He sat on the coffee table in front of me and took my hands in his. "What happened?"

Through sobs and hiccups, I said, "Our father is an evil man."

James's eyes studied me intently, and he gave a brief nod. I wasn't

183

telling him anything he didn't know, but I doubt he knew the depth of depravity that my father was capable of.

"There's something I didn't tell you. Actually, there are a few things I haven't told you. It's not that I wanted to keep them secret or that I didn't trust you, it's just that . . . well, it was embarrassing, and I promised I wouldn't. But now I know the truth, and I really need someone."

"Okay." He rose and grabbed a box of tissue, handing it to me before sitting on the coffee table again.

"Remember that date I had with Max at The Roarke?"

"If I remember correctly, you were saying it wasn't a date."

I shrugged and snuffled, wiping my nose with a tissue. "It was a second date, really. We met and were having fun knowing it wasn't going to go anywhere. He lives in New York and I'm here."

"So it was just a little fling?"

I couldn't decide whether I should nod or shake my head. "That's what it was supposed to be. But we ended up seeing each other more than the two times. We even talked on the phone a little bit."

He tilted his head to the side. "Are you saying you've fallen in love with him?"

I nodded, but a new well of tears came at mentioning my love for Max. There was so much pain at what my father had done.

James's brows narrowed. "What did he do?"

"He didn't do anything. I mean, this whole thing isn't his fault." I shook my head, feeling confused about what to tell him next.

"So what happened?"

"When we left the Roarke, there was a car waiting, and the driver said he was sent from the hotel. So we got in to tour the city and have champagne."

James nodded, and I was grateful that he was patient at how long it was taking me to tell him my story.

"Next day, we woke up, having no memory of anything past the time we got into the limousine."

"Did he drug you?"

"We woke up married."

Any other time, James might've laughed, but he could tell what was going on with me was no laughing matter. "So what happened?" he prompted me again.

"We decided we would get an annulment. But he had to go back to New York and so the process got delayed. During that time, we started talking on the phone and my feelings changed. The first time we were going to deal with the annulment papers, he got called away for an emergency."

I looked down at my hands, my fingers toying with the tissue. "Just before Christmas, he was coming back to visit to do the annulment papers."

"Surely, you weren't ready to stay married," James said gently.

"I knew that no matter what, we were going to have to get the annulment. But because of how my feelings changed, I planned to tell him how I felt and see if maybe we could continue our relationship."

"Did he not take the news well?" James's questioning indicated that he thought Max was the reason for my tears, and that was partially true.

"Just before he was to show up, Dad arrived."

The minute I mentioned that our father, James's expression darkened. "Why?"

"Max and I had agreed that we weren't going to tell anybody we got drunk-married. We were embarrassed by it. Since we were getting an annulment, it would be like it never happened. But when Dad showed up, he told me that he'd arranged the whole thing."

"What?" James looked at me like I was speaking Greek.

"He told me I couldn't get an annulment unless I asked for money because he'd arranged for the marriage. I know it was true because I had tried to hunt down the driver to fill in the gaps of that night and the hotel said they hadn't sent one."

James shot up. "That motherfucker." His hands clenched, and I knew that if my father were there, James would punch him. I doubted I'd do anything to stop it.

"When Max didn't show up that night or call to let me know what was going on, I had a strong suspicion that he'd overheard Dad. I hadn't talked to or seen him until tonight when I served him the annulment papers I filed the other day. He confirmed that he'd heard what Dad had done."

James took a deep breath and sat on the couch next to me, taking my hand again. "Did you explain to Max about Dad?"

"I tried to, but he believes I was part of Dad's scam."

My brother's face morphed into sympathy. He tugged me close, holding me.

I rested my head against his shoulder, glad that he was here for me. "It's even worse than that."

He leaned his head back slightly to look down at me. "What could possibly be worse than that?"

I took a deep breath. "I'm pregnant. And Max says that if Dad and I do anything to make a move on him, he will make sure that we're both put in jail and that he'll take full custody of the baby."

James stared at me, his mouth agape, his eyes wide. Finally, he came to his senses. "I won't let that happen, Amelia. I promise, no one will take your baby."

"James, I don't know what's going to happen. I told Dad that we were getting an annulment, and he got mad. He told me the best I could do is get a divorce because he wanted me to get a settlement and alimony."

James shook his head. "Even if that happened, that would be your money, not his."

I gave him my you-know-how-Dad-is expression. "I'm sure he thought of some way of getting his hands on it. I'm going to defy him, because he's wrong and I have to, but I don't know what he's going to do to me. He'll probably still go after Max. I have no problem with Dad going to jail, but I don't want to go with him. I had no part in it, but I don't know how to prove my innocence."

He wiped tears from my face. "You don't have to prove you're innocent. They would have to prove you're guilty."

"Dad is going to ruin me when he finds out I'm not going to be a part of his scheme. When I realized that, before I talked to Max, I'd been thinking I'd leave Las Vegas and move to New York."

I could see from James's expression that he didn't like the idea of my leaving, and yet he nodded because he understood the situation I was in. "Well, if you love Max, maybe you will be able to prove to him that you weren't a part of Dad's scam and you two can have a future with your baby."

I looked down, pressing my lips together, trying not to start weeping again. "I'm not going to hold my breath for that." I turned to look at James. "You should've seen him. He was so angry. I mean, I don't blame him, but I could see in his eyes that anything we had before was gone. And even then, I'm not sure what he felt for me except perhaps a little bit of affection. I'm terrified he might follow through his threat to take my child. Then again, maybe that would be best. I don't want Dad using my baby as a pawn."

James shook his head. "You can't give your baby away—"

"I would if it kept him safe. If it meant he'd have a happy life. Max's family is like a Norman Rockwell painting."

"No one's life is that perfect. And you're going to be a great mom."

I sighed, feeling so tired. "I had thought if I went to New York, it would be easier to coparent with Max. If the annulment goes through and if I move to New York, Dad has a whole lot less to use against me and Max."

James nodded. "Seems like you have it all figured out."

"Except it could be up to three months before a judge signs the annulment, assuming he does sign. Dad can wreak all kinds of havoc between now and then. I don't know what to do with my business. I have no doubt that he'll try to ruin me. I'm supposed to be making my clients look good, but they're not going to work with a company with scandal or a bad reputation or whatever Dad will do to destroy my business."

"Maybe you should go to New York sooner rather than later. Dad has a lot of power here, but not necessarily elsewhere. He's a giant fish in a tiny pond. He can't go up against the Clarkes in their own backyard."

"I don't know how I could do that. I'd have to sell this place and at the same time try to ward off anything that Dad does to ruin my reputation or hurt my business. New York isn't cheap. I can't afford to lose business."

"Then Max needs to help you."

I shook my head. "He won't do that. He wants nothing to do with me."

Max's eyes narrowed. "What about the baby?"

I shrugged. "Like I said, he threatened to take it from me but at the same time questioned whether I was really pregnant or if it was his child."

James tensed next to me. "He's being an asshole. I know what you're saying, that he has a reason to be mad after what Dad did. But you would never do anything like that and he should know that."

I looked at James. "How would he know that? We haven't known each other very long, and during that time, we've only seen each other on a few occasions."

James held my hand with both of his, looking at me earnestly. "He shouldn't have to know you very long to know that you are a good and decent person. He liked you enough to sleep with you."

I pursed my lips at him. "I don't think affection is very high on the list of requirements for sleeping with somebody."

"Nevertheless, you've been married nearly two months, and only now have you filed paperwork."

"He was out of town."

James shook his head vehemently. "If I woke up married to somebody unexpectedly, I'd be at the courthouse as soon as it opened, with paperwork in hand."

My heart skipped a beat wishing what James was saying were true. But the reason papers weren't filed sooner wasn't because we wanted to stay married. "There were extenuating circumstances."

"No. He made excuses. You don't think a man like Max wouldn't be able to take a day to get to the courthouse and file papers if he really wanted to? Hell, he could hire someone to do it for him. But he didn't."

My heart thumped hard again, but I did my best to ignore it. "It doesn't matter now. Dad changed everything."

James his eyes narrowed. "Where is he staying?"

"Who? Max?"

James nodded.

"It doesn't matter, James."

"The hell it doesn't. Listen, Amelia, I can totally see why he'd be angry and suspicious, but he needs to get over that. You're having his baby, for Christ's sake. And you're right, when Dad finds out he's not going to get whatever he thought he was going to get out of this, he's going to come after you. Hell, he might come after that baby because right now, it's the only solid link between you and Max's money."

A new wave of panic shot through me. "What do you think he could do?" All sorts of scary scenarios flashed through my brain. I looked up at James, clutching him. "He could ruin my business, making me destitute, and then take my child from me."

"He could try, but I'll make sure that doesn't happen. You'd make sure that didn't happen. Even if he ruins your business, you have mad skills someone will pay for."

"He wouldn't let anyone hire me here." I was usually a strong, determined woman. I hated how defeated I sounded now.

"Then you leave. He can be stopped."

"How?"

"Because I know where the bodies are buried. I know every dirty deal he's made or tried to make over the last ten years. More than half of what I do at the company is to monitor him to keep the company safe from all the shady deals and tricks he tries to pull off."

I felt a little glimmer of hope as I looked into James's fierce eyes. "You have to have proof."

"I have enough."

"But I don't. I need to stop him before he tries anything, and I have no leverage. I don't know who picked me and Max up in the car that night, and if I did, what are the chances he'd tell the truth when he's clearly on Dad's payroll? Whatever drug he used on us will be out of our systems, and we don't have the glasses or champagne that probably had the drugs. Plus, until he told me what he did, Max and I thought we had just gotten wasted and married."

"But he told you. You know the truth."

I rolled my eyes. "He'll say that I'm a liar. He'll say I'm trying to put the blame somewhere else so I don't look irresponsible at having gotten drunk-married and pregnant. He hasn't said anything about the baby yet, so I'm thinking he doesn't know, but when he does, that's just more he'll use against me. I have nothing I can use on him."

"I'll hire someone to help." James was normally a smart, practical man, but his confidence in stopping my father was irrational.

"Who are you going to hire that would help us? Dad has his tentacles and minions everywhere."

"I'll find someone somewhere else. I'll find a security firm out of state."

I sagged against my brother, feeling emotionally and physically exhausted. "Thank you for your willingness to do that, but I really think I am fucked."

"We may not be able to stop Dad from doing whatever he's going to do. And maybe Max won't see you for who you really are. But you have me, Amelia, and I'll do whatever it takes to protect you from Dad, even if it means destroying the company."

I tilted my head to look up at him. "You can't ruin your life trying to save mine."

He gave me a cocky smile. "I'd be willing to lose my career to watch Dad crash and burn. I think it would be a worthy trade-off." He checked his watch. "It's going to be January first pretty soon. I know you don't have a lot to look forward to and can't have champagne, but we can be here together."

I sank against him again. "I don't know what I'd do without you, James."

He tugged me close and kissed me on the top of my head. "You'll never have to find out."

CHAPTER TWENTY-THREE

Max

I woke up the morning of January first wondering if this was the first day of what was going to be a shitty year. The new year was usually a time of excitement, of new beginnings, but not for me. I was still married to a woman who got herself pregnant in an attempt to get access to my money. Worse yet, because today was a holiday, I couldn't submit the papers Amelia served me so that the court could set a date to see the judge and have him sign the annulment. If the judge was reluctant to grant the annulment because being drunk wasn't a good enough reason to claim incoherence, then I would file fraud charges against Amelia. I remembered reading on the Nevada State government's website on annulment that fraud and deception were legitimate reasons to get an annulment. Maybe after that, the judge would have her arrested.

Even as I thought about sending Amelia to jail for what she did to me, the image of her staring up at me in horror as I threatened to send her to prison and take the child haunted me. What if I was wrong? What if she really was a victim like she said she was? My heart rolled in my chest, wanting that to be true. But I had no way of knowing the truth, and I wasn't going to take the risk to find out. If I decided to believe her and it turned out she really was in cahoots with her father to gain access to Clarke family assets, that would make me a bigger fool than I already was. There was a saying about once bitten, twice shy, and when it came to Amelia, that was true. Plus, it wasn't like I hadn't been bitten before. Amelia was the third woman to make me look like a fool.

I would've liked to stay in bed all day, but as part of my brother's wedding plans, he and Kate had scheduled a brunch for family and close friends this morning. Why they hadn't flown off into the sunset to have wild sex like rabbits, I didn't know.

Because he and Kate were expected to be there, I knew I needed to go as well. Not showing up would make everyone suspicious and I'd have my mother hovering over me more than it already felt like she was.

So I dragged my ass out of bed and took a shower. I had gotten the impression that this branch would be casual, so I slipped on a pair of jeans, and while I really wanted to wear a Henley, I put on a button-down shirt just in case it was nice casual.

I shaved and took an extra minute to study myself in the mirror. I looked normal, right? I practice a few smiles as a warmup to hiding all the turmoil going on inside me. I didn't want my family to know that my life was so fucked up.

I headed downstairs to the ballroom where the brunch was scheduled. Instead of the full room like we had yesterday, a divider had been pulled down the center, making it a smaller, more intimate room. Rolling my shoulders and stretching my neck, I plastered my smile on and continued into the room. I strode over to my brother who was standing with his arm around Kate, looking like the happiest man on earth. They were talking to a couple who technically weren't family, but close enough. Kate didn't have much family, and her girl-friends were like sisters. Plus, Harper, along with her husband, Noel, were my brother's neighbors. Harper played a significant role in helping Kate and Sam reconcile, so it made sense that they were there.

I sidled up to my brother, patting him on the back. "I'm surprised to see the two of you up and out of bed this morning."

Both Sam and Kate blushed.

"Well, we might still have been except Kate tells me the baby is hungry." Sam looked down at Kate's belly. Her hands pressed over it. She wasn't showing, at least not that I could tell. My understanding was that she was only eight or nine weeks long.

The hair on the back of my neck stood up as I realized that could be how far along Amelia was in her pregnancy. I kicked that thought out of my head. For all I knew, she wasn't pregnant at all. But that thought didn't sit very well either, so I pushed out all thoughts of Amelia and focused on my brother.

I looked over toward the wall where a buffet was set out. "It looks like the baby has a lot to choose from. Are there pancakes?" I looked at Sam pointedly, enjoying joking with him about his obnoxious love of pancakes.

He grinned. "Of course."

"You know, on Christmas, Mom made French toast. There wasn't a pancake in sight."

Sam feigned an expression of horror. "That had to be the worst Christmas ever."

I gave myself kudos for maintaining my smile even though his words were right. It had been the worst Christmas ever.

Kate excused herself to go serve herself a plate. Sam watched her go but didn't follow her. Instead, he turned to me. "Who was that woman with you yesterday at the reception?"

Jesus fuck. He noticed her? "What woman?"

Sam gave me a look like he knew I was giving him bullshit. "The woman with the papers?"

"Oh. Yeah. That was just business."

"On New Year's Eve? At my wedding?"

I shrugged, not wanting to sound like a dick but needing to if I wanted to continue to hide my hot mess of a life. "It was that killing two birds with one stone thing."

His eyes narrowed as he stared at me. "What sort of business?"

I rolled my eyes. "Dude, you should be on your honeymoon. I'll tell you all about it when you're back at work."

"I could tell you what that business was about."

I whipped my head around toward the voice. A man approached us. A man I didn't know. Immediately, my heart sped up and panic grew. Was this the next step of Amelia's and her father's plan?

The man smiled affably, but I could see in his eyes that he had no friendly thoughts toward me.

He extended his hand to Sam. "Congratulations on your marriage. I'm sorry to drop in like this. I'm James Dunsmore."

Sam shook his hand and then looked at me for an explanation.

James then looked at Noel and Harper, who were still standing there. "James Dunsmore."

"Noel St. Martin. This is my wife, Harper." They all shook hands, and James cocked his head to the side.

"Noel St. Martin. The head of Saint Security?"

Noel smiled. "Not anymore. I retired."

James nodded. "Who would I call if I needed to hire someone to look into another person?"

I flinched. Were Amelia and her brother going to hire somebody to investigate me? What the fuck for? She was the one who needed to be investigated. In fact, maybe that was a good idea. If I planned to defend myself, I needed to get some leverage that private investigation could gather.

Noel reached into his pocket and pulled out a business card. He handed it over to James. "Call Archer Graves. He runs the show now."

"Noel has learned to carry Archer's cards around because he has a stellar reputation around the world for his work. Everywhere we go, someone wants to hire him." Harper stared up at her husband with pride. They were yet another couple who found wedded bliss. I wanted to gag.

I turned to James. "If we need to discuss anything further, perhaps we could do it another time."

James shrugged. "I can wait." He pointed his thumb over his shoulder. "I'll be right outside." James looked at Sam and then at Noel and

Harper. "It was nice to meet you. Thank you for the card." He gave me an expectant look and then turned, leaving the ballroom.

Sam watched me, his brow arched. I wanted to go on as if Amelia's brother had never shown up, but I was agitated at the idea of him sitting outside the ballroom where anyone in my family could approach him.

I plastered on that fake smile again. "I'll go take care of this. I'll be right back. I promise."

"Okay, but Kate and I aren't waiting for you. We're on our honeymoon and will be leaving on time."

I gave him a hug. "Understood."

I strode out the door feeling like a thousand eyes were on me. Jesus, I'd grown paranoid as well.

When I stepped out of the ballroom, James was leaning against the opposite wall with one ankle crossed over the other as he looked at something on his phone. He lifted his head as I approached, and this time, there was no attempt at affability.

"What do you want?" I shoved my hands in my pockets because I really felt like I wanted to punch this guy. "I told Amelia that her little plan wouldn't work. Are you in on it too? Are you here to extort money from me?"

James's hand fisted and flexed. Clearly, he wanted to hit me too. "I'm trying to decide what my sister saw in you. All I see is an A-one asshole who knocks a woman up and then threatens to take her child." He nodded toward the ballroom. "I imagine none of the people in there know you're capable of that, do they?"

To be honest, I hadn't known I was capable of it either. "You're lucky your sister and father aren't sitting in a jail cell."

He rolled his eyes. "On what charge?"

"Is everything okay, Max?" I sucked in a deep breath as my mom's voice wafted over to us. I turned and smiled. "Everything's fine, Mom. I'll be back in a minute."

I strode down toward the conference room that Amelia and I had talked in the day before. "We can talk down here."

James smirked. "Just as I thought. The big, wonderful, perfect

Clarke family from New York is far from perfect after all. Are you the black sheep, or are the rest of you full of bullshit too?"

I opened the door and stepped into the room. I returned to the question he asked before. "Your sister drugged me and committed fraud. I could add extortion as well."

Her brother put his hands on his hips and stared at me. "Do you have any proof?"

My jaw tightened.

"You don't. Because if there were proof, my sister would have my father in jail so fast it would make your head spin. While you were here drinking it up and celebrating your brother's wedding, my sister spent her New Year's Eve weeping at my place. My father's going to try and ruin her, and it's all because you were happy to fuck her and knock her up but won't stand by her as her world comes crashing down around her."

I hated how his words seeped into my heart, making me doubt what I'd been so certain was true. Amelia was a con. "I heard them talking."

He didn't seem fazed by that. "And what did you hear, Almighty Max?"

I hated his tone. It reminded me of all the times I'd been taunted as a kid. "They were talking about the plan. About sticking to the plan."

"Who was talking about sticking to the plan?"

I looked away for a moment, getting more annoyed at this discussion. I turned back to him. "Your father and your sister."

"I believe that you heard my father, but you're a liar if you think my sister said anything about sticking to a plan that involved conning you."

I scanned my brain back to the evening outside her door, trying to remember what I heard. He was right. I hadn't heard her say anything, but that didn't make her innocent. "She didn't deny it."

This time, it wasn't just James's tone that suggested I was an idiot. It was his facial expression. "She'd just discovered that her father had drugged her and forced her into marriage. Maybe in your world, that seems normal, but Amelia is still reeling from it. Even knowing the types of things my father is capable of, neither of us ever expected that he would do something like that."

"And yet it happened." I turned away as anger boiled and the urge to punch him grew again. Finally, I turned back. "What do you want from me?"

"I came here to ask you to take her away. Take her back to New York. Away from my father. I can't protect her from him as well as you can."

Was he on drugs? "I don't want anything to do with her."

He stepped away, turning and running his fingers through his hair, as if the intensity was getting to him too. Then he whirled back, pointing a finger at me. "My sister was going to tell you about the baby and that she loved you. That night, you were apparently right outside her door, hearing what my father had done, but did you knock on the door to confront them or protect her?" His gaze raked over me with an expression that suggested I was no better than pond scum. "What about the scam you're pulling on her?"

I jerked back, shocked by his accusation. "I'm not the scammer here."

"Oh? The annulment papers could have been filed almost two months ago, but you dragged your feet. Why is that? I'll tell you why. You like to get your rocks off with my sister. The longer you drew that annulment out, the more often you could fuck her, and when you tired of her, then you could file the papers and be done with it."

I felt pushed back on my heels. Did he really think that? Did Amelia? "That's not true."

"Sure it is. You don't give a shit about her."

Anger boiled up. "I loved your sister." The minute the words were out of my mouth, I turned away, hating that I'd revealed so much.

"Now who's the liar? If you cared even just a little bit about my sister, you wouldn't be over here pouting and whining because a ruthless businessman used his daughter to grift you. A real man would fight. He'd fight for the woman he said he loved."

Confusion filled my brain until I thought it might explode. I turned away, trying to bring a semblance of order to what was going on.

James patted my shoulder as he walked past me. "No worries there, Little Max. Amelia and her baby have me. I'll help her get through this and hopefully put a stop to my father. I can't be sure that he won't try to go after you in some way, and knowing Amelia, she'll try to block him even if it means he hurts her more. My suggestion to you if you don't want my father to fuck with you is to go home and don't look back. Forget my sister and the baby. They don't need you or your money."

"Like hell I'm going to leave my child with you two."

James let out a laugh. "You don't care about that baby."

I stared at him, wanting him to stop, wanting to defend myself but unable to find the words.

"Do you know how many times you asked about her pregnancy or the baby since we started this discussion? Zero."

God. He was right. Shame washed through me.

"According to her, you don't believe she's pregnant, and if she is, you want a DNA test on the baby. So fuck you, Max. Go back to New York and live your pathetic self-centered life. Like I said, Amelia and the baby don't need you or your money."

He walked out of the room, leaving me standing, shaking. He'd painted me as an asshole. If he was right about Amelia, I was being an asshole. But I'd already loved and lost. I wasn't going to open myself up to that again.

That didn't mean I'd abandon my child. No, I would be involved in the baby's life. There was nothing Amelia or James could do about that. But I wasn't going to let James's words get to me. For all I knew, he was part of the scam. He'd probably been sent here to salvage the plan.

I needed to return to the brunch, but there was no way I could enter that room and hide the torrent of emotions swirling inside me. Instead, I headed up to my room, going straight to the minibar for a drink. Sitting on the couch, I tried to calm my nerves. I worked to make sense of what was happening.

I finished my drink and went to the minibar to get more. I'd just downed a shot when there was a knock on my door. I planned to ignore it until I heard Sam's voice on the other side.

Fuck. I still considered not answering it, but of all the people I didn't want to be an asshole to, Sam was it.

I strode over and opened the door, attempting to smile. "I'll be down in just a minute."

He walked in, forcing me to step back. He entered the main part of the suite, going to the window and looking out. Then he turned, giving me a pointed glare. "What the fuck is wrong with you, Max?"

"Nothing." My nerves crackled with agitation again. "Just because our lives were practically joined at the hip as kids, they're not now. Especially when you moved across the country. I've got my own shit."

He nodded. "What shit? And does this affect the business?"

My jaw tightened. I shook my head. "I won't let it."

He gaped at me. "What the hell does that mean? Look, I get that you don't like to share your emotions, but something is going on here, Max. Why won't you tell me what it is? Don't you trust me?"

Shame had me looking down. "It's not a matter of trust. I just need to deal with this on my own."

"Deal with what?" I could tell Sam was getting to the end of his rope.

I shook my head. "You're supposed to be on your honeymoon, Sam. I'm fine."

"You are so far from fine." He laughed derisively. "You can tell me or you can tell Mom. Because if you don't tell me, I'm going to tell her what's going on, and then I'm taking my wife on a honeymoon."

"Don't." I couldn't cope anymore. I just needed time alone to sort my shit out. "Let me deal with this. I don't need you or Mom or anyone butting into my business."

I could've punched Sam in the face and probably not hurt him any more than I just had. The pain of my words showed on his face.

"Butting into your business? You think that's what this is? Fine.

Have it your way." He started to walk past me toward the door but then stopped. "You need to stop using your dyslexia or insecurity you had about it as a kid as an excuse to hide in life. Sharing your problems with family and letting them support you and help you is what family is all about. The only one in this family who isn't his true self is you. You don't let any of us in. When you're like this, Max, you break all of our hearts." He strode to the door, opening it and walking out.

For the second time, I shook with a mixture of grief and shame and anger. I knew he was right. But becoming a person like Sam, who shared his feelings and problems, meant opening myself in a way that I promised I never would. I'd spent much of my life closing that part of me off to avoid being made a fool or vulnerable to others.

Yeah? How's that working for you now? I knew that's exactly what Sam would say if I had spoken those words out loud. It wasn't working, but I still wasn't willing to open myself and risk being made small again.

CHAPTER TWENTY-FOUR

Amelia

I was fast asleep in my brother's guest bedroom when the new year started. When I woke in the morning, I was disoriented, not sure where I was. But then my life came flooding back to me. I was pregnant with my husband's baby, who I was getting an annulment from, because my father ruined my life. I wanted to pull the covers over my head and never come out. But I wasn't a woman to give into depression or hopelessness. And I especially couldn't now with a child on the way. So, I forced myself out of bed. I had a lot to do to prepare for my future . . . and for my father's wrath. I hoped I had time before he discovered the annulment papers had been filed, and I prayed to God he didn't hear about the baby.

I straightened the clothes that I had slept in and made my way to the kitchen where my brother was cooking.

He turned when he saw me. "Happy New Year."

I rolled my eyes.

"I have tea if you like. Or I have coffee, but you're probably not drinking that anymore."

I tilted my head in question. "How do you know so much about pregnant women?"

"We've had a few at work. They always come to me to talk about their leave or possible telecommuting options instead of Dad. Go figure."

I smiled, and it was nice to have a little levity in my life which felt heavy like a lead balloon.

"I'm making eggs and bacon."

I went to the cupboard to get a mug to make my tea. "You sure are being nice to me."

"Consider it making up for all the times I picked on you when we were little."

Thinking of our childhood was bittersweet. Tears came to my eyes, and I set the mug down to give James a hug.

"Hey. It's going to be okay." He wrapped me up, hugging me back. The truth was, James was very rarely mean to me growing up. Not when it became clear that when it came to emotional support, we only had each other.

I released him and heated the water for my tea. Once that was done, I put in the teabag and took my cup to the table to sit.

A few moments later, James brought over two plates with eggs, bacon, and toast. "Eat up. You need your strength to grow my niece or nephew."

I smiled up at him. My life was in shambles, but I wasn't alone. I wondered how I'd ever be able to express my gratitude toward James.

"Do you have plans for today?" he asked as he shoveled up a large forkful of eggs.

"I need to figure out how to Dad-proof my business. In fact, I have to figure out how to Dad-proof my life. I have to figure out what to do when he finds out that I'm not married to Max anymore, and neither am I asking Max for money."

My brother took a sip of coffee. His eyes were intent as he stared at me while he set his cup back down. "Max has a responsibility to this baby. And while Dad may have gotten you guys married, he didn't get you pregnant. You and Max did that all on your own, so Max needs to step up."

I knew he was right, but I didn't want Max involved if it would mean a lifetime of him looking at me with the same disgust that he had yesterday. And I certainly didn't want to live always wondering whether he was going to take the child away from me.

"I can't live my life waiting for whatever Max or Dad or anyone else is going to do. I need to set my own path and follow it. If Max wants to be involved and help out financially, I won't stop him. But I'm not going to go after him if he's not interested."

"If he's not interested in his own child, then he's not the man for you."

I stared at my brother. "Is that your way of saying Dad's heinous actions helped me dodge a bullet?"

James shrugged. "I wouldn't go that far. But as you figured out, attraction and sex are easy. Caring for and respecting someone is a whole other ball of wax."

He wasn't wrong about that. I'd seen a side of Max yesterday that I wouldn't have thought possible.

"What are your plans for today?" I scooped eggs onto my toast and took a bite.

"Not much. I have an errand I want to do this morning, but other than that, I'll probably just be hanging out. You're welcome to hang out here with me."

I shook my head. "Like I said, I need to get all my ducks in a row." With my fork, I toyed with my eggs, hesitating on what I wanted to ask next. "Do you happen to know a good realtor?"

James's gaze lifted to mine. He didn't say anything for a minute, but then he finally nodded. "Yeah, I do." He reached his hand across the table, taking mine. "I hate to see you go, but I understand why you have to. Do you still plan to go to New York?"

I let out a long sigh. I'd only been up for a half hour, but already, I was exhausted again. "I don't know. Max is the only reason to go there, and he was clear that he wasn't interested in me or the baby."

"He threatened to take the child from you. That sounds like he's interested."

I shook my head. "I think he just said that because he was angry and wanted to hurt me." Not that I wasn't fearful that he would follow through. But there was no doubt in my mind that he was speaking from anger and wanting to lash out at the pain he believed I'd caused him.

I finished my breakfast and then gathered up my purse to go home. James gave me another hug. "You can come here and work if you want to. I won't be gone long this morning."

I shook my head. "I need some time alone to sort my head out. If you do happen to think of anything that Dad might do, let me know. I need to come up with a defense strategy. At this point, I think he's capable of anything."

James nodded. "I'll look into hiring a P.I. or something to help us gather leverage against Dad."

My eyes watered as my brother's kindness made my heart swell with emotion. "You're so good to me."

He smiled. "You deserve it, Amelia. You really do."

After one more hug, I headed out the door to a waiting car James had ordered for me while I'd cleaned up the breakfast dishes.

When I arrived home, I got into the shower, washing yesterday off me, and then dressing in a pair of jeans and an extra-large sweatshirt. I made myself another cup of tea and then went into my home office, determined to get my life straight. I couldn't control what Max or my father might do, but I could be proactive in my life. I would do whatever was necessary to protect my business and my baby.

I started by sending every one of my clients a Happy New Year email that included a recap of all we'd accomplished over the last year and what I looked forward to helping them accomplish in the coming year. I had to hope if my father tried to ruin my reputation with my clients, they would remember how much I'd done to help their businesses.

Next, I took another look at my finances to see how long I could live if my business started to tank. I didn't want to let my staff go, but if my father caused my business to falter, I might have to in order to save money that I needed for the baby.

Finally, I researched places I could move to. Places that were out of reach of my father and his cronies but affordable. I also needed to consider places that had a decent job market in case something happened to my business and I decided to get a job. It also needed to be a place with good healthcare and educational systems.

A few hours later, I was too tired to keep working even though my plans were far from being fleshed out. I went to lie on the couch to rest before I took another look at my life to make sure all my bases were covered.

Knocking startled me awake. My eyes opened, and I lay on the couch, listening. The knock came again. I launched myself off the couch, rushing to the door, my heart thundering with hope that it was Max. But as I reached the door, I tempered that hope. There was no way the man who threatened to take my child yesterday was at my door. At least not because he loved me.

I looked through the peephole. James. He stood just outside holding several bags.

I unlocked and opened the door. "Hey. You got your errands done?"

He nodded. "I meant it when I said that you're not alone. I'm here for you."

I tilted my head to study him, wondering what had happened that he felt compelled to remind me of his vow.

"But I'm not here just to support you and stand by your side, Amelia. You and I are going to do this together. We're going to make sure Dad gets what's coming to him. I'm going to make sure that you and your baby are safe and happy."

"You said that before."

He nodded. "I just wanted to make sure you understood. You and I are partners in this now, okay? Together, we'll face whatever Dad brings on. And maybe your baby won't have a dad, but he can have the best fucking uncle in the world."

It was funny how I could smile when I felt so much pain. Perhaps it was the relief in knowing I wasn't alone. The gratitude of knowing my brother didn't just have my back, but he was here with me. By my side. I would've flung my arms around him again, but he was still holding the bags.

"Your words mean everything to me."

He nodded. "It's you and me against the world. Just like always."

I looked at the bags. "What are these?"

"Some of it's food, but the rest of it is supplies. I'm going to work with you on the game plan. And while we need to watch our backs with Dad, we definitely need to go on the offensive. If we do that and are able to drive Dad away, you don't have to move."

"We need to be realistic here, James. Dad is practically an institution here in Las Vegas. He has friends or people who owe him and will protect him."

"I have the name of the man who is running the premier security company in the country. These guys recently brought down a cartel. If they can do that, they can help us bring down Dad. If we're lucky, he'll end up in prison, but if not, we could still make his empire crumble."

What he was saying would take a miracle. At the same time, his words infused me with energy and hope. It would probably go badly, but if James and I were going to go down, we were going to go down kicking and screaming and dragging our father with us.

CHAPTER TWENTY-FIVE

Max

I was supposed to leave Las Vegas with my parents and Vivie the next day, but I had to file the annulment papers, so I was desperately looking for an excuse to bow out of returning with them. I decided I would tell them that I planned to go to Los Angeles to check on the club development while Sam was on his honeymoon. I would have to actually go so I wouldn't be a liar, but I could file the annulment papers tomorrow morning at the clerk's office and then get on a plane and be in Los Angeles by lunchtime.

Later that evening, my parents said they decided to stay in Nevada, wanting to spend more time checking out the sites. Vivie decided she would go to Los Angeles, visiting a friend from college. For once, it felt like the universe was looking out for me. Instead of making a detour to California, I could file the paperwork and then go to the airport and head back to New York. Go back to my old life.

I spent the rest of the night reading through the paperwork Amelia had brought me to make sure there wasn't a loophole or legal statement that would fuck me up. Anyone who was willing to drug a person and force them into a marriage wasn't beyond tampering with legal documents. Although I was no lawyer, and it took me fucking forever to read the papers, everything looked okay to me.

I was at the county clerk's office the moment they unlocked the door to open for the day. As I approached the counter where a woman waited to help me, a feeling of sadness washed through me. I had really thought Amelia was different. For the first time in years, I'd wanted to open myself up to the possibility of love. It had been bad enough to be cheated on and ridiculed by former girlfriends, but what Amelia did effectively killed any ability for me to love.

I remembered thinking Sam was a wuss the way he'd give up on Kate at the first sign of trouble. But now I realized he was the bravest person I knew. To open his heart to a woman who'd actively tried not to love him was crazy. How could he trust that she wouldn't reject him down the line?

Thinking of Sam reminded me of the tongue lashing he gave me yesterday. I was pissed, but mostly, my anger was at myself. He was right. I kept my feelings hidden. But that wasn't anything new. I'd been like that for a long time. He shouldn't have been busting my balls over something that wasn't going to change.

I handed the papers over and left the clerk's office. I stopped outside to order a car to take me to the airport. As I waited for it, I expected to feel free. Once I left Las Vegas, Amelia and our marriage and my humiliation would be left behind. But free wasn't what I felt. I didn't even feel relieved.

The car arrived, and I climbed into the back seat. Thankfully, the driver drove in silence. When I boarded the plane and sat down in the First Class seat, I worked to think of the last few months as a nightmare that I was going to wake up from when we landed in New York. But as the wheels left the ground, I realized that I wasn't leaving all this behind. Not if there was a baby. Was there a baby?

I rubbed my temples, knowing that there had to be one. Amelia had no leverage over me without one. And it wasn't like I hadn't fucked her bare. That would never happen again. From now on, any woman I fucked, I'd be wearing a condom. Maybe two. Then again, I probably wouldn't fuck anyone again. I didn't want to take the risk. I tried to ignore the fact that I couldn't even imagine being with another woman but Amelia.

I sighed, coming to terms with my situation. The baby would keep me tethered to Amelia and whatever play she had next and the scam she was running. Fuck. Why couldn't I have just stuck with my original plan? One woman, one night, and move on.

By the time I reached my apartment in New York, it was close to nine in the evening. Even though it was still early on the West Coast, I was exhausted and decided to call it a night.

Sleep was elusive, but when it did come, it was filled with dreams of Amelia dangling a baby over me, taunting me about how easy I'd been to dupe. About how I had a responsibility. About her draining my bank account dry.

I woke up feeling as tired as I did when I went to bed. What the hell was I going to do? How could I co-parent with a woman who'd used me?

The memory of her brother confronting me swept back into my mind. He told me to forget Amelia and the baby, that they didn't need me. Those words created a kernel of doubt that Amelia was the con woman I'd come to believe she was. But I immediately dismissed it. The truth was more likely that her brother was in on the scam. He'd come to see me to create doubt so that I would demand access to my child, which I had. But even if I hadn't fought for the child, my actions still provided leverage for them to use over me. They could file documents forcing me to pay child support. They could go to the media and paint me as a man who'd abandoned his child. I didn't know how badly that might hurt the business Sam and I had built, but it would kill me on the inside. Maybe it was pride, but I couldn't have them destroy my reputation. I needed to get ahead of this thing.

I remembered Amelia's brother asking Noel St. Martin for information because he wanted to hire him. What were the odds that he was going to hire Noel's company to get dirt on me? Pretty fucking good.

I opened my phone, finding the New York number for Saint Security, and called to make an appointment with someone I could hire to investigate on my behalf.

Two hours later, a thirty-something-year-old man entered my office. He didn't look like the typical investigator or security guy rich businesspeople hired. The closest thing to looking professional was that he wore was a blazer over a T-shirt and worn jeans. His face was rugged, and his eyes looked to be those of a man who had seen a lot in his lifetime. I suspected this man had been with Saint Security back when they were in the mercenary business. Because it was possible that I would need to play dirty, I was glad they'd sent a man who looked like he was willing to bend the rules.

I stood and came around my desk, extending my hand. "Mr. Shepard?"

He nodded. "Dax Shepard."

"I'm Max Clarke. Thank you for coming. Can I get you a coffee or something?"

He shook his head, taking a seat before it was offered. This was a no-nonsense man. Good.

I went back around my desk and sat in my chair.

"I've met your brother," Dax said as he crossed an ankle over his knee as he leaned back in his chair. "He's neighbors with the company founder, Noel St. Martin."

I nodded. "Yes, Noel was at my brother's wedding."

"How can I help?"

"Do you only work here in New York? The work I need done is out in Nevada."

"I started here in the New York office, but then Noel opened an office in Los Angeles, and I went out there with him. Normally, I work out there now, so any work that needs to be done in Nevada, I can do. I'm in New York to check on things in the office here. So, what kind of help do you need?"

I hesitated because in order to let this man know what I needed, I would have to share how I'd been an idiot and been taken in by a woman. It made me look weak. To be honest, if I could let it go, I would. But not doing anything would allow Amelia and her family to hurt others. Plus, I suspected they were the type of people who would go beyond me and try to hurt my family. I wasn't going to let that happen. So if I had to reveal my greatest embarrassment, I would.

"I got caught up in something that's leaving me vulnerable to extortion. I need two things from you. The first is that I need leverage against these people."

Dax gave one quick nod but his expression remained the same. "And the second?"

"And the second is I need to find out what they did to me."

His head tilted to the side. "What do you mean, what they did? You don't know?"

"I was having dinner with a woman, and a limousine driver showed up to give us a tour of the city. But after one glass of champagne in the limousine, I was out until the next morning when I woke up married."

If Dax thought that was funny or that I was a sucker, he didn't show it. "So, you want to find out who drugged you?"

"I know who. The woman and her father, and possibly her brother, were in on it. But I need proof."

"Proof to protect yourself? Or proof to send them to jail?"

Did I really want Amelia to go to jail? Especially if she was carrying my child? Not really. But if she and her family stayed free, who else would they pull this scam on? The reality was, at some point, I would be exposed. Amelia was a social media star. It wouldn't be long before she'd use her platform to hurt me.

"I want them in jail."

Dax nodded. He pulled out a small pad of paper from the breast pocket of his coat. He jotted a couple of notes and then looked up at me. "Names?"

"The woman's name is Amelia Dunsmore. Her brother's name is James, although I'm not sure if he's involved. I do know her father is involved, but I don't know his name."

"And where are they in Nevada?"

The fact that Dax didn't know the Dunsmore family was a reminder to me that I had much more to lose reputation-wise than they did. My family was well known throughout the country. It wasn't because Max and I ran clubs or that my dad and his brother ran the largest real estate company in New York. It was the philanthropic work of my parents and aunts and uncles that made the Clarke name well-known. It was clear to me that the Dunsmore family was well-known in Las Vegas. But he was a big fish in a small pond. With me, they could get money, or perhaps if I had continued with the marriage, they would have attached their name to mine, expanding their credibility and influence. I shuddered to think that I'd nearly been drawn in by Amelia and her lie. If I had told her I loved her and asked for a relationship, how long would it be before she let the truth out? The truth that she didn't love me. The truth that I'd been her mark?

I gave Dax all the information that I knew about Amelia and what happened. When he was finished taking notes, he put his pen and paper back into his pocket and rose from the chair.

"This woman you were with, are you sure she's part of the con?"

I stood to walk him to the door. "I don't know how she couldn't be."

"Was she drugged too?"

I shrugged. "She said she was. But I was out of it. I didn't see it."

"I know this might feel invasive, but the more I know, the easier it is for me to get the information I need."

I nodded in understanding even as my gut tightened, wondering what he was going to ask.

"There was a time when Saint Security didn't care very much about who was paying the bills. We worked with some fairly unscrupulous people. But not anymore. I'm telling you this to let you know that if I think you're going to use it in retaliation or in some fashion that isn't well within the law, we'll have a problem."

"I want to protect myself, and yes, I want them to pay for what they did. But not in retaliation. I want justice and to protect anybody else they could con in the future."

He nodded, seemingly to accept my explanation.

My door blew open, and Vivie strode in.

I arched a brow, not expecting her. She was supposed to be in California.

"Thought you were in Los Angeles?"

She stopped short when she saw Dax standing in my office. "I'm sorry. Your secretary wasn't out there, so I didn't realize you were in a meeting."

"This is Dax Shepard. Dax, this is my sister, Vivie Clarke."

They shook hands. I didn't miss Vivie taking a long look at Dax. She was young and prone to being distracted by good-looking men. I looked at Dax, wanting to make sure he wasn't doing the same to my sister.

His eyes narrowed as he studied her, and then he turned to me. He held out his hand and I shook it.

"I'll be in touch."

I nodded and watched as he strode out of the room.

Vivie watched him until the door shut behind him and then she turned to me. "He's intense. So are you, come to think of it."

I turned away from her because while I just spilled my guts to Dax, I wasn't going to spill them to my sister.

I sat at my desk. "I thought you were going to Los Angeles?"

"I was, except I heard there was someone at my friend's house that I didn't want to see. So I kept my flight. But you weren't on it. How come?"

Shit. "I took a later flight. Sam and I've been talking about building a club in Las Vegas, so I thought maybe I'd stick around a little bit. But then I changed my mind. I'm thinking maybe we should build one in the South. Atlanta, maybe."

Vivie thought on that as she sat in the chair Dax just vacated. "Or Miami."

"I wonder how often the hurricanes cause problems down there?"

"Not enough to stop millions of college spring breakers from showing up." She studied me for a moment. "Are you okay, Max?"

I rolled my shoulders. "Sure. Why?"

Her intense gaze told me she didn't believe me. "You seem tense and unhappy. Mom and Dad noticed too. And Sam, he had some choice words to say about you before he and Kate took off on their honeymoon."

"I'm fine. There's just been a lot going on."

She pursed her lips together, which told me she didn't believe me, but she wasn't going to continue to press me.

We chatted for a bit longer, and then she left, leaving me to stew about my inability to hide what was going on with me. I definitely needed to pull my shit together. Until Dax gave me information that I could use to stop Amelia and her family, I would have to pull off the role of a lifetime. I have to be as good an actor as Amelia was an actress when she made me fall for her.

CHAPTER TWENTY-SIX

Amelia

Every second of every minute of every hour of every day for the next couple of days, I waited for my father to bring the hammer down on me. My father's only virtue was patience except that he used it for evil. He knew that I'd be squirming and anxious, waiting for him to exact his punishment. By the time he popped up and said boo to me, I'd probably stroke out. That's how on edge my nerves were as I sat in the office of Archer Graves of Saint Security with my brother.

I explained what happened with Max and me, and James filled him in on the other details about the type of man my father was.

Archer sat across from us, listening and taking notes. When we finished, he said, "It sounds like your father has a stranglehold on Las Vegas."

"He does," James and I said together.

He looked at his notes, tapping the paper with his pen. "I'm having a hard time seeing how your father benefits from your being married to Max Clarke."

Every time he said Max's name, I winced, knowing I was breaking the promise we made not to tell anyone about our marriage. But at this point, the only way I could protect me and my baby was to be honest with someone who could help, like Archer.

"Your being married to Max gives you a financial benefit, but what about your father?" Archer finished.

"It's not clear to us either, but you can bet my father has a plan," James said. "The possibilities are endless. The first would be that Max Clarke is now his son-in-law and he would use that to benefit himself, whether it's to generate more business, to expand out of Las Vegas, or maybe just to hit Max up for loan."

I nodded. "Our father doesn't do anything that isn't going to benefit him in business, whether that's more money or power and influence."

"What is it that you're wanting us to get for you?" Archer asked.

"I want you to get my father out of my life. Or at the very least, out of Max's life," I said.

James put his hand over mine. "I'm not a lawyer or cop, but it seems like what my father did to Amelia and Max Clarke is against the law, right?"

Archer nodded. "From what you've told me, I see a few things, including kidnapping and fraud."

"He needs to go away for that," James said.

"These crimes are fairly over the top. It's surprising that he hasn't been arrested sooner." There was something about Archer's demeanor that was making me lose hope. Did he not believe us? Or did he think he wouldn't be able to help us?

"That's because he's very good at covering his tracks," I said.

"I'll admit, it's going to be hard to get to him if he has a lot of people on his payroll who are willing to lie and cheat and steal. And those who aren't usually owe him something, or he has something on them."

James squeezed my hand, making me think he was feeling dejected too.

"If we had proof, we'd use it. But I don't know who the driver was that picked us up or how the drugs were given to us, or even who married us. All I know is that it happened. My father was behind it.

He told me so." If my father got away with that, I didn't know what I'd do.

Archer laid his pen down and laced his fingers on the desk, and I felt all hope slipping away.

"He admitted what he did to you once. Do you think he will do it again?"

James laughed. "Course he would. He likes to gloat about his victories."

"Then what we need to do is get him on tape."

I frowned. "You mean like wearing a wire?" He nodded. I looked at James, and he shrugged. I turned back to Archer. "The thing is, if I went to see my father and tried to get him to confess again, he'd see right through me. I've been avoiding him at all costs, not just since this happened, but long before that. He'd get suspicious if I sought him out."

"In that case, you might need to wait for him to come to you. We can help you with equipment and have it ready whenever he shows up." Archer looked from me to James. "The concern, of course, is what will your father do if he finds out? Is he dangerous?"

A chill ran up my spine. I'd never seen my father be violent. I'd never even heard that he'd done anything violent. I suspected he didn't need to be because he had so much leverage over people. But I suppose everybody could be pushed to the limit.

I looked at James, wondering what he thought. He stared back at me, and I could see he was wondering the same thing. How far would my father go?

"I don't know?" I admitted.

"How about we start with having an investigator begin digging around to see what we can learn? Maybe we can find the driver and get him to talk. Or maybe we can find something else. But I think you need to consider that if your father is as wily as you say he is, we may need to get him on tape."

"If we do get him on tape, will it hold up in court?" James asked.

"We'll make sure that it does."

I turned to James again. "Even if it isn't, having it as leverage could help us. Don't you think? We'd have something to hold over him."

James shook his head. "As long as that man is free, he's a danger to all of us. Maybe not physically, but if he knew you had him on tape, he would work even harder to discredit you and ruin you. He'd definitely disown you."

I shrugged. "As soon as he finds out the annulment papers have been filed, he's going to disown me anyway."

James looked down at my stomach, and instinctively, I pressed my hand to protect the baby.

His gaze moved back up to my face. "As long as Max is still connected to you, Dad's going to come after you or him."

He was right. A wave of despair washed through me that I wouldn't be able to protect my baby, much less Max or me. There were many times over the last couple of days when I accepted that truth. This baby was the connection to Max, and my father would use it. The only way he couldn't would be if I gave up all my rights and handed them over to Max. By severing my ties with the child, I'd be able to sever my father's as well. The thought of doing that ripped my soul in two. Yet I knew that if it came down to it, I would do it. I would do anything to protect my baby.

Archer looked at us with sympathy in his eyes. "Where's Mr. Clarke in all of this?"

"He's out of the picture." James said it so intensely that it had me jerking to look at him. Had he talked to Max?

"Surely, he has an interest in getting rid of your father and having your father pay for his deeds?" Archer asked.

I nodded. "He does, but it's much better if I take care of this. I need to protect him. He needs to stay far away from my father."

Archer tilted his head to the side. "Does Mr. Clarke know that you're willing to fall on the sword for him?"

Before I could answer, James said, "He doesn't give a shit. Right now, we need to focus on keeping Amelia safe. We need to put my father away."

Once again, I was looking at James, wondering how he knew so much about Max.

Archer nodded. "Like I said, I'll send somebody to look into this, and we'll go from there."

James and I stood. "Thank you very much, Mr. Graves." I extended my hand to shake Archer's. James did the same.

"Look, I know this is sounding all cloak and dagger, but we need to be careful in how we communicate. My father knows a lot of tech people too. He could very easily find a way to track Amelia's phone or her car or her computer."

James was right. I should've thought of that as well. After all, that's why we were in Los Angeles. It was why we left all our tech gadgets at home and bought burner phones when we arrived in California. It was why we drove instead of flying, which required us to use our identities to travel. We just had to cross our fingers that Dad wasn't watching either of us that closely so that he'd notice we were out of town at the same time. Or if he was, he'd think we were on a vacation.

"Good to know. I will have someone on our tech team set up a fake company, and we'll work it as if we're hiring Ms. Dunsmore as our social media consultant. Of course, we'll have to talk in code, but we'll develop a system so that you'll be able to understand what we're saying. More likely than not, the call will be to set up a meeting about the business arrangement. At that point, we can give you the details of what we've learned."

I was still agitated, but somewhat relieved as well. Archer and his team knew what they were doing. Of course they did. If they were able to take down a cartel. Surely, they'd be able to take down my dad, just as James had said.

James and I left Mr. Graves's office and headed down to the lobby of the building. We ordered a car from the app and had it take us back to our dingy hotel that didn't require real names.

On the drive, I looked over at James. "Did you talk to Max?"

He flinched and looked out the window, telling me that he had. "Why?"

"What did you say? What did you do?" A part of me was annoyed that he'd talked to Max and didn't tell me. Another part of me grieved that a plea my brother might've made on my behalf fell on deaf ears. He hadn't convinced Max that I wasn't a part of my father's scheme.

James turned to look at me. "I went on New Year's Day. He was at some breakfast with his family and the wedding party. I'm not going to lie, Amelia, I loved the way he squirmed when I walked in and he realized who I was."

Sadness filled my chest. "You can't blame Max for feeling the way he does. If you look at it from his point of view—"

James shook his head vehemently. "Anybody who knows you, Amelia, knows you don't have a lying bone in your body. He, on the other hand, is a fucking asshole. I told him to stay away from you and the baby. You don't need him. Whatever you need, you can get from me."

I turned to look out the window, biting my tongue from the need to defend Max.

"He didn't fight for you, Amelia."

It didn't seem possible that my heart could break any more, but in that moment, it did. Max didn't fight for me or the baby. He'd read me wrong in thinking that I would pull a stunt as heinous as what my father had done. But I'd misjudged him too when I thought that he was a good, sweet, and decent man who would do the right thing.

CHAPTER TWENTY-SEVEN

Max

My life was back to normal. At least on the outside. To everyone else, I lived my life just like I had before I'd met and fallen for Amelia. On the inside, though, I was a fucking mess. During the day, when I would think about my predicament, I knew I was doing the right thing. I was certain I was the mark in a grand con by Amelia and her family. There was no denying that I'd been drugged and forced into a marriage. And through that fraud, it appeared as if a child had been created. Amelia and her family needed to pay for that so that they couldn't run the scam on somebody else. I felt certain that Dax Shepard would find the information I needed for justice.

But at night, my dreams told me something else. The pain and horror on Amelia's face when I'd threatened to put her in jail and take the child haunted me. Her brother, James, often showed up in my nightmares as well, emasculating me for not fighting for his sister. The dreams left me feeling alone, so of course Sam and other members of my family would show up as well, telling me I wouldn't be alone if I had the balls to share with them the torment I was going through.

Every morning, I woke up feeling disoriented and confused. I didn't know what was up or down, right or wrong, truth or lies. During the moments when I wondered if I'd had it all wrong about Amelia, that she was a victim of her father too, yearning for her expanded in my chest until I couldn't breathe. It was followed by feelings of guilt and shame about how I'd treated her.

But immediately, I would push that all away because I didn't know whether Amelia was a con or a victim. When I thought back through everything, she could have just as easily been a part of the scam as her father's pawn. What was really fucking me up the most was that I was too much of a coward to find out the truth. To learn if Amelia was the person I thought she was before I learned about the plan, I'd have to open myself up to her. I didn't have the courage to do that.

Four days after meeting with Dax, I got a call that the court date for the annulment was set for mid-February, just a few weeks away. The day after that, Dax called me to report on the progress in my case. As I waited to hear what he had to say, I realized I was equal parts eager to be validated while at the same time dreading the news if I was wrong.

"I can't give you any details, but I can tell you that you're not the only one interested in information about Mr. Dunsmore."

"That doesn't surprise me. I can't imagine I'm the first person that he and his kids have tried to take advantage of." But I would make sure that I was the last.

There was a pause on the line, and it made me wonder what Dax was going to share with me. "I'm in a difficult position here because of privacy and confidentiality."

"What can you tell me?"

"Mr. Dunsmore is a cunning man. There are no electronic breadcrumbs regarding his dastardly deeds. That means no texts, no emails, etc. There are people around him who know what's going on but aren't willing to talk either because he pays them well, or he can hurt them."

My hope of discovering the truth and putting an end to the

Dunsmores' scams faltered. "What about his daughter and son? Are they as careful as their father?"

"Nothing we found suggests that they're involved. Again, I can't go into too much detail, except to answer that one question you had about their culpability in what happened to you. We have no evidence of that. In fact, we're sure they're not involved."

I felt like someone had taken a sledgehammer to my gut. Dax was saying that I'd been wrong about Amelia and James. I couldn't form words. I couldn't breathe. The ramifications of his words filled me with guilt and shame.

"Like I said, Mr. Dunsmore is good at what he does. He runs his organization like a criminal empire. The only way we're going to get him is to have him reveal himself or confess on tape."

"How?" I scraped a hand over my face, having a hard time keeping up with the realization that Amelia was innocent.

"Has Mr. Dunsmore called you?"

"No." Although not a day had gone by when I wasn't waiting for a call or a negative news story about me leaked by someone in the Dunsmore family. Except Dax was telling me it wasn't the Dunsmore family. It was just the father. God. I was the worst. This was the shittiest I'd felt since this whole thing started.

"I don't think he's going to contact you directly, but just in case, I'm going to have somebody from the New York office come over to add an app to your phone that will allow you to record anything if he should call. Like I said, it seems unlikely, but we want to cover all bases."

"What if he doesn't call?" This man had to pay for what he did. I wanted him to pay even more now for what he made me do to Amelia. Not that it alleviated my culpability.

"We have somebody in Vegas who is willing to wear a wire. The thing is, we have to be patient. We can't have her initiate a meeting with him as that would be suspicious."

"Her?" Jesus fuck. My stomach roiled as I realized he had to mean Amelia.

"Like I said, I can't give you any details. You just need to know that we're still working on this, but we have to wait for him to make the next move."

I shot up from my chair and paced my office as dread filled me. "How will you keep her safe? Do you even know what this man is capable of?"

"Mr. Clarke, you hired us because you know we're the best. I would also caution you against making assumptions about what you think we're doing. I told you I can't give you details."

His voice was steady, matter-of-fact. It was clear that he had talked to other clients like this before. But he couldn't sway me from knowing that the woman who was going to wear the wire was Amelia. Who else could it be? She was the only one that her father had revealed his scam to. They were hoping he would do it again. But what would he do if he discovered she was trying to set him up?

The idea of his hurting Amelia took all the wind out of me. I sank onto the couch, unable to stay standing. "She's pregnant."

Dax didn't say anything at first. "I say to you again, you hired us because we know what we're doing."

"If you're doing this because of me, then I want you to stop. I don't want anybody put in danger because of me."

"As I told you earlier, you're not the only person who has reached out to us regarding Mr. Dunsmore."

So he wasn't doing this because of me. He'd said I wasn't the only one wanting Mr. Dunsmore investigated. That had to mean Amelia was the other person. I remembered James asking Noel for Saint Security's number. He must be helping her, but was he really going to let Amelia take this risk?

"I just wanted to give you an update. We're in a holding pattern at the moment, but as soon as Mr. Dunsmore makes contact with our subject, I'll let you know."

He hung up before I could say anything.

I wasn't going to sit here and wait to find out if Amelia's father hurt her. I rose from the couch and grabbed my coat off my chair. I pulled up the rideshare app on my phone to order a car to the airport.

I'd made it halfway across my office to leave when the door opened and my parents walked in.

They stopped short when they saw me.

"Oh, are you leaving? Your secretary said you didn't have any appointments right now." My mom looked at me with concern. In fact, both of them looked at me like they were terrified for me. I gleaned quickly that this visit was going to be an intervention. They probably called ahead to my secretary to find out when I had an opening so that they could ambush me.

"I have to go."

My father stepped into my path. "Max. We've been patient, but you have to tell us what's going on. Are you in legal trouble? Are you on drugs? What the hell is wrong with you?"

"Drew." My mother put her hand on my father's arm, not liking his tone.

"I'm sorry, but we've been watching something unfold over the last few months, and I'm tired of waiting for him to tell us what's going on."

My mother nodded. "We have been patient, Max. We know you don't like to share the inner details of your life, but we can see you slipping away from us. We're not going to let that happen. We're going to fight for you."

Their words filled me with more guilt, which should have been impossible. I was letting them down. Just like I'd let Amelia down. They were going to fight for me like I hadn't fought for Amelia. But now wasn't the time to tell my parents everything that had gone on.

"I can't right now. I have to go." I stepped between them, moving toward the door.

"Where, Son?" my father asked.

I stopped at the open door for a moment. "To Las Vegas." Then I kept going toward the elevator.

My parents followed me.

"What's in Las Vegas?" my mother asked as she and my father stepped into the elevator with me.

I was a grown ass man. I was strong and confident, but in this moment, I felt more emotionally fragile than I had as a child. I could feel the tears of shame and guilt and frustration and panic welling in my eyes. I leaned against the wall of the elevator, bringing my thumb and forefinger up to pinch the bridge of my nose, hoping I could stop whatever breakdown I was about to have.

My mom's hand pressed over my heart. "Max, honey. What's in Las Vegas?"

I let out a shuddering breath. "My life."

CHAPTER TWENTY-EIGHT

Amelia

Anticipation was the worst. Anticipation and uncertainty combined were unbearable. Archer's team had set up all sorts of gizmos in my apartment and an app on my phone to record my father, if and when he came over to confront me about my marriage to Max.

I wasn't sure what frightened me more, that I wouldn't be able to engage one of the recording devices while he was here, or what my father might do if he discovered I was setting him up. Dax, the security man Mr. Graves assigned to us, said that if I had warning that my father was coming, he or someone on his team could remotely activate the devices.

Because there was concern that my father was having my place watched, Dax and his people showed up in a telecommunications van, making it look like I was putting in a new phone or high-speed Internet or something while they wired up my home to record my father. Not only did they set up audio, but video as well.

That was completed several days ago, and now we were waiting for my father to make his move. But the waiting was making me more anxious every day. I found it difficult to work even as I tried to use it as a distraction.

I sat at my desk reading the same social media caption over and over for the last twenty minutes.

My phone rang, startling me. I pressed one hand over my speeding heart as the other picked up my phone. The caller ID told me it was James.

"Hey, James."

"I may have done something stupid."

"What?"

"All this waiting is getting us nowhere. And while the men from Saint Security said they'll stick around for as long as I pay them, there is a limit, don't you think? At some point, they'll need to move on,"

I thought of all the money this had to be costing James. I had wanted to contribute, but he insisted that I keep all my money in case my father did something to hurt my business. I needed to save all my pennies so I could support myself and the child.

I thought of Max because he certainly had a responsibility for the baby, even if our marriage would be annulled in a few weeks. But in many ways, I agreed with James that if Max didn't want anything to do with me, it was best that I let him go. That meant I wouldn't be suing him for child support.

"So, what did you do?" I asked.

"I went to Dad's office and asked him about a rumor I'd heard that you got married, but that an annulment was in process. I acted like I was pissed at him for making you leave the man you married so he wouldn't be suspicious."

My stomach did a somersault and then threatened to rise up. Maybe anticipation wasn't so bad, after all. Because impending doom felt worse.

"What did he say?"

"He acted like he didn't know anything about it, but I could see the wheels turning in his head, the anger that you were defying him. I've let Dax and his team know what I did, but I wanted you to know as well. If Dad doesn't show up sometime today, I'll be surprised."

I nodded, glad that I was sitting down because every nerve in my body was shaking.

"They assured me that they were there and watching the place," James said. I could hear the shaking in his voice. "And I'll be over shortly as well."

"Okay. I'll be ready."

"I sure hope I didn't fuck this up for you, Amelia."

"I'd rather get this over with. The waiting is hard."

When I hung up, I sat at my desk, taking deep breaths to ward off the panic. I knew this had to be done to protect myself and the baby, and even Max. But I'd never been so scared in my life. What did it say about my father that I was terrified of him? I pressed my hand over my belly, looking down where my child was growing.

"I promise you will never be afraid of me."

On wobbly legs, I stood and went to the kitchen to fix myself a cup of tea. Once it was brewed, I sat at my kitchen table and waited.

I had just finished my tea, putting my cup in the sink, when my phone beeped with a notification. It was from the fake business that Saint Security set up to communicate with me incognito.

The campaign has launched. The messages are posted.

I gripped the edge of the sink as I realized this was it. My father was on his way to my front door and the devices were recording.

When the knock on the door sounded, I inhaled a deep breath, trying to calm my nerves. All I had to do was listen to my father rail at me and tell me to go after Max. His disappointment and yelling were nothing new. As long as that was all he did, I'd be okay. He'd never been violent with me in the past, so there was no reason to think he would be now. At least that's what I told myself as I reached for the doorknob to open my door.

The minute it was unlatched, it pushed open hard, causing me to stumble back.

My father barged in. "I told you to stick to the plan."

I was so nervous I could swear my teeth were shaking. Dax and I had practiced different things for me to say to my father. It was important that my father gave away the plan without my leading the conversation. I had to keep my responses vague so that my father would be forced to speak of the terrible thing he'd done.

"You need to go to court and withdraw your annulment papers." He spat his words at me.

I stepped into the room, hoping he'd follow me and move closer to where I knew the recording devises would best be able to capture him. "I can't."

My father's face pinched tight as his dark eyes stared at me menacingly. "You think you can stand up to me, little girl? I gave you the perfect husband. I know you like him."

"It doesn't matter. Max doesn't want to be married to me. He's of no use to you."

My father stepped toward me, and instinct had me wanting to step back, but I didn't want to show fear. If he could tell that my knees were knocking, he might think something was up.

"You think you can go against me? You know what I'm capable of. I can make sure that your business goes down in flames. And don't think that my reach is only in Las Vegas or Nevada. Wherever you go, I will be there. Or you can live a happy, secure life with a man I know you've been fucking."

My breath hitched to hear my father talk to me like that.

"All you have to do is take back the annulment. He must've seen something in you before, although I don't know what." My father's gaze scanned me up and down, looking at me with disdain. "You're not the prettiest woman out there, but he saw something in you, and you need to make him see it again."

"Why are you doing this? It's not like you don't have power and influence. Why are you doing this to me?"

My father laughed derisively. "You? It has very little to do with you. One of my men spotted you with Max Clarke, who has tons of money and influence, and I want a piece of it. Frankly, I don't know why you don't want him. A smart woman would."

I shook my head, wondering if maybe my father was crazy. I wasn't being hyperbolic. I really thought that maybe something was mentally wrong with my father.

I turned my thinking away from my father's mental health to wondering if I had enough to prove what he had done. I didn't think so. He hadn't admitted to drugging us, even if he had indicated that he'd arranged our marriage. So I needed to continue on.

I sat on the couch, hoping I looked nonchalant even though the reason for my sitting had to do with my legs wobbling. "Why did you do it, Dad?"

He stared at me with his hands on his hips, his eyes still glowering at me. "Do what?"

"All that sneaking around and maneuvering?"

His eyes narrowed. "Why?" His suspicious tone made me nervous.

"It just seems like a whole lot of work for a whole lot of nothing. Even if I wanted to stop the annulment or wanted to be married to Max, he doesn't want me. And he's not going to care about anything you say or try to do to him. His power and influence are bigger than yours." The moment that last bit was out of my mouth, I winced.

As expected, my father's dander rose. He pointed his finger at me. "Don't you dare underestimate me. And if Max Clarke underestimates me, he'll learn just how much damage I can do to him. Even to his family."

The Clarke family was well-established, well-liked, but in this day and age, it didn't take much to ruin a reputation.

I decided to take a different route. "I don't know why you think I'd be happy. Even if Max and I wanted to get married, I missed my own wedding. I didn't get to plan it or enjoy it."

He shrugged. "Weddings are overrated and expensive. Honeymoons are better, and from the looks of things, you two didn't need any help in that department."

My skin crawled as I wondered how much my father was able to infiltrate my life. But I still hadn't gotten him to admit that he drugged us and forced us to get married, so I plodded on.

"Considering all the arrangements you had to make, I suspect that this wedding wasn't inexpensive."

He put his hands in his pocket, looking smug. "There were few people who owed me a few favors."

I gaped. "Was there a ceremony? Or was it just paperwork? Is my marriage even legal?"

"Why are you so preoccupied with this? We have an opportunity to capitalize on this. And it's not like it's a hardship. You clearly like the guy."

"This isn't Medieval times, Dad. Today, women like to choose who they're going to marry and be an active participant in it. You took that away from me. It hasn't endeared Max to me, or you. You should just let it go. If you keep pushing this, it's going to get out what you did."

He laughed, and it made me think of a cartoon villain. "Do you think anyone would believe you if you told them what happened?"

"I don't know what happened." I felt I was so close to getting him to say the right words.

He scoffed. "I told you, you experienced the good part. And I know you won't tell anyone what you think happened. You would have already. Max Clark is definitely not going to say anything. It will ruin his reputation. It will make his family a laughingstock."

"Not if we had proof." When I said the words, I stepped far enough out of my father's reach. I watched him closely, wondering how he would respond to my suggestion that we had evidence of his misdeeds.

He gave that same derisive laugh. "What proof? There is no proof."

I stayed silent, hoping he'd follow that up by explaining how he'd been able to hide the evidence of what he did. But he didn't.

Dammit, he was making this hard.

I didn't want to tip my hand, but at the same time, I needed to get my father to say more. If he knew he was under investigation, would he say something to incriminate himself? I couldn't give away that James had hired Saint Security, but maybe I could imply that

Max had. I didn't want to throw him under the bus, but he wasn't here, and it wouldn't be out of the realm of possibility that a man like Max Clarke would hire an investigator if he believed he'd been conned.

"I think Max has hired someone to investigate."

The smugness on my father's face faltered. "He won't find anything."

"How can you be sure? Whoever you paid to help you, Max could pay them more to betray you. You know he could." I worried a little bit about mentioning that he paid money to pull off the scam would be a problem, but I needed my father to come clean.

"He was really freaked out when he couldn't remember the night before. He said something about having blood drawn to see if someone had slipped him a drug," I lied.

"When was that?" My father's demeanor went from triumphant to worried.

"Right after it happened."

My father thought about that and then he said, "It won't matter. Anything he might've consumed would have been out of his system by the next day."

Was that a good enough confession?

"Well, for your sake, you should hope you're right. But if I were you, I'd let this whole thing go. It's not smart to take on the Clarke family. I don't want to be married to a man who didn't choose to marry me."

In an instant, rage consumed my father. He strode toward me, grabbing me by the arms and giving me a shake. "You don't tell me what to do. I've invested too much time and money into this. So what, you were drugged and incoherent during your wedding. Any daughter would be grateful that I had gotten them hitched to a man like Max Clarke. You are going to go to the courthouse to withdraw your annulment, or so help me, Amelia—"

A knock interrupted my father's tirade. We both looked at the door and then at each other.

"Who is that?" he asked.

I shook my head. "I don't know." I hoped to hell that it was Dax and his team.

"Amelia."

My breath hitched as I recognized the voice.

"It's Max. Open up."

I wanted to let Max in because I was afraid to continue to be alone with my dad. But at the same time, I wanted him to go away. Until we had what we needed to put my father in jail, I didn't want him anywhere near Max.

My father's sinister smile returned.

"Why don't you go let your husband in, Amelia?"

CHAPTER TWENTY-NINE

Max

My parents let me go once I promised to fill them in on what was going on with me. I hoped to hell that I'd be telling them about Amelia and the baby.

I'd flown out to Las Vegas many times over the last couple of months, but this trip was the longest flight of all. I'd chartered a flight so I didn't have to wait for the next commercial flight west, and even still, the minutes ticked away like hours. All I could do was sit on the flight and worry. Worry that I wouldn't arrive in time before Amelia had to confront her father. Worried that her father was a dangerous man and wonder what he might do if he found out she was setting him up. Worried I wouldn't have a chance to beg for her forgiveness and tell her that I loved her and our baby. I already knew that I would never be able to forgive myself for how I treated Amelia. But if something happened to her or the baby because I hadn't listened to her, because I wasn't there to protect her, I didn't know how I would live with that.

When the plane landed, I got into the car I'd ordered from a service so that it would be waiting when I arrived. Just like the flight, the car ride to Amelia's townhome took forever. Finally, the driver pulled in front of a row of townhomes. I rushed from the car, making my way toward her home, when all of a sudden, I was grabbed and shoved up against a van.

"Let go." I flailed my arms to get away.

"What are you doing here?"

It took me a moment to realize that the man who grabbed me was Dax Shepard.

"I've come to see Amelia."

Dax released me, but he stood close as if he was prepared to prevent me from getting away. "When I called you and gave you an update, I didn't tell you to come here."

"I don't need your permission to see Amelia." It occurred to me that if Dax was here, Amelia's father was here. "Is it happening now? Is her father here?"

Dax gave a curt nod. "I can't have you going in and ruining it. Her father hasn't revealed enough to incriminate himself."

Just then, a head popped out of the van and gave Dax a thumbs-up.

"What's going on?" I pushed him away so I could get to Amelia's apartment. I didn't care whether her father incriminated himself or not. I needed to see her. I needed to protect her.

Dax grabbed me again. "Hold on. You can go. But don't give away that her place is wired up. My team says we have what we need, so you don't need to agitate him. Just get him out of the apartment."

I nodded and turned back toward Amelia's townhome. As I reached the door, I listened but didn't hear anything.

I knocked. "Amelia." I listened again and thought I heard talking.

"It's Max. Open up."

The door opened, and Amelia stood there, her red hair knotted into a messy bun. Her eyes were tired and at the same time fearful. But Jesus Christ, she was so beautiful.

"What are you doing here?" she asked.

I looked past her to the man standing in her living room. He looked to be in his mid-fifties, even though he clearly spent a lot of time and money on antiaging skincare and hair dye. He looked both smarmy and dangerous.

I brought my gaze back to her. "I'm here to see you." My words felt lame. I should be telling her that I was sorry and how much I loved her.

"Amelia, why don't you let your husband in? I think it's about time we were properly introduced."

She closed her eyes in quiet exasperation. "You should go."

She said it to me, confusing me. Shouldn't her father be the one leaving?

Her phone beeped in her hand. She looked at the text, and then her gaze lifted to me. I saw relief in her eyes. It had to be Dax telling her they had what they needed.

I gave her a smile. "Come with me."

Her father stepped up into the doorway, giving me a fake smile as he extended his hand to me. "Jamison Dunsmore. It's nice to finally meet my daughter's husband."

I looked at his hand and then at him. I wanted to kick his ass, but instead, I turned my attention to Amelia. "Come with me."

Mr. Dunsmore frowned, clearly not liking my rebuff. "I hope this means that your marriage is back on track." He gave Amelia a pointed look. "Remember what I said, Amelia. Make this work."

I stepped back so that her father could leave her townhome. Once again, he put on a smarmy smile. "I look forward to getting to know my son-in-law."

I ignored him, stepping back into Amelia's doorway as her father walked away.

She looked up at me, and I couldn't tell what she was thinking or feeling. Fear and doubt filled my chest, but I knew I couldn't give into it. If she decided she didn't want me, I would have to accept that. Considering how I treated her, I wouldn't be able to blame her.

She stepped back into her home, and when she didn't slam the door in my face, I followed her in, shutting the door behind me.

"Are you okay?" I should have asked that first thing.

Her chin was lifted as if she was being strong, but she still looked shaky. I wanted to reach out to gather her close and tell her that I never wanted to let her go.

"I think I am now. What are you doing here?"

I opened my mouth to answer, but then a knock came on her door. I strode over, yanking it open, ready to give her father a piece of my mind. Instead, her brother pushed past me, heading straight toward her, followed by Dax and a few other men.

"You were fucking brilliant," James said, hugging his sister, filling me with envy that I wasn't the one comforting her. But then he turned to me. "What the fuck are you doing here?"

It occurred to me that while I had been able to figure out that James and Amelia had hired Saint Security to help them deal with Amelia's father, they hadn't realized that I had done so as well. But of course, that wasn't why I was here.

I stood in Amelia's living room with her brother glaring at me while Dax and his men worked to pack up the cameras and listening devices. I wasn't a man to reveal his innermost feelings to himself, much less to a room full of people, but I couldn't wait any longer. Amelia needed to know everything that was in my heart.

I sucked in a breath, praying for the courage I needed. "I love you, Amelia." Maybe I should have started with an apology for how I treated her, but in the end, I led with the thing that was the most important.

Her breath hitched and her eyes widened. James's eyes narrowed further, as if he didn't believe me. Dax and his men were in my periphery, so I didn't know what their expressions were, but they didn't say anything.

I swallowed. "I was probably in love with you from the moment you tried to take my car at the airport."

Her lips twitched upward slightly, enough to give me hope and ease the tightness in my chest. It gave me the courage I needed to continue on. "Waking up married that morning scared the shit out of me."

The hint of her smile faltered, so I hurriedly spoke on, "But your brother was right, there was a reason I dragged my feet in this annulment. I knew that when it went through, I wouldn't see you again, and I couldn't stand that."

To be honest, opening my heart wasn't getting any easier the more I talked, but I continued on. "I haven't had success with women in the past. And when I heard you and your father talking, I assumed the worst because that had been my experience. I'd finally recognized that I was in love with you, and then I heard a conversation that made me believe I was being conned. Again."

She sniffed, and I wished to hell I knew whether her tears were of sadness or hope. What did she think about what I was saying?

"You were being conned, but not by me."

I nodded. "I know that now. I should have known then, but . . . " I looked down because I didn't know how to explain the way my pride and fear had shut me down, had shut her out.

Instead, I said, "I don't know how you feel about me—"

"I love you too, Max."

I opened my mouth to continue my train of thought, but then her words finally seeped into my brain. "You do?"

She smiled and walked toward me. "I do. Probably from the time I tried to steal your car from you."

I smiled as love and happiness inflated my chest. I looked at her brother and to Dax and his men, sure that I had the goofiest grin, but I didn't care.

When I finally looked back at her, I pressed my hand to her cheek. "I'm so sorry about the things I said and did. I hope you'll forgive me and give me a chance." I dipped forward, pressing my lips to hers.

Someone cleared their throat.

"So now that you're going steady, can we get to the business at hand?" her brother interrupted.

I kept my gaze on Amelia's as I straightened. "Okay."

Amelia wrapped her arms around me and held me tightly. "I'm so sorry for what my father did."

I hugged her back. "I'm not worried about him."

"I don't think any of you are going to have to worry about him," Dax said. "Carlton has indicated that your father has said enough to incriminate him. I suppose the question now is how you want to use this information."

One of the men with Dax leaned closer to him and whispered.

"It looks like our men have been able to find some other information about your father's illegal activities. And at least one other person who is willing to report it. Between the three of you and this other person, plus what we have on tape, you have a lot to work with. So are you going to use it as leverage or . . .?"

Amelia's arm stayed around me. "What do you think? You're his mark."

"What do you and James think?"

She twisted around to look at her brother.

"I want him gone, Amelia. Out of our lives." James didn't leave any room for uncertainty.

She nodded. "That could cause problems for the company. What if it can't survive?"

James shrugged. "I'm a big boy. I have options. Dad needs to be in a place where the only people he can hurt are the other inmates who are around him."

"Okay. I agree."

I didn't want to bring up the obvious, but I felt it was important to play devil's advocate. "He'll still have time to try and hurt the two of you. Between the arrest and the trial, he will likely try to do as much damage as he can."

James straightened, lifting his chin. "I can handle it if you can, Amelia."

"I can handle it."

"Hell, yeah, you can. When I realized you were in here trying to get him to confess, my heart practically stopped," I said, pulling Amelia tighter against me.

"Now that all is well, we'll pull this together into a report for all of you. We can help with making the police report, as well. Until he's arrested, I would keep a low profile and not tip your hand. We don't want him running off," Dax said as his men exited the door.

"A report to all of us?" James asked.

Dax nodded. "I'll let Mr. Clarke explain. The team and I will be on our way." Dax followed his men out of the townhome.

Amelia and James looked at me.

"I'd hired them to investigate as well," I said.

Amelia arched a brow. "To investigate me?"

I didn't want to lie, but I had a hard time maintaining eye contact with her and telling her the truth. "I wanted to know what happened that night we couldn't remember, when we woke up married."

Her hand pressed against my cheek. "I don't blame you for your reaction. I'm glad you know the truth. That you believe the truth."

Guilt stabbed in my gut. "I should've believed you when you told me. I just . . . it was like I was having déjà vu. My reaction was an automatic response to being made a fool."

"Amelia is the best woman you will ever meet." James still sounded unsure of me.

I nodded. "I recognize that now."

"If you hurt her again, you and I are going to have some problems."

I nodded. "I understand."

When James left, I tugged Amelia over to the couch. I sat down and pulled her onto my lap. "I need to make amends to you, but I'm not sure what to do."

She wrapped her arms around my neck. "You're here telling me you love me. That's all I need."

I slid my hand to the back of her head and pulled her so that I could kiss her. I wanted to spend the rest of the night—hell, the rest of my life—kissing her, but there was more that we needed to talk about.

"We still need to do the annulment," I said gently. I watched her expression, hoping she wasn't offended or hurt.

She nodded. "I know."

"Do you know why?"

"Because even though we love each other, we're not ready for marriage."

I shook my head. As she sat on my lap with our arms wrapped around each other, I felt as sure as the heart beating in my chest that marriage was in our future.

"It's because that marriage is tainted. Anything and everything that has your father's fingerprints on it, we need to cut out. We need this relationship to be just about us. What we want, when we want it."

Her smile was sweet. Tears welled in her eyes, and I reached up to wipe one of the tears away. "I hope those are happy tears."

She nodded. "They are." Then, her smile faltered slightly, and she stared down at me intently. "What about the baby?"

"I'm happy for the baby. Excited, even." I pressed my hand over her belly. "This little person was made by you and me. It was made because even though I didn't know it at the time, I was falling head over heels for you."

Her smile filled her face again, reaching the depths of her eyes. She leaned forward and kissed me. "When does the makeup sex begin?" she whispered in my ear and then tugged on my lobe with her teeth.

Immediately, my dick was at full staff. "Whenever you're ready, baby."

Our hands were wild as we pulled at each other's clothes. I was crazy with need. Need to touch her soft skin. To taste her body. She must have felt the same because when we were finally free of enough clothes, she straddled my thighs and sank down on me hard and fast.

Our moans filled the room. Then our lips fused together while our bodies connected in the most intimate way possible.

"I wanted to tell you at Christmas that I loved you," I said as I trailed my lips along her jaw and downward, wanting to suck on a sublime nipple, knowing that when I did, her pussy would contract around my cock in the most delicious way possible.

Her hands cradled my face, bringing my gaze to hers. "I did too. And to tell you about the baby."

"I believe you."

A tear fell on her cheek again. "The baby isn't tainted, Max."

"Hell, no, it isn't." I held her closer, wanting her to know how much I loved her and the baby. "This baby would have been made with or without your father's interference."

She smiled. "I was afraid you'd be upset."

"No. How could I be? I forgot a condom half the time." I brought my hand to her cheek. "That was a clue too."

"Clue?"

"That you're the one for me. I never, ever forgot a condom before."

My words seemed to light her up. Like she was recognizing just how important she was to me. "I was on the pill."

"The fact that it failed was a clue too."

She laughed. "I think the spectacular orgasms were a clue."

"No doubt. Are you ready for one?" I slipped my hand between us and rubbed her clit.

She gasped, and her fingers gripped my shoulders. "Yes. But together, Max. I want us to come together."

I removed my hand from her pussy. "Whatever you want, my sweet Amelia, it's yours."

After that, there were no words except for those spoken in the throes of passion. When her body seized, tightening around me, I let go, soaring into bliss with the love of my life.

CHAPTER THIRTY

Amelia

Today was the day. I was going to walk into court to annul my marriage to the man I loved. And I was happy to do it.

Max had been right that we needed to cut anything my father had touched out of our lives, and that included the marriage my father had forced on us. I didn't feel like I was losing a connection to Max because over the last few weeks with Max, I felt certain that we would get married again. When we did, we'd both be conscious. It would be our choice.

After the ordeal with my father, we each got the report from Saint Security, and with Dax's assistance, we filed charges against my father. As expected, my father went ballistic. He did anything and everything he could to ruin me and James and Max, mostly in the court of public opinion.

At one point, Max talked to his brother, Sam, about transferring his half of the partnership to Sam to protect the company. Apparently, Sam told him he was being an idiot. He wasn't worried that my father could damage their business's reputation. And he was right. While I had to talk to all my clients about what they were hearing about my "drunken" night of debauchery that left me married and pregnant, when all was said and done, they believed me and not him. In fact, the more he tried to hurt us, the more the tide turned against him. Others that he'd hurt found the courage to come forward, and business associates distanced themselves. That last bit wasn't great for James, but he was doing all he could to salvage the company.

At the worst of my father's retaliation, Max brought me to New York to get away and also to meet his family. I'd always known my father wasn't a good person, but he and James were the only family I'd known. But then I met Max's family, and I knew that no matter what happened, they would remain my family. His parents took me in like I was one of their own. His sister and I hit it off. We spent a day shopping, and she picked my brain about social media and becoming an influencer while I picked her brain about Max.

We returned home for the court date. We decided that I would go alone because we didn't want the judge to see us together and question the annulment. It was hard for Max and me to be in the same room and not make goo-goo eyes at each other. We believed that if Max didn't show up, the annulment would be granted by default.

I walked into court, and ten minutes later, I left with an annulment. I stepped outside the courthouse, where Max was waiting for me.

I waved the paper at him. "Happy annulment day."

He laughed, wrapping his arms around me and spinning me around. "You know that this annulment is more about getting rid of your father than ending a marriage, right?"

"Right." I gave him a kiss to let him know that I understood why we had gone through with this.

"Good."

He released me and stared at me for a moment. I could see there was something going on in his head but couldn't decipher what it was.

Finally, he knelt down on one knee and reached into his pocket. He took my hand. "I want to do this the right way, Amelia. I want to tell you that I love you and can't imagine my life without you. I want to be coherent when I propose, when we get our marriage license, and especially when we get married."

I laughed. "That doesn't seem unreasonable."

"Okay, then. I love you, Amelia. I can't imagine my life without you. Please tell me that you will marry me."

Oh, my God. I couldn't imagine I'd ever feel happier than I did with Max, but at that moment, I was the happiest I'd ever been. "I will marry you, Max."

He pushed a beautiful platinum and diamond ring on my finger. I noted that it was beautiful, but what was more important to me was the man I was going to marry. The father of our child.

He kissed me and led me back into the building.

"Where are we going?"

"We're going to the County Clerk's office to get a marriage license."

I suspect that Max had pulled some strings because we didn't have to wait in line to get our paperwork.

As we looked down at the paper that we both knew we'd always remember obtaining, he leaned over and kissed me again. "What do you say? Shall we get hitched?"

I felt breathless with happiness and excitement. At the same time, I didn't feel like I could get married without my brother, and I felt pretty certain that his family would want to be a part of it as well. "When? We have to give our families a chance to come."

He thought on that. "Okay, how about we go to lunch at the Roarke, and we can plan our wedding?"

"I love that idea. Almost as much as I love you."

Fifteen minutes later, we were entering the elevator to the Roarke restaurant on the top floor. I was excited to see the three hundred and sixty-degree view of Las Vegas, especially since the day was clear and I imagined we'd be able to see hundreds of miles.

As the elevator doors opened to the restaurant, Max took my hand and led me out. I was surprised by how quiet the restaurant was. I would have thought it would be busy during the lunch hour. He led me over to the window, and we looked out as the restaurant slowly turned.

"If our families were here, would you want to get married now?"

I looked up at him, my heart doing flip-flops in my chest. I nodded, feeling giddy. "Of course."

He put his arm around me and turned us both. As we came around, my brother and Max's family stepped into the main area of the restaurant.

I looked up at Max, tears blurring my eyes because I couldn't contain my happiness. I flung my arms around him and held on. "I love you so much, Max."

His arms came around me and he held me tight against him. "You're my world, Amelia. You and the baby."

A woman I didn't know came to us telling us where to stand. Max introduced her as Serena Roarke, who happened to be married to Devin Roarke, owner of the company that owned the restaurant.

"Technically, they're not family, but my uncle Daniel is married to Devin's sister, so it's like family," he explained.

I shook my head. "You're going to have to draw me a family tree."

He held both of my hands in his. "I'll do that. And sometime in August, I look forward to adding our child to that family tree."

Along with Devin and Serena, Max's aunts and uncles and cousins came too. I worried that James could feel outnumbered since he was the only family I had. But Max's family pulled him in, adopting him as part of their family as well.

With the backdrop of Las Vegas and the Nevada desert behind us, the officiant Max hired married me and Max. When we exchanged vows and rings, said our I dos, and the officiant pronounced as husband and wife, I knew my life going forward would be filled with happiness and joy. The ordeal with my father wasn't done. His trial wouldn't be for a while, and I was sure that even from prison, he would continue to try to hurt me and James, but with Max and the entire Clarke family behind us, I knew that nothing could ruin my happiness.

EPILOGUE ONE

Amelia – Ten Months Later - Christmas

The last ten months of my life have been the greatest. I married the man of my dreams. In August, I bore our sweet little boy, Andrew James Clarke, after Max's father Drew and my brother.

Six months ago, we moved into a larger home that accommodated two home offices since Max was working on building the club in Las Vegas. We lived and worked and raised our boy together. It was perfect.

Today was Christmas Eve, and the happiness continued on. It was a far cry from a year ago when Max had accused me of tricking him into marriage for his money.

I looked down on our son sleeping in his crib. Sometimes, I couldn't believe that my life could be filled with so much love. Andy was proof that my life was real.

A hand slid around me and lips pressed against my neck. "It's hard to take your eyes off him, isn't it?" Max whispered in my ear.

I turned in his arms to hug him. "Thank you for giving me all this."

He smiled. "Don't you know, Amelia? You're the one who's given me all of this."

He kissed me softly, and things slowly heated up. His dick thickened against my belly. I checked my watch, noting we didn't have much time before we had to leave for the company Christmas party. Not Max's company, but James's. The company struggled with my father going to prison. While my brother was doing everything he could to keep the company going, his board wasn't making it easy for him. It wasn't out of any loyalty to my father so much as concern that my father's actions and incarceration were damaging the company too much. They were pushing my brother to fix that but didn't seem to have a lot of faith that he would. Our showing up at the Christmas party, or more accurately, Max's showing up at the Christmas party, was one way to boost James's credibility in the eyes of the company and the others it did business with.

"That will have to wait until later. I need to shower and get ready for the party."

Max gave me a wicked grin. "We could shower together. It would save time and water."

I knew from experience that wasn't true, but at the same time, seeing Max smile at me so seductively, feeling him hard against my belly, it was impossible to say no.

It was a mad rush to the shower. We laughed and kissed until passion took over. Hot water sluiced over our bodies. Steam filled the bathroom. But all I could take in was the hot, hard man assaulting my senses with his hands and lips.

"Max." Like always, he pushed me until edgy and agitated. I needed him to soothe the ache.

He lifted me, pressing me against the cool tiles. "Look at me, Amelia. I love to watch your eyes when I enter you."

I did my best to look at him, but it was hard, especially as he penetrated my body, sending incredible sensations through me.

He grunted as he bucked, filling me. "So fucking good, baby."

"Yes," I agreed, lightly biting his shoulder.

"Speaking of babies."

I lifted my head. "What?"

"When can we have another one?"

I arched a brow. "The one we have is only a few months old."

"He's perfect, isn't he? I want to fill our house with more babies like him."

I laughed, loving how open and loving Max was with me. "Perhaps we could practice a bit longer."

"Like this?" He withdrew and thrust in again, making me gasp at the sweet pleasure.

"Yes. More."

His lips trailed along my collarbone as he moved against me, in me, until we were both gasping and reaching for bliss.

"Now, baby, now."

His words sent me soaring, crying out as pleasure washed through me. Max let go, cried out, and soared with me.

Fifteen minutes later, a knock came on the front door.

"We cut that close," I said as Max zipped up my dress.

"It was worth it." He kissed my neck. "I'll get it. It's probably the troops." Max went to the front door.

I went to check on Andy, finding him awake, watching his mobile. "Hey, sweetie." I picked him and brought him to the living room where Max's parents and Vivie had arrived.

"Where is my grandson?" His mother made a beeline to me.

"He just woke up. Would you like to feed him?"

Max's mother smiled widely. "Would I ever."

It was wonderful to have family with us at Christmas. Max's family was staying with us, and tomorrow afternoon, his brother, Sam, his wife, Kate, and their new baby would be joining us as well. Because we were having Christmas in Las Vegas, it meant that James could be with us too. There was no way to express my gratitude for Max's family's willingness to have the holidays here so that James could join in.

"I think everything's okay," Vivie said with a laugh. "In fact, if you wanted to take the whole night off, or heck, even the whole month, I'm sure Mom and Dad would be perfectly happy to babysit."

"She's not lying," Max's father said as he leaned over his wife's shoulder and kissed Andy on the head.

"A few hours is all we need," I said. The truth was a few hours was all I'd be able to tolerate being away from my little angel.

My brother had gone all out for the office party. He knew he needed to boost morale with the staff, as well as impress members of the board. He had also invited prestigious members of the community, hoping to show off a newer, kinder Dunsmore family business.

The poor guy was working himself ragged to save my father's company. Sometimes, I wondered why he bothered. He was smart and capable. He could start his own company or go be the CEO of someone else's company. But he was dedicated to making this one work. In fact, I think there was a part of him that wanted to make the company his, purge all aspects of my father out of it, sort of in the same way Max and I followed through on the annulment to cut my father out of our relationship.

The guests were drinking expensive champagne and enjoying fancy catered food. They all looked like they were having a good time, except for James, who stood in the corner.

As Max went to get us something to drink, I went over to my brother. "You're doing a great job, James. Look at everyone here. You should smile and not look so sour."

He scowled at me. "You will not believe with those motherfuckers did to me today."

I frowned. "What motherfuckers?"

"The board. I have been busting my nuts for the last ten months, but they still feel like the company is at risk of falling under another scandal."

"We can't help what's going on with Dad."

He rolled his eyes. "Not Dad. Me. They think I'm a risk."

I frowned. "What are you talking about?"

"They're worried that my single status leaves the company open to scandal. They act like I'm a fucking playboy. Do you know the last time I fucked someone?"

"Ah . . . no." And I didn't want to know. Some things didn't need to be shared between brother and sister.

"I don't do anything but work my ass off saving this company, but they think my single status gives the impression that I'm not stable."

"That's ridiculous."

"Maybe you can tell them that."

The board wouldn't listen to me. They'd always dismissed me when my dad was around. That hadn't changed.

Max approached carrying three drinks. He handed me orange juice and seltzer and a glass to James. "You look like you could use this. It's a double shot of scotch."

"I could use more than a double, but I suppose if I had more, my board would kick me out of the company for embarrassing them."

Max looked at me with an arched brow, clearly questioning what was going on with James.

"The board thinks James's single status puts the company at risk for instability and scandal."

This time, Max frowned. "Really? What is your board made up of? Octogenarians?"

James laughed, and it was the first time I'd seen him smile in a long time. "Pretty close to it." He let out a sigh, and then someone from across the room caught his eye. "Can you excuse me? I need to go check in with Reyna."

I nodded. "You're doing a great job, James. Don't let the fuckers get you down."

James waved at my comment as he strode toward a young woman.

Max laughed. "I love it when you say the word fuck."

Thankfully, James was out of earshot when he said that.

I winked at Max. "I know you do." I leaned closer to him, my lips a whisper away from his ear. "I know you like it when I don't just say it, but I do it too."

He groaned, his hand sliding down my back over my ass and giving it a squeeze. "Is there an empty office where we could discuss this further?"

I laughed. "You know, I might consider that, except the board is concerned about scandal in the company. It might not look good if the CEO's sister is caught fucking her husband in one of the offices."

He feigned confusion. "Really? I thought that's the type of thing that happened at Christmas parties. And it's not like we're not married."

"How about we just save that for later tonight?"

"I'll hold you to it," he said.

"You'd better." I held my glass up. "To our first Christmas. It's going to be the best one ever."

His smile was lovely. "To our first Christmas. And to our second and third and fiftieth." He pulled me close. "Last Christmas, I was a broken man. You've healed me. You've healed parts of me that I didn't realize needed healing."

How many times a day did Max say things that made me swoon? Ten? Twenty? I never got tired of it.

"Last Christmas, I was brokenhearted, but you've mended it and then some. I never knew happiness and love like this existed."

"I love you, Amelia. Merry Christmas, baby."

EPILOGUE TWO

James

Christmas was never a Rockwellian picture for me and Amelia. My father didn't have the sentiment gene. Or the loving father one. Christmas was more of an annoyance to him because everything was closed and everyone was at home with their families. The exception had been the company's annual Christmas party. He used this occasion to schmooze and booze with the elite, as well as to remind people that he could ruin them.

This year would be different. My father was disgraced and rotting in jail until his trial after his bail was revoked when he tried to leave the country. Since then, I've been CEO and have done my damnedest to keep the company afloat amid my father's scandal, as well as cleanse it of my father's questionable and ruthless reputation. I knew I was in for the effort of a lifetime. What I hadn't expected was that the board would make it so hard for me. Working with them was like driving with the parking brake on.

They questioned everything I did to clean up the company's act and forge a future without my father's corrupt practices. Was I naïve to think they'd want that? Maybe. After all, the board looked the other way at my father's less than legal business tactics. He was currently in jail for kidnapping, false imprisonment, and fraud for what he did to my sister, Amelia, and her husband, Max. But now he was also being investigated for mortgage fraud. Now all of a sudden, the board was worried about the CEO's reputation?

I wasn't perfect, but I wasn't using people to get what I want at the expense of others. I wasn't inflating assets or low-balling them to manipulate loans or taxes. I wasn't threatening or extorting anyone. No. I was busting my balls to right the company ship that had hit an iceberg and was going to sink without major changes.

To be honest, when I met with the board earlier today, I thought I'd be recognized for getting us to the end of the year. What an idiot I was. Those motherfuckers decided that a single man running the company was a risk. They acted like I was running a fucking bordello out of my office. They saw me as a man sowing my oats, and for some reason, that was bad for a company.

"Single men aren't settled, stable," George Keyes said.

"I don't remember your telling my dad to get married." What a hypocrite.

"Your father had been married. He raised his kids on his own when your mother left." George said that like my father was a saint.

I bit my tongue. They wouldn't care that being raised by my father was like being raised by Rasputin.

Simon Jones nodded, but his expression held sympathy. "You're working hard, James. We can see that."

They all had called my father Mr. Dunsmore, but I was James. Maybe I needed to assert myself more. Be more of an asshole like my father.

"But the company has a lot to overcome, and a single man playing the field doesn't show the sort of stability that our partners and investors need right now," Simon finished.

I hadn't fucked a woman in longer than I could remember. Sex wasn't anywhere in my orbit. But I couldn't very well tell these men that. Not without having them see me as a lesser man than they already did.

"What are you saying?" I asked, thinking maybe I was misunderstanding them. Maybe I was a lesser man.

"You need to get married. Settle down," George said.

I looked at each man sitting at the boardroom table, wondering if they'd taken whatever my father had drugged Amelia and Max with last year.

"What if I don't?"

George didn't blink. "Well, we could remove you as CEO."

I left the meeting. Hell, I left the building and seriously thought about not returning. The only reason I was at this fucked up company Christmas party was that many of the people I worked with were good and loyal workers. They deserved to have someone recognize their efforts after a very difficult year.

So there I was, feeling like Scrooge as company workers and city elites drank booze and schmoozed.

When my sister and Max arrived, she came over to where I was hiding in the corner.

"You're doing a great job, James. Look at everyone here. You should smile and not look so sour."

I scowled at her. "You will not believe what those motherfuckers did to me today."

"What motherfuckers?"

"The board. I have been busting my nuts for the last ten months, but they still feel like the company is at risk of falling under another scandal."

"We can't help what's going on with Dad," she said.

"Not Dad. Me. They think I'm a risk."

She looked at me quizzically. "What are you talking about?"

"They're worried that my single status leaves the company open to scandal. They act like I'm a fucking playboy. Do you know the last time I fucked someone?"

"Ah . . . no." She paled, clearly worried I was going to share my sexual history with her. I wouldn't. There were a few things people didn't need to know about. My lack of orgasms was one of them.

"I don't do anything but work my ass off saving this company, but they think my single status gives the impression that I'm not stable."

"That's ridiculous."

"Maybe you can tell them that." Maybe I'd leave here tonight and never return.

Max approached carrying three drinks. He handed Amelia one glass and another to me. "You look like you could use this. It's a double shot of scotch."

A tanker of scotch couldn't fix what ailed me. "I could use more than a double, but I suppose if I had more, my board would kick me out of the company for embarrassing them."

"The board thinks James's single status puts the company at risk for instability and scandal," Amelia explained to him.

Max frowned. "Really? What is your board made up of? Octogenarians?"

I laughed. "Pretty close to it." Movement across the room caught my eye. My new assistant arrived, and if my life wasn't already a shitshow, she had the potential to make it one. I wasn't lying when I said I hadn't been with a woman in a long time. At least not in person. But from the moment Reyna walked into my office for an interview, she starred in some very nice fantasies. I'd had a satisfying orgasm imagining Reyna on her knees sucking me off while I showered before coming to this shindig. It was wrong. I felt like a perv. But I couldn't remember ever meeting a woman who was the whole package— smart, sexy, and sweet—before. Just my luck, I finally met a woman who makes me feel something, and she works for me, a company no-no. Maybe that was why the board had their boxers in a bunch. Did they notice the few times I was admiring Reyna's ass?

"Can you excuse me? I need to go check in with Reyna."

Amelia nodded. "You're doing a great job, James. Don't let the fuckers get you down."

I strode toward Reyna, my gaze taking in the stunning woman dressed in green instead of red like most of the young, single women here wore. She put off a kind, almost innocent vibe, and yet, she was so fucking sexy.

258

As I approached her, I remembered her sharing some of the challenges she was having in life. It was all financial and mostly at the hands of her family. I could fix that for her. And in return, she could help me.

"How are you this evening, Ms. Pearson?" I asked when I reached her.

She smiled and it was like the fucking sun. "Mr. Dunsmore. Very well, thank you. Everyone has been very welcoming to me."

"I'm glad to hear it. Can I get you a drink?"

"Okay. I suppose one won't hurt. I don't want to embarrass myself in front of the boss."

I wanted to tell her it wasn't the boss she had to worry about. "What's your poison?"

"White wine."

"I'll be right back." As I headed to the bar, my brain worked out logistics that could get my board off my back and help Reyna. The only thing I would have to do would be to convince her to marry me.

Yes! James gets his very own story. This will be a grumpy bo$$hole, secret twins romance. While you wait for that one, how about binge reading the entire Heart of Hope Series here?

When the door slammed behind him, I turned to Max. "What the hell was he saying?"

Max looked confused as well. "I'm pretty sure he just said that Kate is pregnant."

Emotions swirled in a torment in my chest. I was going to be a dad for real. She didn't tell me. For all her talk about honesty, she didn't say a word. Was that also part of her plan? Did she want to punish me for leaving her by breaking my heart and taking my child?

I went over to the bowl by the door and grabbed my keys.

"Where are you going, Sam?"

"I'm going to talk to Kate."

Continue reading THANKFUL FOR US, Sam and Kate's story here.

THANKFUL FOR US (SNEAK PEEK)

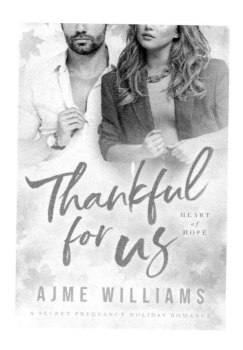

DESCRIPTION

When I say that he broke my heart, what I really mean is that he did something I wouldn't do to my worst enemy.

I hate Sam Wheatly.
I hate him for leaving me, and now for trying to come back into my life.

Yes, he left me for another woman.
A woman he thought was pregnant with his baby.
He didn't just leave me. He also decided to marry that liar.

Well, his life is ruined . . . and I won't let him do the same to mine.
Being born into a wealthy family doesn't give him the green light to come and go as he pleases.

I've built a new life for myself since our breakup.
I cannot allow him to waltz back into my reality and screw everything up . . . especially as my competitor in business.

Holiday season is the best time to show Sam that I've moved on. And I'll prove to myself that I don't love him anymore. I don't . . . right?

PROLOGUE

Kate—Five Years Ago

Beer pong being played by a pirate and a cowboy. Drunken rough-housing between a zombie and a lumberjack. Uncoordinated dancing by a sexy nurse and a gangster. The living room was the very definition of chaos. The family room was quieter, but that was only because the people in there were either stoned or making out.

I'd given up a night of studying for this? I was in a 1980s teen movie, except the party house was filled with college students, not high schoolers. Oh, and it was Halloween.

"Oh, there's Tyler." Janell tossed her hair back and sashayed over to her crush. I had to admit, she made a good Morticia Addams.

When she suggested that we come to this party, I told her I wasn't interested, especially since she'd abandon me.

She promised me she wouldn't, and yet we weren't in the house two seconds before I was trapped between Halloween versions of *Sixteen Candles* and *Fast Times at Ridgemont High*.

It wasn't that I didn't like parties. I did. In fact, until last year, I'd have been enthusiastic about attending an off-campus party open to anyone and everyone. I enjoyed meeting new people and having fun.

But as a college senior, it was time for me to buckle down and set myself up for success once I graduated.

My goal was to get hired in the family business, but my grandfather wasn't going to hand over a position to me simply because I was his granddaughter. He didn't hand over jobs to my older brother Ethan or our cousin, both of whom were in competition to take over the company someday.

My brother Ethan got a job with MacLeod Capital Investment, which I knew would give him the experience needed to defeat our cousin. While my brother and cousin were getting experience elsewhere, I wanted a job within the family company.

I had no illusions about ascending to the top spot.

The truth was, my grandfather, at best, was distant with me, and at worst, disdainful. Still, we were family, and I believed with hard work and smarts, I could earn a position.

To do that, I had to study hard and rock my internship. A drunken off-campus Halloween party was the opposite of working toward my goal.

Still, I was here, so I made my way through the house to the back yard where there were more drunken antics in the pool and yard. But at least it didn't smell like beer or pot.

I found a spot where I wasn't worried that I'd become collateral damage in a drinking game and inhaled a deep breath.

"You look like you've fallen through the looking glass."

I turned, prepared to give my intruder a back-off glare. Unfortunately, it never manifested as I gawked at the blond-haired, green-eyed Captain America. *Holy smokes, he was hot.*

He smirked like he knew I was momentarily stunned by his good looks. "Alice in Wonderland, right?"

Annoyed at my reaction, I schooled my expression back to normal. "Right. I'm surprised you could tell."

I hadn't planned to come to the party, so when Janell pressured me, I didn't have a costume. The best I could manage was a powder blue dress, white stockings, and a black headband to hold back my long blonde hair.

He shrugged. "It's a classic." He held out a red cup. "Beer?"

I made a face. "I'm not really a beer fan."

He tilted his head to the side. "Then why are you here?"

"So my roommate can seduce the guy she's been crushing on since we were freshmen."

He laughed. "I had a roommate like that once."

"What happened?"

"They live together now."

"I guess it turned out for them."

"I guess it did." His green eyes studied me. Once again, I felt bewitched. "So, what is your drink of choice?"

"I'm more of a cocktail gal. But I like wine. Both drinks that aren't served at places like this."

"I saw a bar off the family room. We'd have to brave the stoners and lovers, but I'm willing if you are."

I really should call it a night and go home. Yes, this guy was cute and nice, but I'd promised myself that this year I would solely focus on academics and my internship. I didn't have time for guys.

But . . . I was here, and if I went home now, chances were good that I'd binge watch Netflix instead of studying.

"Sure."

He smiled, and once again, it made my breath catch. It really should have been illegal to look the way he did. "I'm Sam. Sam Clarke."

"Kate Wheatly."

"As in *the* Wheatly family?"

Uh-oh. It took me a while to figure out that it wasn't my radiant personality that lured friends and potential boyfriends to me. It was my family's money.

Of course, my grandfather was stingy with it, so I didn't live as lavishly as people might think. I couldn't wait until I got my trust and could finally be in control of my finances.

"Yes."

He studied me again. "Why the glare?"

"Are you offering me a drink because of my family ties?"

He shook his head. "I don't need your family ties. My uncle is

Daniel Clarke. In New York."

Both Daniel and Clarke were common names, but everyone knew Daniel Clarke from New York like everyone knew Bill Gates or Mark Zuckerberg, although instead of tech, the Clarke family was in real estate.

"That makes your aunt Briana Clarke." I had a list of successful businesswomen that I studied. She was one. I admired her.

Maybe someday, I'd open my own club.

She owned a few now, but I knew the story about how she struggled to find her footing in her family's business, so she said F-it and started her own.

He nodded. "It does. Say, are you accepting my drink offer because of my family ties?"

"Maybe."

He laughed. "Good to know."

"It doesn't bother you that your good looks and money make you a magnet for fake friends?"

He shrugged. "It is what it is. Are you fake?"

"No."

"Well then, how about that drink?"

We managed to get through the crowd and into the family room. The noise and activity were much less than in the living room and back yard, as a few stoned partiers discussed the meaning of life.

"What's your poison?" Sam asked from behind the bar.

"You look like you know what you're doing back there. What's your specialty?"

"I make a killer martini. In fact, my aunt Bri taught me." He pulled out the gin and vermouth and set to work. He found two martini glasses and poured us each one.

He held his drink up. "To *Alice in Wonderland.*"

I clicked my glass against his. "And *Captain America.*"

His cheeks blushed. "I forgot I was wearing tights. Sort of ruins the manly illusion."

I scanned my gaze down his body. He was all manly muscle. "Looks manly to me."

"Come on, let's find somewhere we can breathe and hear each other talk." He grabbed the gin bottle and led me out the front door, where a swing sat on the porch.

We sat and drank and talked. I learned he was studying business at USC. I told him I also studied business but went to his rival college, UCLA. We talked about our brothers, both of whom we were close to. He also had a younger sister who was still in high school.

We both were seniors and were focused on studies this year. He said he'd recently broken up with his girlfriend of a year, and this year, he wanted to have a good time.

In my mind, that meant he wanted to play the field. I was okay with that. I didn't want a relationship either.

On and on, we talked about anything and everything until he leaned closer to me.

"Can I kiss you?"

Yes, please. "Why?"

He gave me his sexy smile as his gaze drifted to my lips. "Because I want to. Don't you want to?"

"Maybe. What about your goal to sow your oats?"

"You said you weren't looking for a relationship either."

I reached up and grabbed the Lycra of his Captain America top and pulled him closer. "Okay."

Our lips met. The sizzle of electricity radiated through me. His lips were soft, sweet, and very thorough.

He tugged me closer. "How do you feel about hookups?"

"Are you saying you want to hook up with me?"

"More than I want my next breath."

His words filled me with a gooey warmth. What woman didn't want to be wanted like that? "On this swing?"

"I'll call for a ride and we can go to my place. I don't have a room-mate anymore, remember?"

I wasn't a virgin, but neither was I a hookup kind of girl. And yet, if I wasn't going to have a relationship, a hookup would be the only way to get my womanly needs met, at least by a person instead of a vibrator.

"Okay."

We left the glasses and gin on the porch as he called for a car. We kissed all the way to his condo. By the time the front door shut, I was so hot and needy I was afraid I might spontaneously combust.

He grabbed my hand and dragged me to his bedroom. Costumes flew off. He pushed me onto the bed while he opened the drawer of his bedside table to get a condom.

Then he looked at me, his gaze roaming over my body. "Why, Alice, you are a wonderland."

"Come explore." I reached up for him. He did exactly that. His hands were everywhere. Followed by his lips. I was a writhing, weeping mess when he finally filled me.

"Fuck . . . so good."

I had to agree. I tingled as his cock touched every millimeter of my inner walls. The friction was sublime. Sam's former girlfriend was an idiot to let this guy go.

He moved in and out, each time picking up the pace. He pushed me up and up until I dangled on the edge.

"Sam . . . oh, God . . . now."

He levered up onto his hands and let loose. He thrust and withdrew, fast and hard, stealing my breath and then launching me over the edge.

He let out a feral growl. "Fuck . . . yes . . . Kate . . ."

When it was done, we lay breathless. I'd had a few good orgasms in the past, but nothing like that. Too bad this was only a one-time thing.

"Will you stay the night, Barley?" he asked.

"Barley?" Did he really forget my name?

"Wheatly, Barley."

I rolled my eyes. It wasn't the first time people had used grain puns on me. "I won't stay if you're going to call me Barley."

"Kate. Will you stay?"

I liked the way my name rolled off his tongue too much. "I thought this was a hookup."

"I don't know about you, but one time isn't enough. No ties. No commitment."

I turned my head to look at him. "Just a night of sex?"

He nodded. God, his green eyes were gorgeous.

"Okay."

One night turned into the entire weekend. By the time Sunday evening rolled around, I didn't want to leave. It wasn't just the sex that had me wanting to stay, though.

Sam was funny and sweet and smart. He was from a prominent rich family, but he didn't put on the airs that so many rich people did. When the weekend ended, I was head over heels in love with him.

Luckily for me, he was too.

By Thanksgiving, I'd moved in with him, which turned out good for Janell as Tyler moved in with her. When May rolled around, my plans to find a job with my family's company had changed. I was going to New York with Sam.

His graduation happened first, and then a week later, I had mine. After my graduation, he took me to the beach where he got down on one knee and proposed.

There weren't many times in my life where I felt incandescently happy. Not just in the moment, but like I'd feel like it forever.

When Sam proposed, I knew my life was set on a course for a lifetime of bliss.

The week before we were to move to New York, we were packing up the condo when there was a knock on the door.

"I'll get it." I went to the door and opened it. A woman about my age stood on the other side. I knew from photos that Sam had that she was his ex, Sandra.

She bit her lip in nervousness. "Is Sam here?"

I opened the door. I suppose it was cattiness that had me wanting to slam the door in her face. No woman liked to have the ex show up. It created self-doubt.

Especially since Sam's stories about her were always positive. They didn't fight. She wasn't a bitch. Their relationship ended simply because it petered out.

"Sam," I called. Then to her, I said, "I'm Kate. Nice to meet you." I reached out my right hand to shake hers. At the same time, I pressed my left hand over my heart, making sure she saw the engagement ring. Catty, I know.

Sam entered and stopped short when he saw her. "Sandra."

"I need to talk to you."

He looked at me like maybe I'd know why she was there. I didn't.

"Sure. Come in." He motioned to the living room that was filled with boxes, but the couch was still sittable.

"I'll give you some privacy." I went to the kitchen, debating on whether I wanted to eavesdrop. I wanted to, but I knew it showed a lack of trust.

They were there a long, long time. If I were a nail biter, I'd have had no nails left.

Finally, I heard the front door shut, and Sam entered the kitchen. He looked completely gutted.

"What's wrong?" I rose and went to him.

He closed his eyes, tilting his head upward. Whatever it was, he didn't want to tell me.

Finally, he looked at me. "She had a baby last month."

I swallowed. "Okay." My mind was taking this to a bad place. I forced myself to wait to react until I had all the details.

"It's mine."

My world wobbled. "Are you sure? You haven't been together—"

"The timing is right. She and I broke up just before school started, but we'd . . . well . . ."

"Had sex around that time?"

He nodded.

I didn't like this, but it wasn't the end of the world. "Okay. So I guess we need to stay in California so you can have visitations. I don't know much about babies, but we can learn together. I promise I won't be an evil stepmom."

I expected relief in his expression. I thought he was worried I'd dump him for having a child with another woman. But I was a realist.

Things like this happened. But I loved him. I knew my future happiness was wrapped up in him.

He looked at me with such pain and regret. "I have to do right by them."

I nodded. "Child support."

He closed his eyes again, and I realized I was missing what he was trying to tell me.

My world tilted a bit more. "What's going on, Sam?"

His hands brushed up and down my arms. "I have to call off our engagement."

I pulled away from him. "What? Why?"

"Because I have to do right by Sandra and the baby."

The meaning of his words finally sank in. "You're leaving me to marry her?"

He shrugged.

"What the fuck, Sam? This isn't the old days."

"I'm sorry."

Two days later, when I went to my grandfather to tell him I wanted a job with the company, he informed me that I had no trust money and no job. Not only that, but he'd also talked all his cronies into not letting me work for them, either. I knew he didn't like me. I hadn't realized he hated and resented me.

I yelled and begged for him to change his mind. Why was he doing this to me?

Finally, he reached into his pocket and pulled out a quarter that he tossed to me. "This is your last handout. Don't spend it all in one place."

I went from incandescently happy to the deepest despair. I lost my love. I lost my money. For a time, I lost myself. Luckily, Ethan was there for me.

When I finally rose from the ashes, I was stronger and smarter. I learned two things. One, trust no one. Two, never be financially indebted to anyone. I carried my engagement ring and my grandfather's quarter to make sure I never forgot.

Keep reading THANKFUL FOR US here.

A NOTE FROM THE AUTHOR

It all started with Juliana and Drew (Sam and Max's parents).

My ex doesn't know that he's got twin sons... and I'm about to meet him... *oops!*
(Yep, the twins are Sam and Max)

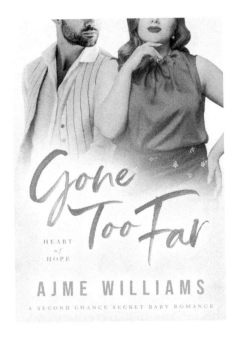

Drew was everything I'd wanted in my life.
And in my bed.
But my dream job waited for me in London.
A huge fight later, I packed my bags and left.
But the two pink lines changed everything.
I took a deep breath and built from scratch.

And now…
I'm watching Drew talk to his sons without knowing they are his.
Read Juliana and Drew's story here.

Want to read more about Harper and Noel? **Get my book, 'Too Complicated' here.**

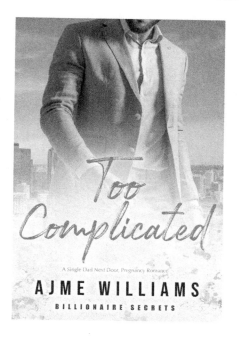

Kate's brother Ethan got his own happily ever after with Lucy in **this** fake marriage office romance. **Get your copy now!**

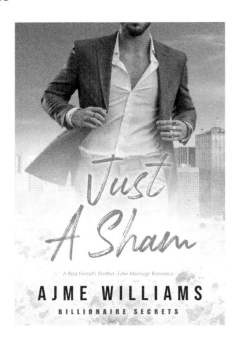

READY TO READ ALL BOOKS IN THE HEART OF HOPE SERIES?

In mood to binge read the entire Heart of Hope Series? GET IT HERE.

All books are steamy, standalone romances packed with heart and heat and promise a very emotional and tear jerking HEA.

Our Last Chance
An Irish Affair
So Wrong
Imperfect Love
Eight Long Years
Friends to Lovers
The One and Only
Best Friend's Brother
Maybe It's Fate
Gone Too Far
Christmas with Brother's Best Friend
Fighting for US
Against All Odds

ABOUT THE AUTHOR

Ajme Williams writes emotional, angsty contemporary romance. All her books can be enjoyed as full length, standalone romances and are FREE to read in Kindle Unlimited .

Books do not have to be read in order.

Heart of Hope Series (this series)
Our Last Chance | An Irish Affair | So Wrong | Imperfect Love | Eight Long Years | Friends to Lovers | The One and Only | Best Friend's Brother | Maybe It's Fate | Gone Too Far | Christmas with Brother's Best Friend | Fighting for US | Against All Odds | Hoping to Score | Thankful for Us | The Vegas Bluff

Billionaire Secrets
Twin Secrets | Just A Sham | Let's Start Over | The Baby Contract | Too Complicated

Dominant Bosses
His Rules | His Desires | His Needs | His Punishments | His Secret

Strong Brothers
Say Yes to Love | Giving In to Love | Wrong to Love You | Hate to Love You

Fake Marriage Series
Accidental Love | Accidental Baby | Accidental Affair | Accidental Meeting

Irresistible Billionaires
Admit You Miss Me | Admit You Love Me | Admit You Want Me | Admit You Need Me

Check out Ajme's full Amazon catalogue here.

Join her VIP NL here.

WANT MORE AJME WILLIAMS?

Join my no spam mailing list here.

You'll only be sent emails about my new releases, extended epilogues, deleted scenes and occasional FREE books.

Printed in Great Britain
by Amazon

15965806R00163